MASKS OF SILENCE

WRITTEN BY

A.K. LOGAN

Preface

In *Masks of Silence*, love begins like a beautiful deception. The world sees a perfect couple with prestige, charm, and control wrapped in silk and stethoscopes. But behind the curtain of civility, something darker breathes. What happens when affection becomes obsession, when protection becomes possession, and when silence becomes the weapon of choice?

Shannon's world unravels one whispered lie at a time. Every secret, every manipulation, every subtle cruelty is another thread pulling her closer to the edge. The mask her lover wears, polished, admired, untouchable, conceals the face of a predator who feeds on her doubt. And in the reflection of his shadow, she begins to question herself.

This is not just a story about love gone wrong. It's about survival of the mind, of the soul, and of the truth buried beneath the ruins of psychological control. Because silence doesn't mean peace. Sometimes, it's the sound of a chaos.

Contents

Chapter 1
Shattered Dreams

Shannon rushed from room to room, gasping for breath, her heart pounding. "Come on, where are they?" she muttered. "Please, not now. Please!" She flung open drawers, knocking over a lamp in her panic. The loud crash of the lamp hitting the floor startled her, but she refused to freeze. She quickly slipped into the narrow hallway, feeling the walls caving in with each frantic step. The flickering light from the broken bulb cast lively shadows that danced in quick, jerky movements along the peeling wallpaper, creating a haunting yet strangely captivating scene. Panic threatened to take hold of her, but she fought it back one trembling breath at a time.

Her thoughts darted wildly, searching for a safe spot under the warped stairs or behind the battered coat rack. Maybe if luck were on her side, she would find the keys in the crawlspace beneath the steps.

A floorboard creaked somewhere behind her in the house, signaling danger for Shannon. She pressed herself flat against the hallway wall, holding her breath until her lungs burned.

In the faint light, she could make out the faint outline of a door left slightly ajar, with footsteps echoing close. She had no choice but to slip inside a doorway in the hall, praying.

The darkness would swallow her, shielding her from visibility and from… *Dennis*.

A wave of nausea grew as Shannon crawled further. Her fingers numb and clumsy, scrabbling against the gritty floorboards. Dust covered her lips. Just as something sharp pricked her palm. She barely registered the sting.

She heard the distant echo of Dennis's voice, something raw, through the walls like a warning.

She squeezed her eyes shut. Trying her best to calm her racing heartbeat. *Think. Think.* The glint of metal caught her eye beneath the radiator. She lunged forward, only to pull out a rusted bottle cap.

She couldn't hide her disappointment, which washed over her like a gentle wave. It left her breathless.

Footsteps grew. Steadily and deliberate. She quietly pressed herself into the shadow of the sofa, her heart pounding so loudly she worried it might reveal her presence.

Shannon, a petite woman with fair skin and dark brunette hair, had married her high school boyfriend, Dennis, when she was only eighteen.

Now thirty, she remains with Dennis, who lost his job as a Phoenix police officer after being let go for misconduct and anger management problems. And now with Dennis out of work, he had become increasingly controlling and displayed narcissistic, abusive behaviors toward Shannon.

Shannon is broken and worn down from the abuse by her husband, but somewhere deep down, she still dares to fight him and rebuild her own life.

Despite exhaustion and fear, her unwavering courage kept her from giving up. She refused to let him take everything, holding onto a determined hope that freedom from his shadow was still within reach.

In the oppressive silence of the night, Shannon forced herself upright, scanning the room with wild, pleading eyes. By the door, just outside the hallway light, her purse was half-open, but no keys were in sight. She hurriedly reached for her purse, still feeling frantic as she searched for her car keys. Stretching out around the hall was Dennis's silhouette. It moved towards the doorway and crept so silently out of the shadows into the light.

A stubborn glimmer of resistance flared within her. She refused to let him take away everything she still possessed, not tonight.

Shannon's shaking hands began fumbling through piles of receipts and tangled cords, but still no keys. Each second stretched longer, and with each second, more fear and anxiety.

She blinked away the tears that had escaped. She quickly wiped them away on the back of her hand.

She cursed herself for ever trusting Dennis. Every corner felt dangerous as the clock ticked, heightening her fear.

In her frantic search, she knocked over a pile of magazines and sank to her knees, clawing beneath the sofa cushions.

A fragile, helpless sound escaped her lips.

What if she didn't find the keys soon?

What would Dennis do to her this time?

How abusive would he be?

Why had she ever trusted this man with her life after so many years of abuse?

Her mind recoiled from the possibility.

Each shadow pressed closer, swelling with threat, while the ticking clock grated relentlessly on her nerves.

But what now held her even stronger than her panic was the cold, creeping certainty: *he would find her. He always did.*

She remembered nights tense with the sound of his boots on tile and waking to his silhouette in the doorway, a dark presence that pressed on her like a suffocating cloud.

She was shivering inside her chest, feeling every muscle tense. Her thoughts fluttered wildly between despair and the urge scream for help. Yet, she knew the walls were too thick and Dennis too quick to catch her cry.

What if no one heard her crying? What if no one cared enough to save her?

Shannon's heartbeat pounded loudly in her ears as she quickly scanned around the room. Longing for anything, a weapon, an escape route, or just a glimmer of hope. With every passing second, as the keys clinked ominously like a countdown, her hope started to fade, and *her chance for freedom was slipping away.*

From the hallway, Dennis's footsteps thudded closer. Unyielding. Unhurried. Heavy with purpose.

Shannon pressed her palm on her mouth. Terrified to even breathe now. Struggling to hold back a sob as she rifled through her purse one final, desperate time.

Then he broke the silence. His voice, low; sending chills down her spine, "Looking for these?" Dennis stood in the doorway. His lips curled into a cold, humorless smile as he dangled the keys just out of reach, the metal glinting in the dim light.

Shannon's eyes widened. "Give them back, Dennis. Please." Her voice trembled, desperate, barely above a whisper.

He took a step forward, blocking the door. "You think you can just run? After all I've done for you? You're not going anywhere, Shannon. You ungrateful bitch."

"Please," she begged, her voice cracking. "Let me go. I can't do this anymore. I can't"

He stepped forward toward Shannon, blocking any hope of escape, his shadow stretching across the floor and swallowing the last sliver of light, "Thought you could sneak away without me finding out. You piece of shit. How dare you try to leave me?"

Dennis was a muscular, well-built man, standing at close to six feet. He had a strong, angular and harsh face. He very rarely smiled. He was possessive, domineering and aggressive.

"You're not going anywhere." His voice was loud and threating, "You owe me, Shannon. You always have."

Her chest tightened. "I don't owe you anything," she managed, tears threatening at the corners of her eyes. "You can't keep me here." Her eyes darted to the door, then back to the keys, her mind searching desperately for an escape.

Dennis laughed, the sound echoing in the cramped space. "Keep telling yourself that if it makes you feel better. But no one's coming for you. You can scream, you can beg, but it won't change a thing. So, Shannon, how does it feel to be trapped like an animal in a cage?

Shannon realized she was utterly helpless when Dennis's anger erupted. His physical abuse was cruel and painful, always landing blows across her face and torso until she collapsed to the ground. Dennis was an expert at physical torture and mind games.

Shannon knew it was impossible to win against Dennis. So, what could she expect this time around? Would he severely injure her or even kill her?

Shannon knew that once Dennis's rage began, all she could do was succumb to the physical abuse. Nothing ever changed, and the vicious physical abuse was ongoing. He continued to prevail in each conflict, getting more abusive and manipulative. She realized that this time was her last chance, and if she did not leave this time, she might not have another opportunity or could face greater harm in the future.

In a rage to survive, she used all her strength to push her arms towards her waist, then upward toward his chin, and right to his throat. Dennis barreled backwards, and she grabbed the keys and runs for the open back door. Her vision narrowing, she forced herself onward, driven by her sheer will to escape.

The world outside was dark and silent, but she didn't hesitate. Her body was moving before her mind could catch up, lungs burning, as she stumbled down the steps and into the driveway.

But even as she drifted at the edge of consciousness, something inside Shannon refused to be extinguished. Time blurred while she couldn't distinguish days from hours. Pain and fear clouded her thoughts.

Yet, she continued toward the car with one thought in mind, but to escape this madness and survive, to reach the car and put as much distance between herself and Dennis.

She reached the car, her heart pounding loudly, and quietly started the engine, her hands trembling a little.

Without daring to glance back, she slowly pulled onto the road, eager to reach the freeway. The soothing hum of tires on the damp asphalt and the steady flicker of streetlights blended into a calming, rhythmic glow.

Every muscle in her body was tense, holding onto the steering wheel tightly, as if this action alone could banish the ghosts behind her. She wasn't sure where she was headed, but with every mile she traveled, she felt herself slowly distancing from the life she was leaving behind, embracing the journey ahead.

Shannon sped down the dark freeway, gripped by anxiety. The tires' steady thump kept her focused as she glanced nervously between the road and headlights behind her. Expecting Dennis to appear at any moment, she drove on, alone in the quiet night.

Each passing exit marked another step away from the chaos and another silent vow that she would never let herself be caged again. It felt surreal to be alone and utterly free, the world outside her windshield stretching out with possibility and promise. She inhaled shakily, letting the cool night air from the cracked window fill her lungs, reminding herself with every breath that she had survived.

Eventually, the adrenaline began to fade, replaced by a deep exhaustion and the faint shimmer of hope. Shannon pulled off the freeway at a small gas station, its fluorescent lights casting a reassuring glow. She parked and sat for a moment, letting her forehead rest against the cool steering wheel as silent tears traced down her cheeks. The world was quiet, punctuated only by the distant rumble of trucks and the chirping of insects. She was safe…for now.

Wiping her face, Shannon knew she couldn't stop for long. She collected herself, checked her surroundings, and leaned forward, rejoining the flow of traffic, heading toward the unknown. Every mile put more space between her and Dennis, and with each turn of the wheels, her resolve grew stronger. She didn't know what tomorrow would bring, but as the road unfurled ahead, she promised herself she'd find a way to start again. She looked forward to a life untethered from fear, where hope could take root.

As she merged back onto the highway, this time, Shannon felt the hum of the engine steadying her nerves. The road ahead was cloaked in uncertainty, but each signpost she passed marked a step away from the chaos she'd left behind.

Tentative rays of dawn began to break through the horizon, illuminating the landscape with pale gold. For the first time in a long while, she was alone with her thoughts, free from the constant threat that had haunted her days and nights.

With every passing mile, the ache in her body eased just enough for hope to slip in. Shannon glanced at the empty passenger seat and allowed herself a small, determined smile. She didn't know where she was headed, only that she was moving forward. The world outside her window felt wide and unfamiliar, but also full of possibilities. She prom-ised herself she'd keep driving until she found a place where fear no longer shaped her life, a place where she could breathe freely and let herself imagine happiness once more.

Chapter 2
New Beginnings

In the days that followed, survival became something more than just endurance. It became an act of reclamation.

Each morning, Shannon woke with a shiver of uncertainty. Despite being away from Dennis, fear was drilled deep within her. Every morning, she would wake up with a growing conviction that every small action mattered. Everyone talks about big wins, forgetting the small, everyday things? The things that, if they didn't exist, could change everything.

She learned to savor the mundane moments alone with no one to tell her what to do. The taste of fresh coffee that she brewed for herself, and the stillness of the night without arguments or regrets.

At first, to settle in a world that was beyond Dennis's control felt foreign, almost untrustworthy. She flinched at unfamiliar noises and double-checked every lock, but with each passing day, the shadows receded a little more. She carefully sketched tentative plans, scribbled lists of groceries along with her dreams and aspirations, carefully mapping out a new path forward.

Sometimes, a simple smile from a neighbor or a brief exchange of words at the corner café would steady her nerves. She felt she had finally found a place that gave her a sweet reminder that kindness still lingered in the world.

The corner café seemed right out of a 1950s movie, its nostalgic charm offering a relaxed escape. The atmosphere inside the café wrapped Shannon in a calm embrace, colored by the soft haze of memory rather than the sharpness of the present.

The walls stood adorned with soft, pastel hues, mint green and buttery yellow. The walls were covered from end to end with framed black-and-white photographs of smiling families, classic cars, and bygone downtown scenes. The floor itself had checkerboard tiles stretching from the door to the gleaming chrome counter. The café's vinyl-upholstered booths in cherry red invited patrons to linger, and Formica tables reflected the warm glow of pendant lights overhead.

A vintage jukebox stood in the corner, pulsating with nostalgia, softly playing old standards like Ella Fitzgerald and Frank Sinatra while playing a soft soundtrack that seemed to shimmer in the soft neon glow. The jukebox's melodies mingled with the hum of conversation and the occasional clink of a spoon against a mug, filling the room with echoes of another time.

Behind the counter, a glass display case displayed fresh-baked pies beneath domed covers, and coffee was poured into sturdy ceramic mugs by a barista in a crisp white apron.

There was a tender simplicity in the air, a sense that life had once moved at a quieter, more deliberate pace. The café was a living memory, a haven shaped by the warmth and resilience of people who knew the value of slowing down, cherishing moments, and finding comfort in the ordinary joys of community.

Stepping inside felt like entering another era, where comfort quietly settled into every groove. It was a gentle refuge from the world outside.

The air carried the comforting aroma of ground coffee and warm pastries, mingling with laughter and the low murmur of easy conversation. It was a place where time seemed to slow, where kindness was served alongside each plate, and where the simple pleasures of yesteryear could still be found, one cup at a time.

The room hummed with the easy sociability of another era, an age when conversations unfolded unhurriedly, laughter was carried across booths, and neighbors greeted one another like old friends. Sitting in a cozy corner café, Shannon was lost in her thoughts as she leisurely enjoyed her coffee by the window. Suddenly, a warm and friendly voice gently interrupted her reverie, catching her attention, saying, "Is this seat taken?"

Shannon glanced up and managed to smile. "No, please go ahead." Her voice felt steadier than she expected.

The stranger, a woman with kind eyes, slight stature, and around the age of mid-thirties, with a stack of library books, settled in. "I've seen you here a few times. You always look so... peaceful."

Shannon laughed softly, surprised by the sound. "It's a work in progress. Some days are better than others."

The woman gave a nod, a glimmer of comprehension shining in her eyes. "I'm Maribel. If you ever want company or someone to talk books with, I'm usually around."

Shannon hesitated, then offered her name. "I'm Shannon. Thank you for the offer. That sounds nice."

It felt like an opening, a thread of connection she hadn't expected to find.

Maribel smiled. "Sometimes the right story, or even the right conversation, can change the day. Or sometimes even a life."

Shannon looked out at the city, the morning light brightening the street. "I think I'm ready for a new chapter."

"Aren't we all?" Maribel replied, raising her mug in a silent toast.

For the first time in a long while, Shannon felt the quiet warmth of possibility. Sitting with Maribel, she dared to picture a future where she might belong, where her story could unfold according to her preferred design.

Shannon's wounds, once raw and aching, slowly began to heal beneath the comfort of new routines and supportive friendships. She found solace in the smallest victories.

The city felt different now, a place that once seemed full of shadows and threats, now revealed itself in a new light,

Shannon built a life from the ashes: she enrolled in classes, staying late at the library to study and determined to reclaim her future. Sometimes, the insidious memories of her husband's abuse crept into her head, but Shannon had learned how to cope with these memories and drown out the dark memories with more positive memories.

She reached out to her sister, reestablishing bonds that Dennis had tried to sever.

Shannon dialed her sister's number, her fingers trembling with anticipation. When the call connected, a familiar voice answered, warm and tentative. "Shannon? Is everything okay?"

A relieved smile broke across Shannon's face. "Yeah, I just… I wanted to talk. If you have time."

There was a gentle pause on the other end, then her sister's voice softened. "For you, always. What's on your mind?"

Shannon hesitated, searching for words that felt foreign after so much silence. "I'm trying to find my way back to myself."

Her sister's breath caught audibly. "I've missed you, too. I never blamed you, Shannon. I just wanted you safe."

Tears pricked Shannon's eyes, bittersweet but healing. "I know that now. I'm learning to let go of the guilt he planted in me. I want to be better sisters again, the way we used to be."

"You already are," her sister replied kindly. "We can take it slow. I'm here, whenever you need me."

Shannon closed her eyes, letting the quiet affirmation settle within. For the first time in years, the thread between them felt unbroken and stronger than before.

"Thank you," she murmured, her voice trembling with emotion as newfound hope wove its way through each syllable.

One rainy Saturday, Shannon sat at her kitchen table and wrote herself a letter, reflecting on her journey from fear to hope.

The action felt empowering and powerful, a declaration that her story belonged, at last, to her.

The letter was bold and intimate proclamation that her story was her own. She carefully folded the letter and placed it in a drawer, then stepped out into the silvery light of the rainy afternoon. Her pulse was calm, unwavering. With each inhale, Shannon felt herself moving further from the version of herself Dennis had tried to shape, and ever closer to the future she was now ready to embrace.

Over the years, Dennis's abuse chipped away at Shannon's sense of self until she felt almost unrecognizable to herself. Even so, she pressed onward, determined to break the patterns he had woven into her life.

Though the past haunted her, Shannon pressed forward, determined to break free of the cycles Dennis had imposed on her life.

She poured herself into healing sessions. Some nights she spent in untangling dark memories from her haunting dreams, while other days she spent journaling her thoughts and emotions.

Step by step, she reclaimed lost pieces of herself, forging new identities and daring to dream of a future that wasn't dictated by fear.

Healing became her mission, with long evenings spent unraveling the past in therapy, days powered by a quiet, persistent hope. Little by little, she reclaimed lost fragments of who she was, nurturing new connections and allowing herself to imagine a future not ruled by fear.

The wounds Dennis inflicted ran deep, reverberating through the quiet moments of her days. His cruelty, both blatant and subtle, had left her guarded, constantly reading the world for signs of danger.

Still, Shannon refused to surrender to despair. She found solace in small victories: a warm conversation with her sister, the satisfaction of a finished assignment, a glimpse of a sunrise from her apartment window.

But trauma has a way of lingering, returning with the force of a storm. There were days the memories pressed so close she could barely breathe. Then there were flashbacks of Dennis's anger, the sharp sting of his words, and the pain he inflicted that left her double over, powerless beneath his fury. In those moments, Shannon reminded herself, she had survived. She was not alone.

The city that once felt oppressive slowly revealed its brighter corners. With every courageous step, Shannon built a new life on the ashes of the old, quietly defiant, ready to move forward even as shadows threatened to pull her back. Shannon created a life from the ashes: she enrolled in classes, spending late nights at the library, determined to reclaim her future. She reached out to her sister, rebuilding the bonds Dennis had tried to break.

Shannon's phone buzzed as she settled into the worn armchair by her window. On the screen, her sister's name glowed, Emma; after a moment's hesitation, Shannon answered.

"Hey, Em," Shannon said, her voice soft but steady.

"Shan! I'm so glad you answered. How are you holding up?" Emma's words came in a gentle rush, threaded with concern.

Shannon drew in a breath, glancing at the gray sky outside. "It's… strange. Some days, I feel like I'm finally free, like I can breathe again. Other days, the past just sneaks up on me. But I'm trying. I really am."

Emma paused, her voice quiet. "I can only imagine. But I see how you've become strong. I wish I'd been there more. I wish I'd known."

"You couldn't have known. I didn't want anyone to see, least of all you," Shannon admitted, her voice trembling.

"I'm here now," Emma replied. "And I'm not going anywhere. Whenever you want to talk, vent, or just sit in silence, call me. Or come over. Remember how we used to eat ice cream straight from the tub and watch bad movies?"

Shannon managed a small laugh. "Yeah. I'd like that. I need that."

"You're not alone, Shan. You never were. And you never will be," Emma said, her words a warm tether pulling Shannon back from her own shadows.

"Thank you, Em. For not giving up on me, even when I almost gave up on myself."

Emma's voice softened, thick with emotion. "That's what sisters are for."

The call ended with a new surge of hope. A quiet hope, fragile but real, and a sense of belonging she thought she'd lost forever, gradually silenced the echoes of the past bad memories and filled the spaces in her mind with the promise of healing.

Another chilly afternoon, Shannon found herself on the phone with her sister, the familiar warmth of her voice a lifeline.

"Are you sleeping any better?" her sister asked gently, hesitating just enough to signal genuine concern.

Shannon exhaled, eyes landing on the steam rising from her tea. "Some nights. Others, I lie awake replaying everything, but… It's different now. I feel like I'm not trapped inside those memories anymore."

Her sister was quiet for a moment. "You sound stronger. I can hear it in you."

"Most days I am," Shannon admitted. "But sometimes I still flinch at things that remind me of him. It's exhausting." Her replied, "I know it is. But you're so brave, Shan. You're giving yourself a real chance this time."

Shannon managed to smile, small but true. "I'm trying. I just want to keep moving forward."

"You are. And when it feels impossible, call me. Promise?"

"I promise," Shannon said. The line between them hummed with silence.

Even as trauma lingered, sometimes striking with the force of a storm, Shannon refused to surrender to despair.

On her worst days, she recalled how far she had come. She had survived. She was not alone. Even as trauma lingered, sometimes striking with the force of a storm, Shannon refused to surrender to despair. The city that once seemed oppressive slowly revealed its brighter corners. With every courageous step, Shannon rebuilt her life on the ruins of the past, quietly defiant, always moving forward, even as old shadows threatened to draw her back.

That was two years ago and much has changed.

Shannon finalized her divorce and has become stronger, more independent.

Life continued to test her resilience with relentlessness and challenges: the grief of her brother's tragic death five years ago, and the heartbreak of losing her child in a car accident three years after that. The aftermath of her bitter divorce and the ongoing turmoil caused by Dennis's actions pushed her to the brink. Yet, she held onto a fragile desire that things would improve.

Sometimes, when you can bear no more, life brings unexpected changes. Shannon thought there was room for a new kind of fairytale for adults with surprising turns of fate.

Her divorce from Dennis was bitter. As a former police officer, Dennis was in control and angry, often using his authority and knowledge of the system to dominate and intimidate.

His abuse came in many forms: direct threats, physical harm, and subtle manipulation designed to undermine her confidence. Finally free from the torment of his control, Shannon looked forward to a brighter and more peaceful life.

Yet life has a way of testing resilience, often striking when you feel you can endure no more.

She has found herself grappling with the aftershocks of her bitter divorce and the fallout from her ex-husband's relentless actions.

Each new challenge pushed her further into a spiral of despair, yet Shannon clung to a fragile hope that things would improve after the divorce. Shannon sat at the small kitchen table, her hands trembling around a chipped mug of coffee.

The silence pressed in until her friend, Maribel, finally broke it. "Have you heard from him again?" Maribel asked quietly, her eyes flickering to the pile of unopened mail on the counter.

Shannon let out a shaky breath. "There was another letter yesterday. No return address, just like before. I didn't even open it. I just... I can't keep doing this, Maribel."

Maribel reached across the table, squeezing Shannon's hand. "You know it's him, don't you? These threats, the way things go missing in your house. Dennis is still trying to control you."

"I know," Shannon whispered, her voice brittle. "Even after everything, he's still there. Lurking in the corners of my head. I thought that when the divorce was final, when I walked away, I'd finally be free. But it's like he's everywhere and nowhere all at once."

Maribel's jaw tightened. "You need to go to the police or contact some of your old friends on the force."

"No! Dennis's friends will be there too. Not a good idea."

Shannon shook her head. "He knows too much. He taught me how easy it is to manipulate the system, how to leave no trace. I won't let him win, but I'm not sure how to fight someone who lives in the shadows."

The two women sat in heavy silence, the air thick with unspoken fears. Outside, a car engine idled, its sound lingering a little too long before fading down the street.

When you think you can no longer take any more disappointments in life, something happens from some magical place to change everything. And you can believe in adult fairytales with some surprising twists of fate.

It was a bitter divorce, and Dennis, her ex-husband, was a controlling, angry, narcissistic ex-cop.

Shannon's fingers twisted in her lap. "Dennis, he's not the kind of man who lets go. He's angry, controlling… years on the force only taught him how to hide it better."

Maribel looked at her, concern flickering in her eyes. "You're talking about Dennis? The ex-police officer? "Shannon nodded, voice trembling. "He always needed control. Even now, it's like he's everywhere, watching. I can't ever fully escape him."

Maribel's jaw set in determination. "You don't have to face this alone, Shannon. We'll find a way."

Shannon said, "He often used sadistic means to control her and get his way. A real jerk who often used his authoritative demeanor and familiarity with systems of power to exert dominance over others." Shannon's voice was shaky, but resolute. "He always finds a way to twist things, Maribel. Sometimes it isn't what he says, but what he does. He is cruel in ways most people wouldn't imagine."

Maribel's eyes narrowed. "Like what? What does he do?"

"He manipulated situations by leveraging his knowledge of laws and procedures by creating an aura of intimidation that leaves little room for opposition. This control could manifest in both overt and subtle ways. Though his style was direct threats, imposing physical harm, and sometimes he used passive-aggressive behaviors designed to undermine confidence." Shannon released a shaky breath, her voice scarcely above a whisper. "What a nightmare he was Maribel. Sometimes I still can't believe I'm free from him."

"In Dennis' personal relationships, he would frequently demand compliance, insisting that his decisions are unquestionable while dismissing the opinions and autonomy of others. Gaslighting could often be a tool he used, making the victim doubt their perceptions or feelings. Moreover, his skills in reading people and situations could be weaponized by being able to identify their vulnerabilities and exploiting them to maintain control for his evil purposes and selfish enjoyment. Outside of his relationships, he acted with a sense of superiority in social or professional settings, using his background to silence, dissent, or impose his will. He relied on surveillance tactics, such as monitoring communication or movements, to keep others in a state of unease. His behavior often stemmed from a deep-seated desire to retain the authority and control he once held in his professional life. You must understand, Maribel, that Dennis's anger was like a storm that never truly dissipated, always hovering on the horizon, ready to erupt without warning." Shannon drew in a shaky breath; her eyes clouded with memories. "His anger was like a storm, Maribel. Even when things seemed calm, I always knew it could break loose without warning."

Maribel's voice was gentle but probing. "Was it always like that? Did you ever feel safe?"

Shannon shook her head slowly. "Never. It was always there, waiting. I'd try to guess his mood, but it never made a difference. One wrong word, one misstep, and suddenly he'd snap. I lived every day on edge, afraid of when the next outburst would come."

Shannon had learned to read the shift in his demeanor. The twitch of his jaw, the narrowing of his eyes, and the way he would close a door with too much force would all alert her to his mood and her safety. These were the harbingers of a tempest she had no power to thwart. His rage was an entity, consuming the air in the room and leaving her gasping for breath, for sanity, and some semblance of safety.

Sometimes, his fury would manifest in words that pierced deeper than any physical blow. Shannon's voice quivered as she spoke, "Sometimes, his fury would come out in words sharper than any slap."

Maribel looked at her, concern etched in her eyes. "What would he say to you?" A shadow flickered across Shannon's face. "He knew exactly how to make me feel small, to twist my own thoughts against me. Sometimes, the words hurt even more than the rest."

The sharp, venomous accusations would come at her like a flood, each one designed to strip away her confidence, her sense of worth, her very humanity. Shannon swallowed, her voice barely above a whisper. "The accusations would come all at once," she said, her hands trembling in her lap. "He'd look me straight in the eye and speak things that made me question my own worth, my own sanity."

Maribel leaned in, concern in her gaze. "What kinds of things did he say?"

A bitter smile flickered on Shannon's lips. "*'You're the reason everything's gone wrong,'* He would say. *'If it weren't for you, none of this would have happened.'* Each word felt like it was meant to tear me down, piece by piece."

Maribel shook her head, her voice gentle. "That must have been so hard, Shannon."

"Especially when we lost our child. He blamed me." Shannon's eyes distant. "It stripped me of my confidence and made me feel like I was nothing. He knew exactly how to make me feel small. You're worthless. You ruined everything, you piece of shit." He would spit out, directing his anger toward me.

Shannon would stand frozen, her mind desperately searching for a way to defuse the situation, though she knew from experience that nothing she did could placate him once the storm had begun.

Maribel reached across the table, her voice low. "Shannon, nobody deserves to be spoken to like that. Did you ever try to tell anyone what was happening?"

Shannon hesitated, her fingers tightening around her mug. "I tried, once. But people didn't want to see it. They'd say, *'He seems like such a good man,'* or *'You must be exaggerating.'* After a while, I stopped even trying to explain."

Maribel's eyes flashed with anger on Shannon's behalf. "You were isolated."

"Completely," Shannon admitted, her expression bleak. "It was as if I was screaming in a soundproof room. I lost track of who I was."

Maribel nodded. "But you're here now. You're safe. That counts for something."

A shaky laugh escaped Shannon. "Safe is a relative word. Some days, I still feel like I'm looking over my shoulder."

Maribel squeezed her hand, silent but steadfast beside her as the memories pressed in, dark and heavy. He was angry at her for losing his job on the Phoenix Police force and for them to lose their home. Shannon drew in a trembling breath; her eyes fixed on her mug.

Maribel's brow furrowed with concern. "He told you it was your fault?"

Shannon nodded quietly. "Every chance he got. It was always something I'd done wrong, some reason he had to remind me I'd ruined his life."

The anger was always directed at Shannon, and was mostly violent outbursts and physical abuse, as well as emotional and psychological abuse.

Dennis's fury was an unrelenting tide, crashing over Shannon without pause. His accusations haunted her thoughts. Everything was directed at her. Each accusation came laced with venom, each violent outburst carving deeper into the fragile remnants of her spirit. His rage was a storm she could never escape, and Shannon felt as though she was trapped in an eternal night, with no dawn in sight.

Maribel's voice was gentle but insistent. "Shannon, you know none of this was your fault, right? No matter what he said, what he did. It was never on you."

Shannon managed a hollow shrug. "I want to believe that. Sometimes, I almost do. But then... something happens. Like last week, I found the window in the back room cracked open. I know I locked it." Her words trembled, dissolving into a nervous laugh.

Maribel squeezed her hand tighter. "You're not imagining things, Shannon. Has anything else happened?"

Shannon paused, swallowing hard. "Letters. Anonymous ones. They started after the divorce. Just a few words here and there, nothing direct, but enough to keep me up at night. And sometimes, I see cars parked outside. Not neighbors. I can feel them watching. It's like I can't ever let my guard down."

Maribel's eyes darkened with worry. "Did you call the police?"

Shannon nodded. "They made a report, but there's never any proof. Dennis knows how to be invisible. He's always been good at hiding in plain sight."

A silence settled between them, heavy and unspoken. Maribel finally spoke, "You don't have to keep doing this alone. It's time to stand up to him, Shannon. To make sure he knows you're not afraid anymore."

Shannon glanced out the window; the lines of her face etched with exhaustion and defiance. "I'm tired of running, Mare. I just want to live. I want to walk in my own garden without looking over my shoulder."

Maribel offered a small, encouraging smile. "Then let's start there. One step at a time. You're not alone. Not anymore."

A faint glimmer of hope flickered in Shannon's eyes as she nodded resolutely. "No more running," she whispered. "It ends now."

Strange occurrences without explanations were happening. Cars she didn't recognize would linger near her home, their presence a silent reminder that she was being watched. Items in her house would occasionally be moved, leaving behind subtle signs of intrusion that left her questioning her sanity. The feeling of being hunted grew unmistakable, casting a shadow over every small victory she had achieved in rebuilding her life.

Determined to protect herself, Shannon made the painful decision to uproot her existence repeatedly, moving from one house to another in various neighborhoods to shake off the looming presence of Dennis or whoever might be behind the threats.

But no matter how far she fled, the fear followed her, like an unwelcome phantom refusing to be exorcized.

Despite her efforts and the occasional police investigation, no definitive evidence surfaced to pinpoint Dennis or anyone else as the culprit.

***

Shannon sat across from the detective, her hands clenched in her lap. The sterile office hummed with fluorescent light, while Detective Alvarez glanced up from the folder, the lines around their eyes suggesting both fatigue and skepticism. "Shannon, you said the car was parked on your street for three nights in a row. "Shannon nodded, her voice raw.

"Yes. The same dark sedan. No plates that I could see. And last night, someone moved my gardening tools. It's not the first time."

Alvarez scribbled a note. "You're sure nothing was taken?" Nothing's missing, just...moved. It's like someone wants me to know they've been inside," she said, her throat dry. "And the letters, they keep coming. I gave you all of them."

The detective hesitated, then offered a practiced, reassuring tone. "We take these reports seriously. But without a suspect or witnesses, our options are limited." Shannon's composure wavered. "You don't understand. This isn't just random harassment. Dennis, my ex-husband, has done this before. He thrives on making me feel unsafe."

Alvarez closed the folder gently. "We are monitoring your neighborhood, and we've increased patrols. We'll also request a review of nearby traffic cameras." Their gaze softened. "But if you remember any new detail, no matter how small, please call me directly." Ms. Sullivan.

Shannon looked down at the business card, Alvarez pushed across the table, the weight of her isolation pressing in again. "I just want it to stop," she whispered. "We're doing everything we can," the detective replied, "but stay vigilant. Sometimes, the smallest details can break a case."

Shannon nodded, but as she left the precinct, the answers still seemed as distant as ever.

Shannon learned to adapt, becoming hyper-vigilant, locking doors twice, keeping curtains drawn, and memorizing the patterns of her surroundings.

Yet, amid this relentless game of cat and mouse, she began to realize that running was no longer enough; it was time to confront the ghosts of her past rather than merely evading their reach.

The turning point came one evening in her garden, a space she had claimed as her sanctuary. As dusk settled, Shannon noticed a movement in the shadows, a fleeting figure retreating into the tree line. Her heart raced, but instead of succumbing to the panic that had governed her actions for so long, she resolved that this was where the running ended.

In that moment, Shannon decided to reclaim her life not as a victim, but as someone ready to fight back against the forces seeking to break her.

No longer defined by survival alone, Shannon began crafting a path toward thriving, a fierce defiance of those who sought to keep her shackled by fear. She would no longer let Dennis, or the specter of his threats, dictate the terms of her life. It was a resolution born of courage, determination, and the painful lessons she had inherited and endured. Shannon was ready to rewrite her story on her own terms.

Shannon stopped expecting her life to be peaceful and tranquil, while she felt like she was walking on eggshells to please others.

Her father had the same temperament, and he kept a tight ship when it came to his family. This is where Shannon learned that to survive; she needed to be quiet and please others.

Dennis's abuse was multifaceted, a harrowing combination of physical violence, emotional manipulation, and psychological warfare. The physical abuse left Shannon with more than just bruises; it carried the deeper, invisible scars of fear and powerlessness that lingered long after the wounds healed. His violent outbursts were unpredictable, making Shannon feel as though she was constantly walking a tightrope, fearing that the smallest misstep could lead to yet another storm of rage.

But what Shannon didn't realize was that her persistent unease wasn't just a phantom of her trauma. Dennis's threats were real and not empty words spoken in anger.

Fearing for her safety, Shannon made the heartbreaking decision to uproot her life and move repeatedly, leaving behind the fragile comfort she had begun to rebuild. The police were of little help, their investigations yielding no solid leads, and their reassurances ringing hollow in her ears.

Dennis, cunning as ever, knew how to slip through cracks in the system, staying just out of reach while making her feel perpetually hunted. She had to adapt, becoming her own protector in a game of shadows where the stakes became her life.

But the real twist came late one evening, as Shannon stood in her garden, relishing the solitude she had fought so hard to reclaim. As twilight deepened in her garden, Shannon stood alone, alert to every sound. Suddenly, a branch snapped in the shadows. Her pulse quickened. "Who's there?" she called, her voice steady despite the tremor in her chest. A pause hung in the air, thick with tension. Then, a figure melted further into the darkness. No answer, only the rustle of leaves.

Shannon's jaw clenched. "I'm not running anymore," she said aloud, voice stronger this time, as if daring the darkness to answer. "You don't get to decide how my story ends."

The night was silent, and Shannon experienced an internal change, developing a sense of determination.

Here, in the soil she had nurtured and claimed as her sanctuary, Shannon resolved to make her stand.

She whispered, "This ends here. I will not let fear rule me any longer."

The breeze moved, dispersing her words, but resulting in a strong resolve for the woman who chose not to be affected by the past.

She first thought the soft rustle was just the wind but soon spotted a shadowy figure by the tree line. Her heart was clenched as she froze, the realization dawning on her that she was not as alone as she had believed. That night, Shannon resolved that running would no longer define her story. She now had the opportunity to reconstruct her life, not merely as a survivor, but as an individual prepared to address the longstanding challenges she faced just as her mother had done in confronting her father.

Shannon often reflected on the parallels between her own life and her mother's, finding an unsettling familiarity in how they had both endured abuse in silence. Shannon saw now that her mother's quiet endurance of her father's harshness was not strength, but a means to survive under his anger and control.

As a child, Shannon watched her mother tread carefully around her father to avoid his anger, a survival strategy

Shannon later brought into her marriage with Dennis. Like her mother, she had learned to appease, to endure, and to shrink herself in the face of another's dominance, believing it was the only way to preserve what little stability she had.

It wasn't until Shannon found herself trapped in the same patterns, repeating the cycles of fear and submission, that she truly saw her mother's silent suffering mirrored in her own. The realization was both painful and liberating. Shannon knew she could no longer follow the same path. Her mother's story was a warning she endured but never truly lived, showing the price of surviving without facing reality.

And so, as she stood in her garden that fateful evening, Shannon resolved to break the chain, to redefine what strength meant for herself. She would honor her mother not by making her sacrifices but by carving a new narrative. One where her survival was no longer enough, and thriving became the ultimate act of defiance.

Her schedule was composed of morning walks, evening reading sessions, and extensive time spent in her garden. For Shannon, life had not always been peaceful.

Shannon's life had always been a careful balancing act, orchestrated to appear steady even when turbulence churned underneath. After leaving her position at the hospital and her marriage, she had managed to construct a new, quieter life, a world defined by routines, familiar faces, and a garden that served as both sanctuary and metaphor for her rebuilding.

For Shannon, solitude was not merely an absence of others; it became the canvas upon which she painted the contours of her reclaimed life. It defined her world in profound ways, shaping her sense of identity, resilience, and peace in the aftermath of her turbulent past. Solitude was her sanctuary, a space untainted by judgment or fear, where she could lay bare her emotions and shift through the fragments of her soul. It offered her the silence necessary to confront the shadows of her past while nurturing the seeds of healing and self-discovery. This quiet retreat allowed her to untangle the complexities of her experiences, transforming moments of pain into threads of strength.

Her solitude was not without its complexities. It carried the weight of lingering ache, a reminder of desires unfulfilled and risks untaken. It was both a refuge and a challenge, an invitation to find strength in independence while grappling with the yearning for companionship she had long buried. It defined her world as one of introspection and quiet triumph tapestry of peace woven with threads of resilience, self-care, and the occasional pang of longing.

Solitude, for Shannon, was never simply an absence of others. It was an intentional reclamation of her own space, a quiet act of courage in the face of her past trials. It had become evidence of her resilience, a sanctuary she had built for herself, brick by careful brick.

Chapter 3
The Pedestal

Now Shannon had an opportunity to break out of her solitude and meet new people. But she was not sure if she was ready for this bold move.

The invitation sat on her kitchen counter for days, a glossy reminder of the life she once knew. She had come close to discarding it multiple times, convincing herself there was no point in clinging to a past that had already moved way past her… without her.

And yet, something held her back.

It was nostalgia. A need to prove to herself that she had truly healed. Or it was the faint hope that stepping into that world again might offer unexpected closure, or a new sense of direction.

Attending the event wasn't an easy decision for Shannon. She hesitated. She had become adept at finding reasons to decline, but this time, she couldn't justify the excuses. Not to herself. Not now.

She pulled an old dress from the dark shadows of her closet. The fabric of the dress whispered to her of her past life and a bold, unspoken challenge yet to come.

But then the invitation arrived, a gala fundraiser hosted by the hospital where she had once served as an administrator.

Her initial instinct was to decline. To push the glossy card aside as another relic of a past life she had left behind.

Yet, something stirred within her faint whisper, reminding her of the possibility of connection. She thought that one evening spent among others could reopen doors to a part of herself she had long kept locked away.

Stepping into the elaborately decorated hall, Shannon felt the weight of the past tugging at her edges. The bittersweet familiarity of a world she had left behind. But yet it has somehow followed, and she stood at the doorstep of her very own past.

She made her way through the crowd with practiced grace, exchanging polite smiles and nodding to former colleagues, but keeping her distance as if threading through a maze she wasn't quite ready to solve.

Shannon did not intend to pursue another romantic relationship. Following considerable personal recovery and reflection over the years, she had found solace in quiet contemplation and the stability of her routines. She had lost too much in love. The risk was too high for her to take a chance again.

Shannon lingered at the edge of the ballroom, her fingers tracing the rim of her glass, eyes scanning the glimmering crowd with practiced detachment.

A man approached with easy confidence in his stride. "You look like someone who's seen dozens of these events," he said, offering a tentative smile. Her mask had worked. "Found any secrets to surviving them?"

Shannon glanced up, surprised by the warmth in his tone. "I've learned that people-watching is an art form," she replied, her lips curving in a cautious smile. "And that the canapés always taste better than the speeches."

He chuckled, the sound low and genuine. "I'll keep that in mind. I'm Scott, by the way."

"Shannon." She extended her hand, steady yet reserved.

For a moment, they stood together, the noise of the gala receding. Scott broke the silence.

"What brought you here tonight, if you don't mind my asking?"

She hesitated, then shrugged. "Curiosity, I suppose. A chance to see if the world had changed or if I had."

"I think sometimes it just takes one night to tell," Scott said softly.

Shannon met his gaze, a flicker of something unguarded passing between them. "Maybe tonight is the *one night* that will surprise both of us."

Scott smiled, his eyes reflecting a kindred hope. "I'd like that."

And so, amid the swirl of laughter and music, their conversation unfolded, tentative, honest, and alive with the fresh promise of something new about to bloom.

Scott was a polished, articulate, retired chief of surgery who wore his confidence like a tailored suit. He said he came from a small Midwest hospital where he was the chief of surgery and decision maker for all the nurses. He was now the chief of surgery for one of the largest Phoenix hospitals and one of the largest organ donor hospitals in Arizona.

They talked extensively about their history and goals, and she thought he saw who she was. *Or so she thought.*

From the moment they met, there seemed to be an instant connection. The attraction was mutual, showing clear chemistry.

Scott's instant attraction to Shannon wasn't rooted in superficialities or fleeting charms; it was something far deeper, something that resonated with the man he had become after years of navigating the demanding corridors of hospitals and the complexities of life.

In Shannon, he found a quiet strength that mirrored his own strength, forged not in loud declarations but in the quiet resilience of someone who had faced life's cruelties and learned to rise above them.

Her poise captivated him immediately. It wasn't the kind of elegance that drew attention to itself but rather the understated grace of someone who had found beauty in survival.

Shannon's demeanor, a blend of composure and vulnerability, spoke to Scott's yearning for authenticity, an unguarded connection in a world where facades were the norm.

Her smile, while warm, carried a trace of guardedness that hinted at stories untold. It was a kind of complexity that intrigued him to know her more rather than repelled him away from her.

But more than anything, it was her presence, a calm yet commanding aura that filled the room without the need for fanfare.

To Scott, Shannon represented a balance he had long sought: depth without pretension, strength without aggression, and a sense of self so deeply rooted that it invited rather than demanded attention. It was as though, in meeting her, he had glimpsed a reflection of his own hopes of finding someone who could truly see him, beyond the titles and achievements, and meet him in a place of mutual honesty.

As the evening unfolded, the gala seemed to shrink from its grandeur, becoming just a simple backdrop to the unfolding connection between Shannon and Scott.

Their conversation, which began with light humor and observations about the event, soon deepened. Scott's gentle yet inquisitive manner coaxed Shannon to reveal fragments of herself she hadn't intended to share, her thoughts on resilience, the quiet victories she found in her garden, and the way she had learned to appreciate moments of stillness.

Scott glanced at the painting behind Shannon, then back into her eyes. "Do you ever think art imitates life, or is it just wishful thinking on the artist's part?"

Shannon smiled, amused by the question. "The best art reminds us of what we've survived. Sometimes it's personal. And sometimes it's just a beautiful chaos."

Scott nodded, his expression softening. "Beautiful chaos," he repeated her words, "I like that. I suppose that's what Life can feel like that, too. Less structure, and more… possibility."

She chuckled. "I imagine it takes courage to step into that kind of freedom."

He tilted his head, considering. "Sometimes. Other times, it feels like I'm wandering through a garden I didn't plant, hoping I'll recognize something familiar."

Shannon's gaze lingered on him, "And have you found anything worth keeping, so far?"

Scott's lips curved into a gentle smile. "Tonight, I have. What about you? Do you tend to your own garden?"

She looked away for a moment, the flicker of vulnerability passing through her smile.

"Every day. Some days I find flowers. Other days, it's just thorns. Sometimes both together. Even the thorns teach me something."

He met her honesty with his own. "I respect that. Most people hide the thorns."

Shannon shrugged lightly. "Maybe that's why I notice someone who doesn't."

Their laughter, subtle and sincere, mingled with the music. For a moment, the world outside their conversation faded, leaving only the warmth of connection and the gentle unfolding of trust.

Scott, in turn, shared glimpses of his own journey, the toll of years spent in operating rooms, the weight of decisions measured in lives saved or lost, and the hollow spaces retirement had yet to fill.

Scott glanced down, tracing the rim of his glass. "You know, I spent years in operating rooms, chasing precision. Sometimes I consider that retirement could bring a sense of ease, although there remain aspects of life that are unfinished."

Shannon's eyes softened, curiosity and understanding mingling in her gaze. "Is it the decisions you miss, or the certainty?"

He considered this, then shook his head gently. "Neither, really. It's the moments in between the quiet after a life is saved or lost, when you must face yourself. Those are heavier than I expected."

She nodded, letting a silence settle, comfortable and real. "We all carry those spaces. It's what we choose to do with them that matters."

Scott offered a small, grateful smile. "And sometimes, it helps to talk to someone who understands."

His genuine vulnerability struck a chord with Shannon, drawing her to his depths as he explored hers.

Scott, on the other hand, had emerged from decades of a demanding career, his life defined by precision and control. Yet beneath his polished demeanor lay a yearning, a quiet desire to reconnect with something genuine, something unguarded.

A pause lingered between them, charged with honesty just shared. Scott broke it first, voice gentle, "Do you ever wonder how different life might be if we could set down those burdens, just for a while?"

Shannon's lips curved in a wistful smile, "Maybe. But our burdens shape us as much as our joys do. The trick is not letting them weigh us down so much that we forget the lighter parts."

He nodded, eyes tracing the lines of her face with newfound admiration. "You seem to manage that balance. How?"

She tilted her head, considering. "I plant things literally and figuratively. In my garden, in conversations, in small moments of kindness. It's not always enough, but it helps me remember there's new growth after hard seasons."

Scott let out a soft chuckle. "I like that. I could use a bit more planting, myself."

Shannon met his eyes with kindness. "You already are just being here and talking matters, more than you realize."

Their words hung in the soft hush of the evening, a promise of understanding quietly taking root between them. When their eyes first met across the crowded gala hall, Shannon felt a flicker of something unfamiliar a curiosity, a quiet pull toward this man whose presence seemed both commanding and inviting.

Scott, equally intrigued, noticed her poised yet understated elegance, the way she navigated the room with a grace that belied the weight she had carried. It wasn't a love-at-first-sight moment, but rather the beginning of a subtle dance, an unspoken dialogue that would unfold in layers neither of them anticipated.

Scott approached her not with grand gestures but with sincerity, his words carefully chosen to complement rather than overwhelm. "You look like the kind of person who appreciates a good story," he remarked, his tone light but not flippant.

Shannon, slightly caught off guard but warmed by his approach, replied with a smile that carried a trace of her guarded heart. "Well, that depends on the storyteller," she had said, a touch of playfulness in her voice.

Shannon leaned in slightly, "I've always preferred stories you earn, rather than the ones you buy."

Scott, the best stories are the ones that unfold when you least expect them. Like this conversation.

Shannon warned him she was a tough critic.

Scott, replied, he would do his best to rise to the occasion.

Shannon, "Why did you come tonight, Scott? Are you an art lover, or just here for the spectacle?"

Scott, "A bit of both, I suppose. I appreciate art, but I was hoping for something unexpected. And you?"

Shannon: I came for the cause, but I stayed for the company.

Scott replied, "That's the best reason I've heard all night.

Shannon laughed, "You're good at this making people feel at ease.

Scott said, "Years in the operating room teach you the value of steady hands and calm words. But this—talking to you—feels different. Easier, somehow".

Shannon, remarked," I think that's because we're both still learning how to let go of what we can't control."

Scott looked into her eyes saying, that was the real story tonight.

Their laughter mingles with the distant hum of the gala, and for a moment, the world beyond their conversation fades into the background.

It was the kind of interaction that could have ended there a fleeting moment in a sea of social formalities.

But for Scott, there was something in Shannon's response that sparked a deeper interest. And for Shannon, Scott's confidence didn't feel like bravado; it felt earned, layered with experiences she didn't yet know but wanted to understand.

Their first real conversation wasn't about themselves but rather about the world around them. The art auction happening at the gala, the thematic elements of the night's decor, and the absurdity of certain bids. Their laughter attracted attention from others, but neither appeared to notice as they continued their conversation.

It was when Shannon realized she had barely touched her dessert that she understood how captivated she had been.

Scott's approach to Shannon was deliberate yet unhurried. He didn't rush to impress her with grand declarations or flashy anecdotes. Instead, he listened, truly listened to her. At the end of the evening, Shannon found herself offering Scott her number, a gesture of that surprised her more than it did him. Their connection was steady, like a thread weaving through the fabric of their lives.

Their first coffee date revealed layers of mutual curiosity, Scott sharing anecdotes from his years in surgery, Shannon opening up about her journey toward self-reclamation. Each word exchanged felt like a steppingstone, leading them to places they hadn't ventured alone.

Shannon asked, "Do you ever wonder if this whatever we have might be more than coincidence?"

Scott replied, "Sometimes I do. Sometimes it feels like there's a current running between us, something I can't quite explain."

Shannon, "You mean chemistry?"

Scott, "Exactly. Not the kind you read about in romance novels, but something quieter. Like the way you laugh, and I can't help but join in, even on my worst days."

Shannon, "Or how do you somehow remember all the little things I mention, even when I barely remember saying them."

Scott, "It's strange, isn't it? How comfortable it feels. As if we've skipped a few steps and landed in the middle of something real."

Shannon, "It's not always easy, though. There's this tension, like we're both holding back, afraid the spell might break."

Scott, "Maybe that's what chemistry really is knowing there's risk but wanting to see what happens anyway."

Shannon, "I like that idea. That we're both here, willing to find out."

Scott, "Then, whatever this is, let's not rush it. Let's see."

To him, she was a mystery, one he felt compelled to understand. Not conquer. It was this very complexity that drew him closer.

For a man like Scott, who had spent his life in the pursuit of precision and control, Shannon represented the very thing he hadn't realized he was missing: a connection that felt unforced, genuine, and refreshingly real.

As the days turned into weeks, their connection deepened in ways neither had anticipated.

Twice a day, like clockwork, Scott found himself compelled to reach out to Shannon once in the morning, as the world stirred awake, and again in the evening, when the day had settled into a quieter rhythm. Their calls became a ritual, an unspoken agreement that linked their lives in small but significant ways.

For Scott, these moments of contact were more than idle conversation; they were a lifeline to something that felt startlingly rare and refreshingly genuine.

He found himself drawn not only to Shannon's perspective on life and her capacity for hope but also to the way she listened, truly listened, in a way that made him feel understood without judgment. Her voice carried warmth that lingered, a quiet reassurance that reminded him he wasn't navigating the complexities of life alone.

"Twice a day," Scott mused on the phone one evening, his voice carrying a gentle warmth. "I find myself waiting for our calls, Shannon. It's as if my mornings and evenings are missing something if I don't hear from you."

Shannon laughed softly, the sound brightening Scott's quiet living room. "You make it sound as if I'm your daily dose of medicine," she teased. "But I'll admit, I've started looking forward to these moments too. Feels less like routine, more like… comfort."

Scott let the silence linger, savoring the subtle intimacy. "It's more than comfort," he said quietly. "I never thought a conversation could feel this genuine. You listen in a way that makes me feel understood even when I feel I'm not making much sense."

"I know what you mean," Shannon replied. "Sometimes I think I've spent so much time listening to others, I forgot how much I needed someone to really hear me. I guess we're both learning to let someone in… again."

Scott smiled, picturing the way Shannon's words always seemed to wrap around him like a soft blanket. "You've got a way of making the world less complicated, you know? Just by being yourself."

Shannon's voice softened. "That's the trick. Letting things be simple. Letting life's beauty find us in the quiet moments."

Their conversation drifted, easy and unhurried, each word weaving another thread in the fabric of their quiet connection. It wasn't just Shannon's stories of nurturing her garden or her reflections on the simple joys she had reclaimed that captivated him. It was the unspoken understanding they shared, the alignment of values and dreams that bridged the spaces between their worlds. She had a way of grounding him, of reminding him that life's beauty often lies in its quieter moments.

Each call became a touchpoint, a brief yet meaningful escape from the solitude that had settled into Scott's post-retirement days. It wasn't just Shannon's stories of nurturing her garden or her reflections on the simple joys she had reclaimed that captivated him; it was the unspoken understanding they shared, the alignment of values and dreams that bridged the spaces between their worlds. She had a way of grounding him, of reminding him that life's beauty often lay in its quieter moments.

For Shannon, the regularity of Scott's calls initially felt almost disarming, yet she quickly grew to cherish them. His voice carried an ease that put her at peace, his curiosity about her day, and an echo of the care she had long stopped expecting from others.

What struck her most was his consistency, a man who, despite a career spent in the unpredictable chaos of surgery, now sought stability in the smallest gestures of connection.

And while she hadn't expected to let her guard down so quickly, she found herself looking forward to those moments of shared laughter and mutual exploration, as if they were stitching together a bond she hadn't dared to hope for in others.

Together, their conversations wove a quiet intimacy, each call a new layer in the tapestry of a relationship that was becoming as natural as it was transformative.

Scott, "Do you ever wonder how something as simple as a phone call can change the course of your day?"

Shannon, "More than I used to. It's like… each time we talk, the day feels a little lighter. Sometimes I catch myself waiting for the next call."

Scott, chuckled "I know the feeling. There's comfort to it. Like finding a rhythm during all the noise."

Shannon, "I didn't think I'd open up again, but with you, it feels different. I want to continue where things ended before, not start over."

Scott, "We're just old enough to appreciate what matters, and brave enough to reach for it."

Shannon smiled, "I like that. Brave enough to reach for it."

Scott, "So, should we make a pact? Twice a day, no matter what, we check in. Even if it's just to say hello."

Shannon, "Deal. But only if you promise to tell me the best part of your day each time."

"Only if you promise the same."

"It's a deal, Scott."

"Then I guess we're in this together."

Scott, in turn, shared glimpses of his own journey, the toll of years spent in operating rooms, the weight of decisions measured in lives saved or lost, and the hollow spaces retirement had yet to fill. His words carried a vulnerability that resonated with Shannon, not because they were heavy, but because they were authentic. She found herself drawn to layers of him, much like he was discovering her layers.

Scott, on the other hand, had emerged from decades of a demanding career, his life defined by precision and control. Yet beneath his polished demeanor lay a yearning, a quiet desire to reconnect with something genuine, something unguarded.

It was as though, in Shannon's presence, he could finally loosen the armor he'd worn for decades, allowing comfortable silences to fill the spaces between their sentences.

In those unhurried pauses, he noticed the effortless clarity of her laughter and the way her gaze lingered on him, as if searching his face for a half-remembered story they might have once shared.

With each exchange, Scott felt something within him begin to thaw, an unfamiliar warmth, quiet but insistent, reminding him that, perhaps, it wasn't too late to rediscover the kind of joy that comes not from accomplishment, but from simple, honest connection.

Scott's approach to Shannon was deliberate yet unhurried. He didn't rush to impress her with grand declarations or flashy anecdotes.

Instead, he listened, truly listened to her words.

Shannon felt it in the way her pulse quickened whenever he entered the room. It wasn't just his polished exterior or the quiet authority in his voice; it was the way he drew her out of her fortress of solitude, coaxing her into conversations that sparkled with wit and depth.

For Shannon, chemistry involved not only physical but also intellectual aspects, leading her to consider the possibility of renewed emotional connections.

For Scott, chemistry was equally compelling, but it manifested differently. He admired Shannon's resilience, her unspoken strength that shone through her vulnerability. He found himself captivated by her laughter, which broke through the layers of sophistication he had carefully cultivated. Shannon wasn't like the other women he had known she was tender yet fierce, intelligent yet unpretentious.

It was this paradox, this balance of contradictions, which kept him coming back to her, week after week, despite his reservations. Yet, for all their mutual attraction, their chemistry carried a tension, an undercurrent of unspoken truths.

Shannon longed for the kind of intimacy that would confirm Scott's feelings, to dissolve the invisible wall between them. Scott, burdened by his past and the lingering effects of his surgeries, felt the pull of connection but hesitated to let it deepen.

Their chemistry, vibrant and raw, was both a gift and a challenging undeniable force that could either bridge the gap between them or expose the cracks in their fragile bond.

Their chemistry was not the kind that blazed uncontrollably, burning bright and fast. Instead, it was a slow, mesmerizing fire, glowing steadily, illuminating corners of themselves they hadn't dared to explore for years. It was in the way their conversations spiraled into the early hours, each word unraveling layers of their past, their hopes, their hesitations.

For Shannon, there was a thrill in discovering that Scott's confident exterior masked uncertainties and dreams as fragile as her own.

Scott found Shannon's genuine honesty and her unwillingness to hide her true self to be a rare and captivating authenticity.

Their connection went beyond words. It was the way Shannon instinctively reached for Scott's arm during a moment of shared laughter. It was the slight pause before Scott answered her questions, as if he measured each response to honor her curiosity.

Even in silence, they communicated a glance across the table at a crowded restaurant, the shared amusement watching a waiter fumble a tray, the mutual understanding that there was something extraordinary simmering between them.

Shannon couldn't help but marvel at the synchronicities that seemed to pulse through their every interaction. Scott remembered her favorite wine, surprising her at dinner with a chilled bottle of Sauvignon Blanc.

She, in turn, noticed how he always preferred sitting by the window, soaking in the view. These gestures, though subtle, built a bridge of mutual attentiveness, one gesture at a time.

Even their disagreements served to strengthen their bond.

When Shannon questioned Scott's philosophical ideas, he continued the discussion and listened as her viewpoints added to his own.

Scott: "You know, I never expected anyone to push back on my theories about free will quite so eloquently."

Shannon, "Well, someone has to keep you honest. Besides, it's fun watching you rethink your conclusions."

Scott, "You call this fun? Most people would call this an argument."

Shannon, "Only if you're afraid of a little intellectual sparring. I prefer to think of it as… mutual growth."

"You make a compelling case, counselor. That's why I look forward to these debates as much as I do to our quiet moments."

"That's because you know I'll challenge you and still bring you coffee afterward."

"Exactly. And I wouldn't trade that balance for anything."

The friction was exhilarating, their ideas colliding in a way that left them both exhilarated rather than exhausted. It was this delicate interplay of passion and respect, of contradiction and complement, which lent their connection to a depth Shannon hadn't thought possible.

She laughed, surprised by the gentleness in his voice, the way he looked directly into her eyes.

That night turned into a coffee date.

Coffee turned into dinner.

Dinners turned into weeks of long talks on the phone and conversations that peeled back the ache she had been carrying for too long.

Scott spoke of philosophy, medicine, and his time abroad. He made her feel intelligent, desirable, and cherished. Shannon, who had once felt invisible, began to glow under his attention. Her friends noticed. She noticed.

Scott idealized her from the start, calling her "a rare woman," "a treasure," "one of a kind."

Scott, "You know, I meant what I said, you're a rare woman. Truly, one of a kind."

Shannon, "Careful, Scott. Flattery like that could make a woman believe she's a treasure."

Scott, "That's because you are. I've never met anyone like you."

But even in his flattery, there were walls. He kept their time limited, seeing her only once a week, always citing paperwork, travel, or golf outings with colleagues or family. Shannon rationalized it.

He was busy. He had a life before her.

But more than anything, it was her presence, a calm yet commanding aura that filled the room without the need for fanfare.

Despite Scott's infatuation with Shannon, their romance fell off.

His hesitation about a physical relationship was overly concerning to Shannon since she was looking for a physical relationship to bring them closer intimately. The lack of physical intimacy is something Shannon craved, and she felt was important for someone her age. At 48, she was not willing to live a celibate life.

For four months, there were no advances beyond brief, formal kisses. No intimacy. No deep physical connection other than sharing a bed with him. There was no sexual advances.

It made her wonder if he was genuinely interested or if she was simply another flattering distraction.

Scott's reluctance to make physical advances on Shannon stems from a deeply personal and vulnerable experience, his past battle with prostate cancer, and the subsequent surgeries he underwent.

Shannon softly speaks, pausing thoughtfully before saying, "Scott, I've noticed you sometimes pull away when things get close. I hope you know you can talk to me about anything."

Scott looked down, fidgeting softly with his hands, as he hesitated to speak. "It's not easy for me, Shannon. There's something I've been meaning to tell you, but I haven't found the right moment."

Shannon softly says, "Whatever it is, you don't need to be afraid. I care about you truly. Just say what's on your mind."

Scott's voice wavered a little as he spoke. "A few years ago, I was diagnosed with prostate cancer. I had to go through surgery, and… it changed things for me. Physically."

Scott's statements are a blend of genuine vulnerability and a calculated approach to maintain emotional distance while ensuring that Shannon remains emotionally connected. They highlight his struggle to navigate trust, trauma, and intimacy in the wake of his past experiences.

Shannon, leaning across the table with a warm smile, "Thank you for telling me. That must have been so hard to face, and even harder to share."

Scott sighs in relief, releasing a breath he had been holding, "I haven't tried… I mean, I haven't been with anyone since the surgery. I'm not sure what's possible anymore. I worry you'll think I'm not interested in you, or that I'm pushing you away, when really, I'm just… scared."

Shannon gently squeezes his hand with a warm smile. "Scott, what matters to me is you, the whole of you. We'll figure this out together, at whatever pace feels right. Thank you for trusting me with this."

Scott, managing a small smile, "That means more than I can say. I just want to be honest, even if it's messy or hard sometimes."

Shannon reassured him, "Honesty is all I ask. We'll take things one day at a time, together."

Shannon's heart twisted. Her empathy kicked in, instantly drowning her in her doubts. She took his hand. "Thank you for telling me, "She whispered. "I'm so sorry you went through that."

He nodded solemnly. "It's hard to talk about. Most women don't understand."

These medical procedures significantly impactedhis physical capacity for intimacy, leaving him uncertain about whether he could fulfill that aspect of a relationship. This uncertainty has weighed heavily on him, influencing his behavior and interactions with Shannon.

Rather than openly confronting these challenges, Scott has navigated this sensitive issue with a mix of vulnerability and emotional distance.

By sharing his medical history, he seeks Shannon's empathy and understanding, building a connection based on trust.

However, his actions, such as offering her a guest room instead of sharing his personal space, reflected his hesitations and the lingering insecurities tied to his medical condition.

This careful balance suggests that Scott is still grappling with the trauma and emotional impact of his past while trying to maintain a semblance of control over their relationship.

Scott's approach reveals a complex interplay of seeking closeness while guarding his autonomy, shaped by his fears about physical intimacy and its potential impact on their connection.

Scott's insecurities about sexual performance are intertwined with his history of prostate cancer, and its aftermath has far-reaching emotional and psychological effects that cause Scott to prevent intimacy from developing.

In that moment, Scott had shifted the dynamic. What had been emotional distance was now framed as vulnerability. What felt like detachment became something noble, almost tragic. His words made Shannon feel special that he trusted her enough to share his physical disability, and her nurturing instincts surged to the surface.

It was a masterstroke. He now had her sympathy, her patience, and her emotional investment without offering his own heart fully in return.

Scott's approach was a win because it allowed him to create a dynamic where Shannon felt deeply connected to him without requiring him to reciprocate in equal measures.

By presenting his vulnerabilities, rooted in his medical history, Scott shifted the perception of his emotional distance from being neglectful or detached to being noble and tragic.

This reframing not only elicited Shannon's empathy but also positioned her as a caretaker. This role compelled her to remain emotionally invested in him, despite his lack of genuine intimacy or passion.

Furthermore, this strategy allowed Scott to maintain control over the relationship by setting boundaries.

He used selective vulnerability to draw Shannon closer, while simultaneously crafting conditions that kept her at arm's length, both emotionally and physically.

This ensured he could protect himself from further insecurity while keeping her invested in the idea of connection. By portraying his reluctance as a product of trauma rather than disinterest, Scott avoided scrutiny and built an emotional shield that prevented Shannon from questioning his actions.

It was a calculated and deliberate move that left her feeling special and needed, all while ensuring he remained in control of their dynamic.

Weeks later, he invited her to his home on the hill, a modern house with expansive windows and a breathtaking view of the city lights. He had dimmed the lights, lit candles, and placed soft music on the stereo. Wine was served, accompanied by a fire that provided a warm and ambient backdrop. The air was thick with the scent of jasmine and anticipation. It was seductive, romantic, like a scene from a movie.

Shannon felt herself drawn in, captivated by the illusion. Shannon glanced around the softly lit room, the candle flames flickering shadows along the windows. She hesitated, her voice gentle. "This is beautiful, Scott. I never imagined… all this."

Scott poured her another glass of wine, his eyes not meeting hers. "I wanted tonight to feel special for you. You deserve that."

She smiled, but there was a nervous edge to it. She let the silence linger before continuing, "Sometimes, I wonder if I'm doing the right thing. If I'm… enough."

He set the bottle down, turning to her with a solemn expression. "You are. All of this," he gestured to the fire, the music, the view, "it's because I want you to feel how important you are. Even if I can't… be everything you might want."

Her eyes softened. "You're giving me what you can. I understand." She reached for his hand, squeezing it gently. "And I'm here, Scott. I'm not going anywhere."

He squeezed back, a faint smile touching his lips. "That means more than you know."

The fire crackled softly as the city lights shimmered below, and for a moment, the performance and the reality blurred, leaving only the fragile truth between them. It was everything she thought intimacy should look like, but still, something inside her made her tense.

The tenderness felt choreographed and practiced. But she silenced that voice since she didn't want to be suspicious. She wanted to believe this was real.

Later that evening, as the fire died down and the city lights blinked below them, Scott turned to her and said, "You're welcome to stay the night if you'd like. I have a beautiful guest room downstairs. I don't sleep well with people next to me, so it's easier this way."

Her trust in him, built on the foundation of shared vulnerabilities, now felt precarious, a delicate balance between genuine connection and orchestrated detachment. Scott's actions, though wrapped in layers of tragedy and tenderness, seemed to carry a calculated intent, leaving Shannon to grapple with a growing sense of uncertainty.

Was this a relationship based on mutual understanding, or merely a carefully constructed facade designed to keep her tethered while he held her at arm's length? These questions swirled as she lay in the guest room and the perfection of her surroundings only amplifying the emptiness in her heart.

The request felt odd, formal, almost clinical.

But again, Shannon quieted that gut instinct.

Scott's request seemed odd because it lacked the warmth and natural flow one might expect in a romantic setting. It was devoid of spontaneity, instead carrying an air of calculated control.

The formality of his statement inviting Shannon to stay the night but immediately clarifying strict boundaries about sleeping arrangements stripped the moment of intimacy and replaced it with structure. It subtly communicated detachment, cloaked under the guise of vulnerability.

The discrepancy between his earlier seductive ambiance and his abrupt invitation emphasized the oddness.

The dimmed lights, the soft music, the crackling fire, all choreographed to evoke romance. Yet his actions and contrasted clinical tone and impersonal approach towards her painted a different story of who he was portraying.

It was as if he had crafted the scene to draw Shannon emotionally, only to erect an invisible barrier when she reached out for a genuine connection. The request felt like a performance, carefully curated to maintain control while giving just enough to keep Shannon hopeful without fulfilling her emotional and physical needs.

What lies beneath this oddness is a deeper, calculated strategy. Scott's behavior reflects a need to maintain control over their dynamic.

By presenting himself as vulnerable, he garners Shannon's empathy, positioning her as a caretaker rather than a partner in a mutually fulfilling relationship. The seductive ambiance, while romantic, serves as a tool to draw her closer emotionally.

However, his abrupt and impersonal boundary-setting acts as a mechanism to keep her at a safe emotional distance, ensuring he retains dominance and avoids exposing himself to genuine connection or risk.

Scott's actions are manipulated under the guise of trust.

As Shannon lay in the guest room, rest eluded her. The silence pressed in, broken only by the soft clink of pipes somewhere deep in the house. She heard muffled footsteps in the hallway, Scott, moving restlessly.

Unable to sleep, she padded to the doorway and found him standing by the kitchen window, nursing a glass of water.

Shannon cleared her throat gently. "Did I do something wrong?"

Scott turned, his face half-shadowed by the dim light. "No, not at all," he said softly. "I just… I need things a certain way. It's nothing personal."

She hesitated, searching for his expression for any trace of warmth. "Sometimes it feels like you're close, but not here. I just want to understand."

He set the glass down; fingers tense around the rim. "It's complicated. There are things I'm still working through. I wish I could be different, but it's just… safer for me like this."

"Safer?" she echoed, her voice barely above a whisper.

He nodded, glancing away. "When people get too close, it all falls apart. I can't risk that right now."

Shannon bit her lip, wanting to reach out, but suddenly feeling oceans away. She nodded, letting the silence settle once more before returning to the guest room, questions swirling in her mind.

The next morning, before the sun had fully risen, Scott knocked on the guest room door. "I have numerous tasks to complete today," he stated with an urgent tone that precluded further discussion. "If you could be up and ready by six, I'll walk you out."

There was no coffee. No breakfast. Just a rushed farewell and the promise, "I'll call you later."

It became a pattern. Week after week, their time together felt guarded and structured. She would be formally invited, kept at a distance, and then politely dismissed.

Why did he do it? Shannon couldn't understand. Was he afraid of intimacy? Was it truly his health? Or was he simply maintaining control by giving her just enough to keep her hopeful?

Shannon stood in the doorway of the kitchen one evening, her hand resting lightly on the frame. "Scott, can I ask you something?" He didn't look up from his phone. "Sure."

"Why do you always keep me at arm's length? Even when we're together, I feel like I'm reaching for someone who isn't really there."

Scott sighed, rubbing his temples. "It's not that simple, Shannon."

She stepped forward, searching his face for answers. "Then help me understand. Is it me? Or is there something you're not telling me?"

He hesitated, glancing away. "I have a lot going on. My health, work... Sometimes it's just easier not to let people in."

"Easier for you, maybe," Shannon replied, her voice barely above a whisper. "But it makes me feel like I'm the only one trying. Like I'm the only one who cares."

Scott closed his eyes, as if he was stealing himself. "You're one of the few people who really get it. I just sometimes don't know how to be what you need."

Shannon felt tears sting her eyes. "All I need is honesty, Scott. If you're afraid, say you're afraid. If you want distance, tell me. But please, don't keep giving me hope only to pull away again."

He looked at her, at last, his expression softening. "I don't want to hurt you. But I can't promise I'll ever be different."

She nodded, the silence heavy between them. "Then maybe I need to stop hoping you will."

She ignored the sting. She had waited too long for affection to question it now.

Shannon had spent years convincing herself that love, the kind of love she yearned for, was a prize worth chasing, even if it meant enduring the sharp edges of someone else's brokenness. She carried within her the quiet ache of always being the one who gave more, the one who waited longer, the one who held on tighter. It was a story she had lived too many times, a story born of an emptiness she couldn't quite name but recognized in the hollow spaces of her heart.

If only Scott had been different and met her halfway. If he had physically tried to love her, not just showered her with fragments of attention that sparkled like promises. It could have been a turning point, a chance to rewrite the narrative of always being the one just out of reach.

Shannon clung to the threads of his fleeting tenderness, weaving them into a tapestry of hope, while trying to make sense of his aloofness.

Scott sat at the edge of the sofa, his fingers nervously tracing the seam of a cushion.

Shannon, arms crossed, leaned against the window, watching the dusk settle over the city.

Shannon replied, " Scott, sometimes it's like you're here, and then suddenly, you're gone. Do you even notice how that feels?"

Scott, "It's not that I want to hurt you. I just… I'm not good at this. At being what you need."

Shannon, "But you are, sometimes. And those moments are what keep me hanging on. I see something in you, Scott, something gentle. And then, it slips away again."

Scott: "I wish I knew how to hold onto it. I wish I could be that person for you, always. But I don't know how."

Shannon, "I keep telling myself that if I try harder, if I give more, you'll see How much this mean to me? To us."

Scott: "I do see it, Shannon. I do. And I don't want to take it for granted. I just… sometimes, it feels like I'm standing on the outside of my own life, watching it happens."

Shannon: "I want to believe you. I want to believe that those moments mean something, that they're not just in my head."

Scott: "They mean something. But I'm scared I'll let you down, over and over."

Shannon, "And what am I supposed to do with that? How long can I keep hoping for something you can't promise?"

Scott reached for her hand but stopped short. Silence stretched between them, heavy with unspoken longing and regrets.

Scott, "Maybe you shouldn't have to. I need to figure out what I can give before I ask you to keep waiting."

Shannon nodded, her eyes stinging with unshed tears. Again, she was in a relationship with a man who played with her emotions. How could she get him to care about her feelings?

In her mind, she was the healer, the one who could mend the fractures he carried. She was the one who smoothed over the jagged edges of his past with her unwavering patience.

Each moment of sweetness, every whispered confession or glance of vulnerability, became a relic to treasure, a fragile artifact that proved, at least to her, that he was worth saving.

She saw their connection not as it was, but as it could be, if only she tried harder, gave more and understood deeper. She believed that her love, relentless and nurturing, could fill the gaps where he faltered. She could transform his guarded heart into one that throbbed with unrestrained affection. She wanted to be the force that pulled him from his darkness, the one who made him whole again, as if her presence alone could stitch together his broken pieces.

But in holding onto this fragile story, Shannon was sacrificing herself. Each time she poured more of her energy into deciphering his moods, excusing his distance, or justifying his push-pull behavior, she was giving away parts of herself she could never reclaim.

She told herself that love required sacrifice, that intimacy meant enduring the sharp edges of another's pain. Yet deep within her, a quiet voice whispered of exhaustion. She was carrying the burden of his struggles while growing weary from carrying the weight of his struggles as if they were her own.

She replied to the moments he seemed to soften, the rare instances where his walls crumbled just enough to offer her a glimpse of what lay beyond. Those fragments felt like promises, assuring her that her patience and tenderness were worthwhile. Shannon wasn't just fighting for Scott's love; she was fighting for the validation that she could hold onto something good and fragile, that her passion could endure the trials and emerge victorious.

One evening, watching the sunset of the Arizona sky, Scott reached out emotionally.

Scott said, "Shannon, I know I haven't made this easy. Sometimes you deserve better than the mess I carry around."

Shannon replied, "It's not about 'better,' Scott. I just... I want to feel like I'm not the only one holding this together."

Scott looked away, his jaw tense. "I wish I could be the person you see when you look at me. I want to, more than you know. But it's like I keep getting in my own way."

Shannon's voice softened, a whisper. "I'm not asking you to be perfect. I just want to know you're trying not just for me, but for yourself too."

A heavy silence settled. Their hands lingered inches apart on the table, neither quite brave enough to close the gap.

Scott: "I've gotten so used to shutting people out, it feels safer than letting someone in. But when I see you, I see how much you give. I feel like I should be more for you."

Shannon: "I can't be the only one fighting for us, Scott. Loving you shouldn't mean losing myself."

Scott: "I know. I'm afraid that if you stop fighting, I'll lose you. But I'm also afraid that if you keep pushing, you'll lose yourself."

Shannon looked at him, eyes glistening with hope and resignation. "Maybe love isn't about saving each other. Maybe it's about standing together, both of us whole, not broken halves."

Scott nodded, his voice barely audible. "I'd like to believe that's possible."

Their words lingered in the air, delicate and uncertain, as if the answer rested somewhere between letting go and holding on.

It wasn't about him; it was about her.

About proving to herself that she was enough, that she could love deeply and make it matter.

Yet in chasing this story, a truth lingered just beneath the surface, painful and unspoken: sometimes, no matter how tightly you hold onto something fragile, the act of holding is what keeps it from ever truly becoming whole.

And yet, as each fleeting interaction with him dissolved into hurried exits and half-hearted reassurances, she found herself clinging harder, desperate to prove to herself, and to him, that she could make this work.

It wasn't him; it was about the story she was desperate to believe, the story of her own worth, of her ability to hold onto something fragile and make it whole.

She ached for validation, not in the fleeting kind offered by kind words or soft glances, but in the enduring kind, the kind that stays, that fights, which chooses her every time. And so, she ignored the warning signs, smothering her doubts beneath the heavy blanket of her longing.

She told herself that love required patience, which understanding someone else's pain was part of the price of intimacy. But deep down, she wondered if she was simply bargaining with her own loneliness, mistaking scraps for sustenance.

Somewhere inside, she knew the truth; she had placed Scott on a pedestal not because of who he was, but because of what she needed him to be.

Shannon realized she avoided reality by thinking love required hardship and her self-worth relied on endurance. She had built this narrative over the years, layering it with the echoes of past rejection and the scars of unreciprocated affection. It was a script she knew by heart, one in which she always played the role of the giver, the fixer and the one who stayed when everyone else walked away.

But this truth, the one she was only beginning to confront, whispered a different story. It suggested that love was not meant to be a battlefield where she had to prove her resilience or a puzzle where she had to solve someone else's wounds to find her happiness.

Love, real love, was supposed to be mutual, a space where two people could stand as equals, each offering their whole selves without fear of diminishing the other. And yet, she found herself terrified of this idea.

Because if love wasn't something she had to fight for, if it didn't come with struggle and sacrifice as its currency, then what had all her pain been for? Then was love worth holding?

This truth was not an easy one to accept; it unraveled the very foundation she had built her identity upon. It told her that the love she deserved wasn't the kind born from proving her patience through someone's indifference, but the kind that met her halfway, without her needing to stretch herself thin.

It whispered that she had been so busy justifying the scraps she received that she hadn't allowed herself to imagine a feast. It told her that the love she sought wouldn't demand so much from her that she lost herself in the process.

And as she turned these thoughts over in her mind, a new fear began to surface. a desire hidden by her need for affirmation.

She feared that letting go of Scott would mean letting go of the story she had told herself, the story that she could be the one to save someone, to transform their darkness into light. That story had been her anchor, her proof that she could matter in a world that often made her feel invisible.

In its absence, what remained of her identity?

The answer, though still hazy, began to take shape in the quiet moments when the ache of loving him felt heavier than the joy of his occasional tenderness. It emerged in the silences when she no longer had the energy to excuse his distance or to convince herself that his fleeting attention was enough. It hovered in the air like a question she wasn't yet ready to answer; what if the love she had been chasing wasn't worth the pieces she was losing in the process?

This truth, as painful as it was, held a kind of power.

She was counseled to prioritize self-respect rather than compromise. It challenged her to relinquish the idealized view she had constructed, not only for Scott but also for the version of herself who perceived love as an achievement to be attained.

She realized that stepping down from her position and leaving could be a thoughtful decision motivated by self-respect rather than by loss.

The fall from a self-made pedestal was shattering, but it was also the beginning of something else. She no longer had to protect the walls of her heart. She had built a strong foundation that could finally hold the weight of her own love.

At last, she had come home to herself.

Shannon wanted to prove she could be loved while remaining positive despite challenges.

"I just want to make this work," she whispered to herself, as though pleading with the universe to validate her hope. She clung to the fleeting moments of tenderness, holding onto his compliments like fragile shards of light amid a storm, each replaying a quiet prayer that love could triumph over the chaos within and around her.

To acknowledge any other explanation would imply that she had been deceived. Her mind would not allow her to go there. Shannon had promised herself she'd never let that happen again.

But sometimes, the most dangerous pedestal is the one we build ourselves. From it, the fall is always shattering.

Because to accept anything else would mean admitting that all her sacrifices, all her quiet endurance, had been for nothing. The thought clawed at her like a shadow she couldn't escape, wrapping around her every hope and filling the spaces in her mind with relentless doubt. Shannon vowed never to lose herself again, but the pedestal she built wasn't just for Scott, it was for her hope that she mattered, that her pain had meaning. Without it, she feared collapse, and the fall felt crushing and final.

Chapter 4
The Cracks Beneath the Surface

Shannon sat at the edge of the bathtub, towel wrapped tightly around her, steam curling in the air like smoke from a dying fire. The mirror had fogged over, but she could still make out the faint outline of her reflection. Blurred. Distant. She couldn't recognize her own reflection anymore. The change happened so gradually. It was almost impossible to notice at first.

Scott had walked into her life with the smoothness of a practiced illusionist. He was a retired chief of surgery from a small Midwest hospital. His aura screamed calm authority. The kind of man who used words like "legacy" and "reputation" with reverence, as if he were responsible for preserving some great tradition. He commanded obedience, masked by gentle eyes and polite speech.

Their first few dates felt like scenes from a movie she didn't know she'd auditioned for. Elegant dinners, long philosophical talks, weekends spent at his serene hilltop house. It truly captured everything the books describe. It's like experiencing what they've written about firsthand.

Scott always knew just what to say, just what to give. Just until he didn't.

The first red flag was so small it almost went unnoticed. Shannon had planned a dinner with her two closest friends at a restaurant near Scott's home and invited him to join. It was casual. But he hesitated. Then he agreed to meet her friends.

But when he arrived, everything changed.

He greeted her friends with calm politeness. His smile was too measured. His tone is overly formal. The man was too hard once laughed freely with her now spoke like a visiting professor giving a lecture on restraint.

Her friends exchanged glances, their expressions subtle yet unmistakable. After he excused himself to take a call, Cassandra leaned in.

"He's… intense," she said carefully.

Elena didn't even bother to mask her concern. "There's something off about him. Did you see how he corrected you about the wine pairing?"

Shannon brushed it off, defending him automatically. "He's just used to being… in control. It's his medical background. He's very precise."

But that night, she noticed something she hadn't before: how he subtly steered the conversation, how he inserted backhanded compliments, how her words seemed to shrink when he was near. The man she believed was helping her rise was pulling her down instead.

Over time, instances like that multiplied. And the speed at which they multiplied was rapid.

Scott would ignore her text for hours, then accuse her of being needy and clingy. He dismissed her work in wellness coaching as "cute," once calling it "emotional fluff." When she spoke about starting her podcast, he scoffed. "Another platform for wounded women to whine?"

She tried to rationalize it. She tried to justify everything he did or said. *Maybe he was under stress. He had back pain. He had issues he didn't talk about with health problems he waved away, sometimes contradicting himself.*

One day, he claimed he had a neurological condition; the next, he denied ever saying it. There was an air of mystery around his medical history as if his illnesses were a private currency, he used to buy sympathy or escape responsibility.

But what really unsettled her the most wasn't just the confusion. It was how much she doubted herself. She found it hard to believe herself now.

She found herself apologizing for things she hadn't done, checking her tone before every sentence, withholding thoughts she once shared freely. Her world had grown smaller. Each move filtered through Scott's moods and unspoken rules.

In quiet moments, Shannon would flash back to her childhood, the nights when her mother sat in the dark kitchen, crying silently over a man who claimed he loved her while destroying her spirit. The feeling was starting to grow on her. It was all very familiar now. The realization sent a knot in her stomach. The silence after small cruelties was eating her up alive. Their relationship was so damaged that she began longing for something real and something safe.

She didn't say it aloud yet, but the thought had taken root: *This man is not who he pretended to be. Something is not right here, and I am not sure what he is hiding.*

That night after the dinner with her friends, Shannon lay in bed next to Scott, wide awake. Though they finally agreed to share one bed, there was still no intimacy. She could hear his breathing, consistent and measured. She could feel the weight of his presence even across the bed.

She stared at the ceiling, reflecting on the evening, how he had subtly dismissed Cassandra's story about her promotion, how he'd corrected Elena on a statistic about cardiac arrest, even though it wasn't relevant, how he rolled his eyes when Shannon laughed a little too loud.

Then came the silence in the car afterward, which was long, frigid, and measured with meticulous precision. "You always must make everything about you when you're around them," he'd finally said, voice tight. "You perform."

It hit her like a slap. She turned toward him, confused. "Perform?"

"You know what I mean. It's exhausting and shallow."

She didn't argue. She didn't cry. She just nodded slightly, as if receiving notes after a failed audition.

The next day, there was no apology. He simply acted as if nothing had happened. Scott said, "I'm dealing with a lot of stuff right now, and I need time to process things."

The apology was backhanded and coated in implication. If she hadn't been so sensitive, it wouldn't have happened. If she only understood him better, there wouldn't be so much tension.

He made her feel like she was always one step away from losing him, and she became an expert at self-censorship. She stopped telling stories that made her feel bright. She stopped bringing up her podcast. She stopped laughing too loud. She stopped being herself.

Shannon's friend, Rachael, started asking questions. "Why don't you bring him around anymore? Why are you so quiet about him now?"

Shannon lied to her friend and said, "Things were fine, just private." But inside, the gnawing grew and with it her suspicions.

She started journaling again. Making sure she had the pages hidden in the back of a drawer, like forbidden truths: "I don't know who I am around him anymore. Sometimes I think he's sick, but other times he just uses sickness to keep me here."

One night, Shannon sat in her car outside his place after an argument, her hands gripping the steering wheel long after the engine stopped. She had asked about his headaches and why he refused to see a neurologist.

His answer: "Don't question me. I know more about this than you ever will."

She remembered staring at her reflection in the rearview mirror, whispering, *You must wake up.*

So, she kept wondering why she was here. Why didn't she leave?

Then the truth stood face to face with her. Stared in her eyes. Because with fear, there was also hope—*hope that he would change*. Just maybe she could love him into health. That it wasn't as bad as it felt and that she was making something out of nothing.

That maybe… it was *her.*

Scott started using other tactics to manipulate Shannon. The gaslighting started slowly, like poison in water.

At first, it tasted odd. But then, it was all normal.

But cracks were beginning to show. Shannon was starting to ask questions not to him, but to herself, dangerous questions. The kind that brings whole illusions crashing down and makes you take notice of your actions.

There were days when Scott was magnetic and charming. His activity was manic. He was talking a mile a minute about plans for travel and a business idea. He wanted Shannon to agree with his plans.

He even spoke about them buying a vacation home, and they'd renovate it together. He would seem intense at these times and energetic, and other times solemn and cold. Day after day, his moods and reactions became unpredictable.

He'd stay up all night rearranging his kitchen or researching foreign markets for property investments he never followed through on. Shannon once found him at 3 am re-cataloging every bottle of wine in his cellar.

When she asked why he wasn't sleeping, he said, "I don't need sleep. I'm operating at a different frequency than you. You wouldn't understand. You're an emotional pedestrian. I'm experienced and much more superior."

She laughed nervously, unsure if it was a joke. He didn't smile back.

The next day, he was as cold as ice. He wouldn't respond to her texts. When she called, he answered with a sigh. "Why do you always need something from me?" he muttered. "Can't you just let me be?"

These swings high and then low began to define their relationship. At first, Shannon mistook them for moodiness, a kind of creative temperament. But over time, she noticed a pattern that was harder to dismiss.

When Scott was up, he was invincible, God-like. He would shower her with praise and intensity. He talked about jetting to Paris for the weekend. Promises that never happened. Or building a retreat center in Tuscany. He even talked about her becoming the face of a new wellness brand that he had been researching online.

But when he crashed, the darkness swallowed everything. He'd go silent. Or worse, cutting, and sarcasm. He'd mock her dreams and call her unstable. Accuse her of betrayal if she didn't match his energy exactly as he wanted her to.

"You think you're so intuitive," he snapped one night when she asked gently if he was okay. "You're not. You just want control. "She stood there, stunned that it had come from nowhere. The emotional whiplash was unbearable and exhausting. She had fallen in love with two men living in the same body, one intoxicating and the other terrifying.

Shannon began to research late at night, bipolar and other mental illnesses. She read about bipolar disorder and its symptoms, which included rapid cycling, grandiosity, paranoia, and denial of the illness. She checked all the boxes silently, wondering: *"Is this what's happening to Scott? Is he aware of these actions? Is that why he won't get help? Is he in denial, or doesn't know at all?"*

One evening on his patio, watching the sun sink into the trees, Shannon decided to address his mental illness. She tried to identify his bipolar actions by saying, "I've noticed your energy shifts sometimes," she said, cautiously. "Not just moods. Whole days where you're soaring, then… not. I worry you might be hurting."

He turned sharply. "You think I'm crazy?"

"No. I think you're hurting," she said. "There's no shame in that."

He stood up, walked inside, and locked the patio door behind him.

She stayed outside for an hour until he unlocked it without a word. That was his punishment was pure silence. After that, she never mentioned it again.

Shannon had planted the idea, and it had taken root. He had a mental illness, and he knew it just didn't want to accept it and work on it. He clearly didn't care who he harmed in the process.

Scott had mastered the art of distortion. If Shannon mentioned a confusing event, he'd insist she remembered it wrong. If she told him how much his behavior hurt her, he'd respond with, "You're always overreacting," or "That's not what happened. You're twisting things again."

His words began to evolve into weapons, honed sharper with every exchange. What initially felt like fleeting moments of frustration gradually revealed themselves as calculated attempts to diminish her.

A small comment on her outfit, "You're really wearing that?" would spiral into hours of her questioning her taste.

A casual dismissal of her career aspirations, "You're lucky anyone even notices your work." These words began chipping away at her confidence. These weren't outbursts; they were precision strikes, meant to land softly, but linger painfully.

The hardest part wasn't his words, though. It was the way he delivered them, so uncaring and cruel, as if he were merely stating facts. Scott turned Shannon's insecurities into his playground, every interaction a subtle reminder of her perceived shortcomings.

Yet, each time she tried to address her feelings, he made her feel like the villain. "You're so sensitive," he'd say, shaking his head in mock pity. "I can't joke around with you anymore." Everything he said would become a joke.

She began to dread his presence as much as she craved his approval. The duality of his charm and cruelty kept her in a constant state of emotional whiplash, unsure of which Scott she'd encounter on any given day. Every time she found herself on the verge of leaving, he'd reel her back in with a promise, a touch, a fleeting kindness that made her believe, for just a moment, that he could change.

But deep down, Shannon was beginning to understand. These weren't jokes, weren't misunderstandings or bad days for Scott. They were patterns, calculated patterns that reflected more about him than they ever did about her.

It was this pattern, along with the dismissal of her feelings, the recycling of thoughtless gifts, and the disarming punishment of silence, that eventually carved out a new clarity for Shannon.

This clarity was painful, but it allowed her to finally see through the cracks that Scott tried so desperately to cover.

His gestures, whether physical or emotional, were never about her. They were about maintaining his image and masking the hollowness of his own inability to give from the heart.

Shannon determined the areas of her life that needed improvement and identified aspects that required further consideration. This realization wasn't immediate, nor was it dramatic. It unfolded like a quiet revelation. It was like a seed of self-worth taking root in a barren field. Scott continued to manipulate and distort Shannon's reality.

Piece by piece, she was losing touch with herself. She was a chess piece in his life to be manipulated at his will. Her world was becoming a chessboard, and he held all the moves to win.

Scott never truly gave Shannon anything from the heart. There were no flowers, there were no handwritten notes, no gifts that showed he had listened or cared about her soul. What he offered instead were the leftover things others had given him, items of no emotional value to him, but dressed up as if they were tokens of thoughtfulness. Scott planned each of his gestures with the intention of recalling and using them in the future. Nothing was ever unconditional.

Shannon began to understand that she wasn't in a relationship; she was in psychological negotiation. One where the currency was her silence, her compliance and her erasure. Even the intimate moments felt transactional. It really depended on how he wanted things to be.

Once, after a minor disagreement, he didn't speak to her for four days. When she broke down and begged him to tell her what she had done wrong, and all he had to say to her was, *"You should know."*

That was the turning point. Not loud, not dramatic, but internal, quiet, and seismic.

It was the first time Shannon wrote in her journal, in thick, shaky pen: *"This is not love. This is not normal. Something is very wrong here."*

She was convinced a lot was wrong, but she wasn't ready to leave quite yet. However, she began to detach emotionally and physically from him.

Shannon wrote in her journal that night: "My soul is stirring, and I yearn to be loved and recognized. I don't want to be invisible."

Shannon wrote the next day in her journal, "Once a woman wakes up, the world around her may appear unchanged, but every detail begins to shift under her gaze. She starts to see the cracks in the facade and hear the echoes of her own voice calling out from the places she had abandoned. The lies she had accepted as truths begin to unravel, thread by thread, and the chains of expectation that once felt unbreakable start to loosen. A waking woman moves subtly at first, testing the strength of her newfound clarity. She doesn't always announce her awakening to the world. Because it isn't for the world. It is for her. She learns to stand in front of the mirror, meeting her own eyes without flinching, and asks the questions she has been avoiding. *"What do I want? Who am I when no one is watching. Where did I go?"* When did his voice became louder than my own." Every small reclamation becomes a victory. She stops apologizing for the space she takes up, the air she breathes and the dreams she holds close. She begins to draw boundaries, not walls, but lines etched in steel that no one can cross without her permission. She doesn't find her strength at once. It's in the quiet moments, the choices no one else sees, letting the phone ring instead of rushing to explain, saying *"no"* without guilt, or simply giving herself permission to rest. *The power of a waking woman is not in her anger, though it may burn quietly within her."*

Shannon realized that it is up to her to quit settling for crumbs. She begins to understand that love should not be something she must plead for, nor should respect be something she has to earn by devaluing herself. Shannon realizes her worth was always hers, independent of anyone else's approval, and it is up to her to take back her power and strength.

Her awakening is not the end of the story, but the beginning of something vast and unknowable. A world of possibilities opens before her, not because the world itself has changed, but because she has.

As Shannon steps forward, her soul no longer stirs but soars with wings to fly and be free. And once a woman begins to wake up, with that realization, nothing can stop her from being her own woman.

Chapter 5
The Invitation

Scott's offer to travel for a vacation lingered in Shannon's mind like a puzzle; she couldn't quite solve it. "Just us. Someplace quiet," he had said. No timeline. No details. No warmth.

She should have felt excited.

But instead, she felt… managed like scheduling a case file. It was the kind of offer that should have felt romantic. Instead, it felt tactical and controlled.

When she brought it up again days later, his mood shifted. "I said, I'd think about it," she reminded him gently.

"You overthink," he replied flatly. "That's always been your problem."

The correction landed like a scalpel, precise and cutting. Shannon had heard variations of it her entire life. As a girl, from her father. Later, in the arms of men who mistook her sensitivity for weakness. But from Scott, it felt colder like a clinical judgment rather than a moment of impatience.

She learned that everything with Scott had a layer beneath it, a dual meaning. He never yelled at her directly and never insulted her outright. But his tone could reduce her to silence, and that silence was starting to take root inside her.

Scott's travel plans always piqued and held Shannon's interest. "Someplace quiet, away from all the noise," he'd murmur, planting the seed without any commitment. His tone was deliberate, like a fisher casting bait. "I'll let you know when I've worked out the details," he would add with a slight smile, one that never reached his eyes.

It felt less like an invitation and more like a reward dangled before her like an unspoken promise that was tied to how well she played her part. Based on how well she acted and how agreeable she was towards him. But only if she earned it. She would only be considered deserving if he believed she had earned it.

When Shannon pressed for clarity, like dates and plans, Scott would pivot with an air of quiet authority. "I said I'd think about it," he'd say, his voice calm, measured, stripped of any any warmth. "You always want everything mapped out immediately. That's not how I operate."

It wasn't a refusal, but it wasn't a promise either. It was a dangling carrot, a calculation, a move to keep her hoping and keep her striving for approval. The offer became less about the destination and more about the message it carried; *behave, meet my expectations, and you might be worthy of my time.*

And as Shannon stood at the edge of his calculated ambiguity, she realized how the simplicity of *just us* had altered into something fraught with judgment, with conditions, with the weight of proving her worth.

Shannon's sense of anticipation twisted into unease, a constant undercurrent that hummed beneath every interaction with Scott. The invitations are always vague, always just out of reach, becoming mirrors reflecting her uncertainty about herself. Alone in her apartment, she found herself rehearsing conversations in her mind, searching for the right words, the gentlest approaches and ways to remain agreeable without erasing herself. She started to measure her responses, to trim the edges of her honesty and offering up only what she thought he wanted to see.

But the more she tried to fit herself into his mold, the more she felt herself shrinking and her colors fading into the background. There were moments, brief and electric, when she almost voiced her longing for clarity and her need for genuine connection. Yet the memory of his clipped responses kept her silent as she was unable to find words to respond and not getting an abrupt reaction out of it.

The days blurred together, each one marked by an ever-present sense of waiting: for a text, for a sign of tenderness and for any small gesture that might reassure her.

But the reassurance never arrived. What came was only more ambiguity.

Shannon felt caught between hope and resignation and unable to let go, yet afraid of holding on. She wondered when her life had become an audition for someone else's affection. A series of tests she had not agreed to take.

When his message finally appeared, "Hey. Sure, what's up?"

Her heart thudded in her chest. She hesitated only a moment before typing, letting honesty guide her fingertips.

Shannon said, "I've been thinking about the trips you mentioned. I like the idea, but I wish we could talk more openly about plans. Sometimes it feels like… like I'm waiting for permission to get excited."

Several seconds passed. She could picture Scott, jaw set, weighing his words.

Scott replied, "I just don't see the point of planning everything. Our lives are unpredictable. I like to keep things open to change."

Shannon wrote, "I understand that. But for me, having something to look forward to isn't about. Control. It's about feeling included. I want to be part of the conversation, not just a bystander."

Scot replied, "It's not that I don't want you involved. I just don't want pressure, that's all."

She drew a deep breath, grounding herself.

Shannon replied, "It's not pressured to want clarity. It's about feeling like we're in this together. It feels like I must earn the time that I spend with you. I want to share it."

There was a long pause. The cursor blinked. Scott's next reply was shorter.

Scott replied, "I need to think about that."

Shannon replied, "Okay. Take your time. I just needed you to know how I feel."

She set her phone down, the silence in her apartment finally feeling less like a cage and more like a space she could breathe in. Yet, somewhere quiet, a new resolve was kindling.

She read old journal pages searching for traces of her old self. Beneath the doubt and longing, she found a pulse of defiance. A quiet promise to herself; she would not disappear. Not for Scott; not for anyone. Shannon continued to yearn for more than a dangling invitation. She started to wonder what it would feel like to invite herself to her own life, to her own happiness with no permissions required.

Each time her phone buzzed, she jolted with hope, only to see it that is was not Scott. Was it a weather alert, a reminder for a bill, or anything but the warmth she craved?

Gradually, she stopped rehearsing their conversations. The need to edit herself dulled, replaced by a cautious curiosity. What if she said exactly what she felt? What if she stopped waiting for permission to want more? How long would she have to be all calculated around him? When could she be herself?

She started to write again, not in her journal hidden away in the drawer, but in a notebook left open on the kitchen table. Fragments of honesty poured out onto the page; her frustration, her longing, the ache for simplicity and the clarity she yearned for in a romantic partner.

She wandered through her days in a muted haze, yet somewhere inside, a stubborn ember of self-preservation fumed. She caught herself picturing weekends alone. But now it was not a punishment, but a possibility. She was looking forward to her solitude and pampering time. The idea of letting go of the chase,and of stepping back from the constant vigil for crumbs of affection, grew less terrifying and more like freedom. It wasn't that scary after all.

But somehow the hope for Scott's approval still lingered. Her heart still held hope as persistent as dawn after a sleepless night.

When her phone finally chimed with his name, her pulse raced, but her fingers hovered over the screen. She read his message carefully, weighing each word, the meaning beneath the casual tone. "Trust me," he wrote. She folded the message into her memory, uncertain whether it was comfort or caution.

As the days drifted, she could sense the tides shifting, the space between them stretching thin. Yet, for the first time, she wondered if the distance wasn't just his doing. Maybe, quietly, she was learning to let go.

Shannon stared at her phone, the blue light painting gentle shadows across her face. She took a breath, typed, and hit send on her computer.

Shannon, "Hey, do you have a minute to talk?"

A minute later, three grey dots appeared.

Scott, "Hey. Sure, what's up?"

She hesitated, fingers trembling slightly.

Shannon, "I've been feeling a bit lost. About us. About... where we're going."

A pause. The dots flickered, vanished, then returned.

Scott "You're worrying too much again. I told you, I don't like to plan everything out."

Shannon replied, "I know. But sometimes I just want to know if we're moving forward, or if I'm just standing here waiting. Maybe waiting alone."

Scott, "Why does it have to be so defined? Can't we just enjoy what we have?"

Shanno replied, "Because I need to feel like I matter. I don't care about what the world says, labels matter to me. I need to know where we're headed. Like I'm not just waiting for you to decide if I fit."

There was a longer silence this time.

Scott replied, "You do matter. But this is how I am. I need space. You need to trust that."

Shannon replied, "I want to trust you. But I also want to trust myself. I can't keep guessing where I stand."

Scott, "You're overthinking this. You should try to relax a little."

Shannon, "And maybe you should try to see what it feels like for me."

Scott didn't respond right away. The silence lingered, heavy yet clarifying.

Shannon, "I just want honesty, Scott. I need to know if we're in this together, or if not, then I want to know that I'm on my own."

Scott, "I'll think about it."

As the conversation faded into stillness, Shannon felt the familiar ache of uncertainty, but also, the faint glow of her own voice, steady and real amidst the fog.

Chapter 6
The Slow Withdrawal

Scott started to pull back in careful, small steps.

A canceled dinner here. A late reply there. A string of vague texts: "Busy today," or "Need some space."

Each time he resurfaced, it was calm, and calculated warmth. "You're important to me, Shannon. But I live in a different rhythm. You need to trust that."

She began to doubt herself. Her instincts. Her timing. Her tone. *Could she not fit right into his rhythm? What was she doing wrong? Everything? Was she too needy? Too emotional? Too available?*

He never directly said it. Because he didn't have to.

She sat alone, her thoughts circling like restless birds around the same questions. *Was she enough for him? Could she ever be? Will she ever be?* The doubt distressed her, an ache for which she could find no remedy. She began to fear that Scott wasn't just retreating into himself. But now he was pulling away from her to make room for someone new, someone who didn't ask, didn't need, didn't push too hard against the walls he'd built and someone who just co-existed with out demands.

When Scott smiled at her now, it felt transactional, as if he were measuring her responses against some invisible scale of worthiness. She wondered whether his pauses and absences were test runs for a future without her. The thought chilled her, settling deep into her bones. His love (or what she thought was love) had started to feel conditional, precariously balanced in her ability to exist within his rules.

And if she faltered, even once, what then? Will she be considered? Would her efforts to hold on to him crumble into dust?

These questions stayed with her, unspoken, even as Scott's text messages arrived with their cryptic warmth. The words reassured but hinted that her value lay in how well she fit his story. Shannon didn't want to lose him, yet she felt herself already losing pieces of herself, one doubt at a time.

She adjusted. She waited. She gave him the benefit of the doubt. Again, and again, he disappointed her.

Her journal entries grew darker.

"It's like loving a ghost. He's a present, but not here. I don't know what I'm chasing anymore. I just know I keep waiting for the version of him that makes me feel seen."

Shannon sat on the edge of the couch, phone in hand, watching Scott as he scrolled through unread emails. A dense silence settled between them.

Shannon replied, Scott, can we talk? I just… I don't know where we stand anymore.

Scott, What do you mean? I told you, everything's fine. I'm just busy.

Shannon, But you're always busy. Or tired. Or somewhere else in your head. I just want to understand what's changed.

Scott, Nothing's changed. You worry too much. Can't we just have a quiet night for once?

Shannon: I'm not trying to start anything. I just miss the way we used to talk. Lately, I feel like I'm reaching for someone who's slipping away.

Scott, You're overthinking it. I just need space, Shannon. That's all.

Shannon, Space is fine, but I can't tell if you even want me here anymore. I feel… invisible.

Scott, You're not invisible. I said you're important to me. Is that not enough?

Shannon, I want it to be enough. But sometimes love isn't just words, Scott. I need to feel it too.

Scott replied, You're asking for more than I can give right now.

Shannon, I already knew that.

The silence settled again. Heavier than before. The words had been building walls instead of bridges between them.

She felt hollowness creeping into her once vibrant world, like ink bleeding into clear water, subtle at first, until it colored everything. Her laughter became softer, less spontaneous, as if she were afraid of drawing too much attention.

The things that once brought her joy, her favorite books, long walks, the way her friends' voices overlapped in cheerful chaos, felt muted now, distant echoes of a life she couldn't quite touch.

Shannon found herself avoiding mirrors, afraid of what she might see. Not the physical changes, but the absence of the person she used to be. She could no longer recognize herself in the mirror. She was looking for the woman who laughed easily, who spoke with conviction, who didn't question her worth with every passing glance or text that was disappearing. She whispered to herself in moments of solitude, asking where that version of her had gone, and whether Scott's world had simply swallowed her whole.

Even her interactions felt stripped of color. She typed responses to friends and deleted them before sending them, worried she might be saying too much, too hones and too much to handle. Her voice, once steady, now weakened in conversations, with a tremor betraying her uncertainty. She hesitated to share her thoughts, fearing they might disrupt the delicate balance she was trying so hard to maintain. The effort to exist within Scott's orbit, to be exactly what he needed, had left her unmoored and floating aimlessly in a sea of self-doubt.

Shannon felt she was living a fractured fairytale life. Where she felt like she was continuously falling down the rabbit hole, like Alice in Wonderland. In this situation, she was following the rabbit without a clear destination, similar to her experiences with Scott.

The fact that he was not seeing her as who she was, but rather someone to feed off.

"I think I'm disappearing," Shannon said, as she recognized the profound toll this relationship was taking on her mental well-being.

Each day seemed to blur into the next, marked only by the gentle ache of longing for the woman she once knew. In quiet moments, she would trace the outline of her reflection in the darkened window, searching for traces of that lost vitality. The world outside carried on with its neon lights, city noises, and the promise of possibility. Yet she felt herself growing pale and fading into the background of her own life.

Sometimes Shannon wondered what it would take to reclaim her own light. Could she gather the scattered pieces, or had she left too much of herself behind in the spaces between Scott's words and silences? The uncertainty lingered, heavy and persistent.

But beneath the doubt, a small ember of hope remained, whispering that maybe she was still there, waiting to be seen, waiting to come home to herself.

Chapter 7
The Vegas Trip

Their getaway to Las Vegas marked a turning point in their relationship. Shannon had carefully arranged dinners and tickets to shows, while Scott managed the hotel and flight bookings. Everything seemed fine and planned out.

But, from the outset, something felt off. Scott hadn't reserved seats for them together on the plane, and he arrived late at the airport, offering only a brief explanation about his driver's tardiness.

Something just did not seem right. He was cold and distant. He didn't at all seem to be excited about the romantic weekend like she was. His mood was off and not fun.

After arriving at the hotel, she noticed he just wasn't peppy and excited about being in Las Vegas with all the glitter and excitement of the fast-paced movement. His mood was down and distant, and he was more interested in going up to the room than playing craps or slots.

He suggested that they go up to their room and get things together and luggage sorted out. She agreed, as usual. They proceeded into the elevator for the sixteenth floor with luggage in tote.

Once inside their hotel room, Shannon noticed a palpable shift in Scott's demeanor. He grabbed several bottles of pills from his duffel bag and locked himself in the bathroom without a word. It struck her as odd that one bag contained his haphazardly packed clothes, oddly heavy on socks but missing essentials like a jacket, despite the chilly January nights.

Shannon waited by the window, watching the neon lights of Vegas far below. The hush from the bathroom was heavy, punctuated only by the dull hum of the shower. When Scott finally emerged, his towel draped loosely around his shoulders, she gathered her courage.

Shannon, "Scott, are you okay? You seemed… off, even before we got here."

Scott avoided her eyes as he tossed the towel onto the chair, trying to seem casual. "Just tired from the flight. You know how I get. The city's a lot."

Shannon hesitated, studying him. "You know, you could have told me if you weren't feeling up for this trip. We didn't have to come."

Scott's jaw tightened. "It's not the trip. I just want to relax tonight. Why do you want to pick at every little thing?"

Shannon took a slow breath, feeling the tension knot in her chest. "I'm not trying to pick. I just… I want to understand you. I feel like you're shutting me out."

Scott shook his head. "Not everything is about you trying to fix me, Shan. I can't be how you want me to be all the time. Sometimes I just need space."

Shannon's voice was barely a whisper. "You don't have to do it all alone."

He glanced at her then, the briefest flicker of vulnerability in his eyes. "Maybe I do."

She stepped closer, lowering her voice. "Are you sure? Because it doesn't feel like we're in this together anymore. And in relationships, people are in it together for everything."

Scott let out a tired sigh, running his hand through damp hair. "You always want answers. I don't always have them. Can't we just… not talk about it tonight?"

Shannon nodded, her heart sinking. "Alright. No more questions. Just… let me know if you need me, okay?"

He gave a curt nod, already turning away. Shannon watched his retreating figure, feeling like the thin wall between was t glass, clear, but unbreakable.

Shannon noticed that the other bag was even more puzzling. It held nothing but prescription medications, a collection that seemed far too extensive for someone who had claimed perfect health and was more like a drug dealer. Shannon couldn't get her mind off them. The question kept coming back to her, *what were all these drugs for?*

While Scott was in the shower, Shannon glanced through his duffel bag and discovered a collection of medications, including antipsychotics, mood stabilizers, and anxiety drugs.

She recognized them from her brother's treatment for bipolar disorder. Other medications were unfamiliar, but she knew enough to be concerned. This didn't seem like the collection of someone responsible for managing their health. It hinted at something darker and more troubling, and a definite red flag for Shannon to be concerned.

Shannon wondered if Scott was bipolar or had a personality disorder, especially since he kept it hidden from her. She noted his restlessness, insomnia, mood swings, and emotional withdrawal. Was he also struggling with addiction or self-medicating?

The discovery made her feel more convinced that Scott's unpredictable actions weren't just little personality quirks, but possibly indications of a more serious, untreated condition.

Shannon waited until Scott had settled onto the edge of the bed, scrolling absently through his phone.

She kept her voice gentle, careful, "Scott, can we talk for a minute?"

He didn't look up, just muttered, "About what?"

She hesitated, the words catching in her throat. "I—um, I noticed the medications in your bag. There's a lot, and some I don't recognize. Are you… okay?"

Scott's fingers tightened around the phone. His jaw set. "Why were you looking in my bag?"

"I wasn't snooping," she said softly. "I was getting out the charger and saw them. Scott, I'm worried. These aren't *just* for sleep, right?"

A muscle twitched in his cheek as he set the phone down. "They're for anxiety. Sleep. Stress. The usual."

She looked at him for a moment before responding. She studied him, unwilling to let it go. "Scott, some of those are serious medications. Are you seeing someone about this? Is there something you're not telling me?"

He stood up abruptly, pacing to the far side of the room. "You always must dig, don't you? Always looking for something wrong with me."

Shannon's voice trembled. "I'm not trying to accuse you. I just want to help you and be there as much as possible. If something's going on, if you're struggling with anything, we can get through it together. But I can only help if I know about it."

His eyes flashed, sharp with defensiveness. "I don't need your help, get it? I don't need anyone's help. I can handle it."

There was a long silence, heavy and brittle as glass. Shannon forced herself to meet his gaze. "But you're unable to handle it, right? Not really. Not in my dictionary."

Scott's expression flickered, pain and anger mixing. "Just drop it, Shannon. I don't want to talk about it."

Shannon swallowed, her heart aching. "If you ever do feel like talking, I'll be here. I'm sorry, but I can't keep pretending everything's fine."

Scott turned away, his silhouette tense against the dim hotel light. "Sometimes pretending is the only way I get through the day," he said quietly.

Shannon nodded, defeated but resolute. "I just hope one day you'll let me in. Until then, I can't keep pretending."

Later that night at dinner, Shannon broached the topic of the drugs again. Scott's reaction was swift, icy, and dismissive. He just dismissed her with some excuse that he had just traveled that way and used them when he needed to sleep.

He told Shannon she was overanalyzing again. "So, what are you, a narc spying on me?" he coldly said as he dismissed her once again.

But the tension in his jaw and the way his hands gripped the edge of the table at dinner revealed something different about him.

She suddenly understood that his biggest fear wasn't about the illness itself, but rather the worry that someone might discover the truth he had spent so much effort trying to hide. It was a blunt reminder that he valued his facade more than their connection. Additionally, he valued and prioritized secrecy over revealing his vulnerabilities to her. He was looking for a future with just someone to pass the time.

Shannon didn't press further that night, though the revelation sat heavy in her mind. She began to see their dynamics in a new light, not a partnership, but as a carefully managed charade.

Scott's unwillingness to confront his struggles, his insistence on control at all costs, made it clear that he would rather push her away than have his secret known. It was a bitter realization that while she had been fighting for their connection, he had been fighting to maintain his facade.

As Shannon shifted through her thoughts, she realized how much of herself she had sacrificed in this relationship. The Vegas trip had brought to light not just Scott's secrets but her own silent compromises. She was like a dimming candle, whose light had burned out. Every unanswered question, every deflection, every distant gaze added to a growing pile of emotional debris she couldn't avoid anymore.

She spent the evening pacing the room, her mind racing with questions she wasn't sure she wanted answers to. Was his coldness a shield or a prison? Were the walls he built around himself to keep others out or to keep himself from collapsing entirely? And more pressingly, could she be the one to keep holding him up when her own foundation was crumbling?

That night, lying awake next to someone who felt more like a stranger than ever, Shannon came to an unsettling conclusion; she wasn't disappearing because Scott was erasing her. She was fading away because she had stopped fighting to exist within herself.

That evening, Shannon and Scott made their way to a magic show at a casino nearby. As they walked, Scott grew irritated by the new pedestrian routes, grumbling about the longer distance and blaming Shannon for choosing that path. His irritation only grew, more irritating casting a shadow over what Shannon had hoped would be an enjoyable outing.

Even as they finally reached the theater, his sour mood continue to manifest itself, making it clear that nothing she did could ease his dissatisfaction.

Scott always enjoyed the attention when the focus was on him. That evening, the audience chose Shannon to help the magician perform on stage. He had a 30-minute magic presentation in which Shannon assisted him on stage and with the audience. Shannon got a lot of attention from the audience with questions asking her if she was just a guest from the audience or his partner in real life. Scott was not incredibly happy with Shannon's limelight attention on stage, and he told her so later.

On their way back to the room, Scott's frustration finally spilled out. "You really seemed to love being in the spotlight tonight," he muttered, his voice sharp with annoyance. "I thought this weekend was for us, not for you to perform for a crowd."

Shannon stopped for a moment, stung by his words. She did not know how to get him to open up and enjoy the time in Vegas.

Even as the trip progressed, Scott's icy demeanor showed no signs of thawing. Shannon felt like an intruder in a story she thought they were writing together. The emotional chasm between them yawned wider with every passing hour, and the glimmers of warmth she once held onto seemed extinguished.

At breakfast the next morning, Shannon tried to make conversation, mentioning the vibrant energy of Las Vegas and suggesting they explore the local sights.

Scott, however, barely looked up from his phone, his responses clipped and perfunctory. Any effort to close the gap felt challenging, yet it reflected a heartfelt desire to connect and understand futile moods. An awkward silence settled over the table, broken only by the faint clatter of cutlery against plates as Shannon pushed her food around, appetite long forgotten.

As the hours unfolded, Scott's restlessness became more apparent. He spent extended periods staring at his phone, occasionally stepping outside for hushed phone calls that he brushed off with vague explanations. Shannon spent hours with Scott in the hotel lounge while he drank wine and called family members and friends from his phone. Too exhausted to pry further into his moods, she spent the day alone in the hotel lounge, watching as couples strolled by, laughing and holding hands, none of them burdened by the weight of unspoken truths.

That night, surrounded by the tang of cologne and cheap perfume, Shannon drifted through the casino, tossing unfocused bets at the craps table while Scott loudly proclaimed his gambling skills. The smoky haze of cigars and cigarettes hung thick in the air, closing in around them. With every roll of the dice, their exchanges grew emptier, stripped of the warmth and connection Shannon so deeply craved.

In that moment, she realized she was little more than a fleeting figure in Scott's restless games. Shannon decided that she would never know when her turn would end or on what number she'd finally land in their relationship.

By the time they returned to the room, Shannon knew deep in her heart that this trip wasn't saving their bond. Instead, it was exposing the fractures that had always been there, lying dormant beneath the surface.

Vegas, with all its glitter and tinsel, could not transfer that feeling into their relationship. Instead, Shannon felt more alone on this trip than she had felt back at home with Scott. Shannon noticed he was distant and preferred to be by himself. He went downstairs early in the morning and said he needed his space for a few hours without her.

Prior to that morning, before he got out of bed, Shannon noticed several women calling him on his phone, asking where he was and what was up with him. Shannon wondered if he was bored with her looking for excitement elsewhere, which would make him feel whole again.

Shannon realized he must be seeing other women, leaving her questioning her place in his life. He showed no romantic interest, avoided intimacy, and rejected her advances. What were they to each other?

Shannon had hoped that this weekend away would help them reconnect romantically, but that just was not happening.

By the time Sunday morning rolled around, Shannon found herself staring out the hotel window, watching the sunrise with its painted hues across the Las Vegas skyline. The city with its pulsating activity seemed to mock her relationship with its lack of luster and romance. While her spirit felt drained and exhausted from trying to make him entertained and happy.

Scott hadn't come back to the room that nigh till early in the morning and she hadn't bothered asking where he'd gone. Even if she asked, she knew the answer wouldn't bring her peace.

The realization hit her all at once: she couldn't force him to be the partner she needed, nor could she continue sacrificing her self-worth in the hopes that he might change.

As she packed her suitcase, the weight of the decision settled heavily on her shoulders. Walking away wouldn't be easy, but staying would only deepen her unhappiness.

When the time came to leave, Shannon's insecurities solidified. No matter how dazzling the surroundings in Vegas are, she could not make that early romantic spark return back into their relationship. She needed to make a decision whether to leave or stay.

The truth, once shadowed by wishful thinking, now stood stark and clear before her; it was time to let go and choose herself.

Shannon had come to an undeniable conclusion; Scott would never be the romantic partner she had envisioned, the one who could bring laughter and warmth into her life. Instead, his indifference, the growing emotional chasm between them, and the subtle dismissals of her attempts to connect clarified a painful truth. Now she knew Scott was a man caught in his own orbit, unable or unwilling to embrace the shared intimacy and companionship Shannon longed for in her heart.

This realization wasn't just a disappointment; it was the final thread unraveling the fabric of their strained relationship. Heading to the airport for Phoenix, Shannon glanced back at the hotel as they entered the taxicab with the realization and truth of the future of their relationship. Questions filtered through her thoughts like "What was I doing with this man? He was beyond saving. This man was not fixable."

As the taxi merged into traffic and the city's skyline receded, a strange calm settled over her. Watching Scott preoccupied more with his phone and messages this weekend clarified her position in his life and his priorities. It was up to her to move away.

They rode in silence, the air between them thick with words unspoken and roads untraveled. In that hush, Shannon's heart no longer clamored for something more.

Instead, for the first time in months, she felt the faint but steady beat of her own courage. Whatever came next, it would be chosen not out of fear or loneliness, but with the quiet strength of someone who had finally remembered their own worth.

Chapter 8
Friends Fade, Doubts Grow

Elly and Cassie noticed the change first. Shannon was quieter. Harder to reach. She spoke less about Scott, not due to a lack of content, but because it no longer felt safe to share.

At brunch one Sunday, Cassie leaned across the table. "He's not building you up. He's whittling you down. One inch at a time. Shannon, can't you see what he has done to you?"

Shannon looked away, making excuses, "He's just guarded. He's had a hard life."

Elly was more direct. "We're not judging him. We're watching you vanish. We're watching you disappear. Come back to us before you've gone too far that no one can reach you."

That night, Scott texted her: "Your friends may feel apprehensive about changes. They don't want to see you grow. That's common when people stay small."

Shannon read the message several times. Something inside her stirred. But she didn't answer. Scott's words, though innocuous on the surface, carried an malicious undertone. His message aimed to make Shannon question the intentions of her friends and her own perceptions. By framing their concern as reluctance to see her *grow*, he positioned himself as the sole advocate for her evolution, subtly implying that her friends were regressive forces holding her back.

There was a calculated precision in his approach. Scott didn't outright demand that Shannon distance herself from Elly and Cassie; instead, he planted the narrative of them being "threatened by change." A phrase that disarmed Shannon by making her feel as though her friends might be envious of her relationship with Scott. It was a masterstroke move for Scott to try an alienate Shannon from her friends. One that didn't overtly push Shannon away from her friendships but made her question their intentions suspiciously.

Shannon, "Scott, I noticed you seemed a little distant when I mentioned brunch with Cassie and Elly. Is something bothering you?"

Scott replied, "Not at all, Shannon. I just want you to be aware, you know, sometimes friends don't always react well when someone close to them starts growing or changing. It's natural for them to feel a bit left out."

Shannon, "You think Cassie and Elly feel left out? They've always supported me."

Scott, "Of course, they care for you. But sometimes people worry they'll lose the old connection as you step into something new. They can't help but see your happiness as a threat to the way things used to be."

Shannon replied, "I don't know… Cassie's never seemed jealous. She's always cheered me on."

Scott, "I'm not saying she's jealous. Just… sometimes support can come with strings attached, even if nobody means for it to. They're afraid you'll change so much that the friendship won't feel the same."

Shannon, "I've never thought of it that way."

Scott, "Just something to consider. I only want what's best for you. If you ever feel like they're holding you back, you know I'll always be here supporting your growth, no matter what."

Shannon, "Thanks, Scott. I'll… keep that in mind."

Scott's goal in isolating Shannon was rooted in control. By weakening her trust in the people who had been her support system, he stripped her of the external anchors that could challenge his behavior or offer alternative perspectives. Their voices, once comforting and familiar, had become barriers to her growth and their relationship. Scott knew that to maintain dominance in Shannon's life, he needed her world to revolve entirely around him. His words operated like slow erosion, breaking down both her sense of self and her relationships with others. Through his manipulative tactics, Scott was systematically dismantling her individuality and her connection to those who cared for her.

Scott is deliberately distancing Shannon from Elly and Cassie, who serve as her anchors of emotional support and clarity. By framing their concern as jealousy and portraying them as obstacles to Shannon's growth, Scott is sowing seeds of mistrust and doubt. This alienation is subtle yet powerful, as it forces Shannon to question the intentions of people who genuinely care for her well-being. The result is a growing isolation that leaves Shannon more vulnerable to Scott's influence.

Hoping to ease the growing tension, Shannon invited Scott and her closest friends, Cassie and Elly, for a relaxed evening together. She wanted Scott to witness firsthand the sincere bond she shared with them, believing that their warmth and support might help him feel less uneasy. By bringing everyone together, Shannon wished to show that she could cherish her friendships without compromising her relationship with Scott, and that is all parts of her life could coexist in harmony.

Scott, "You know, Cassie, you're such a strong personality. I can see why Shannon looks up to you. She's always talking about how you've been like a sister for her."

Cassie, "Well, that's what friends do, Scott. We've always supported each other. Shannon's been there for me just as much as I've been there for her."

Scott, "That's great, but sometimes, strong personalities can cast a shadow. Do you ever think Shannon feels... boxed in? Like, she's hesitant to branch out because she doesn't want to disappoint you."

Shannon, "What do you mean, Scott? Cassie's never made me feel that way."

Cassie, "Of course not. Shannon, you know I want the best for you, no matter what direction you choose."

Scott, "Oh, I didn't mean to cause trouble. It's just something I've noticed. Sometimes when people care deeply, it can unintentionally feel like pressure. Growth can be hard when you're trying to keep everyone happy."

Shannon, "I've never thought of it like that..."

Cassie, "Shannon, don't let this twist things. You don't need to question my intentions. I'm here for you, always."

Scott, "I know you mean well, Cassie. It's just that sometimes, even the best intentions can hold someone back. Shannon's really blossoming lately, and it's beautiful to watch. I just want her to feel free to explore that."

Shannon, "I guess... I need to think about everything."

As the scene unfolds, Shannon finds herself torn. Cassie's words are steady and reassuring, yet Scott's insinuations plant seeds of doubt. The dialogue is more than words. It's a delicate dance of manipulation, where Scott positions himself as the advocate for Shannon's independence while subtly casting her dearest friend in a questionable light.

Cassie's intentions are pure, but Shannon's trust starts to waver.

Scott's behavior is not only about isolating Shannon but also about reshaping her perception of herself. His remarks and behavior aim to erode Shannon's self-confidence and independence. By disregarding her feelings, belittling her emotional vulnerabilities, and positioning himself as the arbiter of her "growth," he is eroding her vibrant individuality. Shannon's self-worth now depends solely on Scott's perspective.

Scott's calculated precision in communication reveals his intent to exert control without overt confrontation. His remarks, such as "threatened by change" and dismissive language about her emotional experiences, serve to destabilize Shannon's trust in herself and others. This quiet manipulation ensures that Shannon begins to rely solely on Scott for validation and guidance, further diminishing her capacity for independent thought and action.

Finally, Scott's actions aim to make himself the sole constant in Shannon's life. He is not just alienating her from her friends or undermining her individuality; he is reshaping her reality entirely. Shannon's identity is changing due to Scott's influence. Her world is becoming smaller, darker, and centered around him, leaving little room for her own growth or the impact of others.

This erosion, both external and internal, highlights the dangerous dynamics at play in their relationship. It speaks to the manipulative strategies employed to isolate, control, and diminish another's sense of self and connection to the people who genuinely care for them.

Shannon began to retreat, not because she doubted Elly and Cassie's love for her, but because the act of confiding in them started to feel disloyal. She couldn't untangle the threads of manipulation from genuine concern, leaving her increasingly isolated prey to Scott's narrative that painted her friends as stagnant forces unable to comprehend the depth of what they shared.

In the end, Scott's tactics weren't about alienating Shannon from her friends; they were about reshaping her reality. He wanted her to see him as the only constant in her life, the foundation upon which everything else rested. Shannon, like her friends, was losing her vibrant individuality under Scott's influence.

Chapter 9
Pieces of the Puzzle

One night, while discussing childhood memories, Shannon mentioned feeling abandoned as a child. Scott laughed. Not cruelly, but casually. As if it were an overreaction.

"You women and your daddy issues," he said. "You want men to fix what your fathers broke. It's exhausting. "Her breath caught. "I'm not asking you to fix me." Her breath caught. Scott leaned back, a faint, calculated smirk on his face, as though her words amused him rather than challenged him. "That's the thing, Shannon. You don't have to ask. It's what you're doing, whether you realize it or not."

The casual dismissal in his tone sliced through her defenses. Shannon felt the sting of his words reverberate, their weight pressing against the fragile barrier she had constructed to protect herself. Yet, there was something more manipulative in his response and a subtle assertion that her independence was a façade. He implied that her very existence revolved around him, whether she wanted it to or not.

His gaze remained a bit longer on her due to the mixture of empathy and undeniable arrogance. "You've built your world around me, haven't you? I mean, look at how much you depend on me for clarity, for validation. It's exhausting, yes, but also... predictable."

Shannon's pulse quickened as her mind grappled with the manipulation embedded in his words. She realized that Scott wasn't merely responding to her; he was rewriting the narrative, positioning himself as the protagonist in her story while relegating her to a supporting role. His calculated charm packaged dominance in a way that seemed reasonable, but it wasn't.

She looked away, unable to meet the gaze that sought to consume her. His words felt like chains, locking her into a reality she didn't recognize as her own. A small but persistent spark of rebellion remained in her mind. She realized she could take control of her own story, despite his influence.

Scott's remark about *women and their daddy issues* was not just an offhanded comment. It was a glimpse into the calculated way he sought to diminish Shannon's feelings and experiences, reducing them to cliches that stripped them of their significance.

In framing her vulnerability as a burden, Scott effectively dismissed her pain while positioning himself as the one who holds the power to absolve or exacerbate it. This casual cruelty served a dual purpose. It simultaneously undermined Shannon's sense of worth and strengthened his role as the architect of her reality.

But his words seemed to hold a deeper meaning beyond just dismissing the idea. As Shannon reeled from the sting of his comment, Scott's reference to *you women* hinted at a broader strategy. It suggested that he might already be seeking others to fill the role that Shannon currently occupied. By generalizing her emotions into a collective stereotype, he subtly de-individualized her, reducing Shannon from a unique partner to just another interchangeable figure in a pattern he could replicate. It was not just a statement about Shannon's perceived flaws, but a veiled declaration of his ability to replace her should she cease to serve his needs.

Shannon couldn't shake the feeling that she was struggling to make sense of her feelings. She was trying so hard to reconcile the man she thought she knew with the actions that increasingly revealed his true intentions.

Scott wasn't just reshaping her life; he was preparing for the possibility of grooming others to step into her place. His charisma, his calculated charm, and his ability to manipulate emotions were tools he had used before and would use again. Shannon was beginning to see that her relationship with Scott might not be unique, but rather a chapter in a pattern of control and exploitation.

Her realization was both freeing and overwhelming, a mix that felt deeply personal and intense. Shannon valued mutual respect and understanding in relationships, but Scott used these principles as tools for control, disguised as affection. Her eyes opened to the patterns in his behavior, the masterful orchestration of charm, dismissal, and emotional withdrawal designed to keep her tethered while he remained aloof.

What really stood out to her was how all of it was so carefully planned and thought out. Scott wasn't reckless or impulsive at all. Every word, every laugh, every moment of casual cruelty was deliberate, a part of a larger strategy to mold Shannon into someone who doubted her worth and depended on his validation.

She realized it wasn't about losing Scott, but about how he saw people as interchangeable, like puzzle pieces in his game.

But even as she felt overwhelmed by this realization, a gentle determination started to grow inside her.

For the first time, Shannon felt the stirring of rebellion against the narrative Scott had imposed on her. She thought of Elly and Cassie and their unwavering love and concern. Shannon saw the threads of hope they offered, a reminder that she wasn't alone and didn't have to remain ensnared in his shadow.

Scott's world was one of dominance and manipulation, but Shannon was starting to see cracks in the foundation he had built. She gradually rediscovered herself, facing fear with determination. She hadn't yet escaped his grasp, but she was beginning to understand that she could reclaim the vibrant individuality he had tried to suppress.

It was time to rewrite her story. The one where she was the author of her own fate. She was no longer a character in Scott's calculated script.

Yet, Scott's words persisted, steeped in a sense of foreboding. They indicated that, to him, Shannon was dispensable.

Instead, she was part of a cycle and one he could perpetuate with someone new when she no longer fit into the mold he had crafted for her. She acknowledged that Scott had led her to believe that a replacement was inevitable.

That night, he turned his back on her in bed. Not in anger, but because he didn't care about intimacy or closeness. Shannon felt alone and lonely for his attention as she stared at the ceiling, the darkness pressing down like a weighted blanket.

It was the first time she let herself say it, even silently: *Something is wrong with this man.*

Scott's behaviors, as described, show patterns that could be associated with various psychological tendencies such as narcissistic traits or manipulative control strategies. His calculated charm, dismissal of Shannon's emotions, and the subtle way he undermines her sense of individuality point toward a personality that thrives on dominance and external validation.

Scott's behavior was like the pieces of a puzzle I was just starting to put together, and the picture slowly emerging wasn't what I had hoped to see. His charm, which once seemed so genuine, now felt more calculated and a skill he seemed to use with careful intention. Every time he dismissed her feelings or made casual comments about "you women" or "anxieties," it didn't seem random. It felt like a conscious choice. He gradually shifting her perception, little by little.

Shannon couldn't ignore how he reduced her to a stereotype, brushing aside her pain like it was something trivial, something universal to all women, and somehow expected. It hurt in a way that stayed, not just physically, but emotionally, because it made her feel invisible and like she didn't matter, as if she could be replaced at any moment. She felt like just another placeholder in a role; he could easily recast her without hesitation whenever she no longer fit into his script.

She couldn't shake the feeling that this wasn't her story. It was his. A script he'd written long before she arrived. She was beginning to see that she wasn't meant to be more than a chapter in it.

There was darkness in him, one that thrived on control. I couldn't help but feel curious about whether his power stemmed from making her stay close, uncertain, dependent, and feeling like she could be replaced.

She hated how easily he could make her second-guess herself. She hated how it worked. He had this ability to dismiss her fears while positioning himself as the authority on her emotions. It wasn't just cruel, it was strategic. The worst part was that she was aware of his devious behavior, and yet she did nothing. She could feel it in every one of her doubts. It showed up in her actions, as she tiptoed around him to accommodate his needs and ignored mine.

Scott wasn't just someone who had hurt me. He was someone who had taught me, unintentionally, that my pain didn't matter to him and my emotions were a hindrance.

Scott's behaviors began to mirror the unpredictable and volatile patterns she had read about in bipolar disorder. His sudden shifts from charm to cold detachment, the calculated way he dismissed her emotions one moment. Then he buried her under clinical, caring observations, the next, felt eerily like the manic highs and depressive lows she imagined bipolarity might manifest. His fluctuating grip on control and those brief moments of vulnerability only made her feel more uneasy.

What terrified her was the realization that Scott's actions aligned with a mental health condition that was incurable and lifelong. Though he carefully masked his manic episode with his charm and wit, his aloofness indicated depressive withdrawal.

Shannon found herself questioning both his intentions and her own perception of reality. Was she dealing with a person whose instability could spiral unpredictably, leaving her perpetually braced for the next turn, or was it darker, more sinister?

This realization struck a deep chord of fear within Shannon. If Scott's behavior was due to bipolar disorder, she might never fully understand his moods, motives, or control.

Worse still, it forced her to confront a chilling possibility: that his power over her didn't come from deliberate manipulation, but from something intrinsic, uncontrollable, that might never change.

The idea that her life could remain tethered to this whirlwind of instability was enough to send a shiver down her spine. It wasn't about Scott anymore. It was about the shadow his behavior cast over every aspect of her sense of safety and self.

Shannon was now convinced that Scott's actions weren't random or careless; they were intentional. I could see how he had groomed me into a role where I relied on him, where my autonomy slowly vanished. He was preparing for the moment he could move me aside for someone else, as if I were nothing more than an interchangeable piece in his life. Every gesture of charm felt calculated, every dismissal of my feelings was a tool to keep me uncertain, dependent, and small. It wasn't about his control over me; it was about his ability to maintain a facade of strength and dominance at the expense of my sense of self. The realization was devastating, but I couldn't ignore it any longer. I saw how he maneuvered, how he carefully positioned me to rely on him, to question myself. It wasn't always obvious at first, but the signs were there: the way he charmed his way through every situation, his dismissive responses to my fears, the subtle digs that chipped away at my sense of self. It felt like he had rehearsed these moves, like he knew exactly how to make me feel small, uncertain, and replaceable.

I couldn't ignore the patterns I was seeing. His words, his tone, his timing all aligned to keep me in check, to keep me doubting myself while he maintained the upper hand. Watching him, I started to realize that his charm wasn't warmth; it was a mask. His concern wasn't genuine; it was a tool. His refusal to acknowledge my emotions wasn't indifferent; it was intentional. He thrived on control, on the power that came from keeping me dependent and questioning my own reality.

What struck me most was how deliberate it seemed, as if he had perfected this routine long before I'd ever stepped into his life. It was planned, not spontaneous or impulsive. As I pieced it together, I began to see that his dominance wasn't power over me; it was about preserving an image of himself that left no room for vulnerability or equal partnership.

Scott's behavior defies a single diagnosis or pattern. His actions might span multiple psychological tendencies, blending narcissistic traits with deliberate manipulation and other underlying factors. Understanding the "darkness" within him would require a thorough psychological evaluation, but what is clear is the profound emotional impact his behaviors have had on Shannon.

Shannon, understanding Scott's behavior was not an exercise in analyzing his actions, but a journey toward reclaiming her own sense of self. Every new realization about his manipulative tendencies slowly chipped away at the comforting image she had held of him. It revealed a harsh truth: his charm was just a superficial veneer, his concern was a carefully calculated tool, and his control was a deliberate effort to systematically weaken her independence.

Shannon began to recognize the strength in her own awareness. The clarity she found in his patterns of behavior gave her the courage to confront the emotional toll of their relationship. It was no longer about understanding Scott; it was about understanding herself, her limits, and the boundaries she needed to set to preserve her autonomy.

The turning point came when Shannon decided to confide in her trusted friends about her experiences. She realized Scott's influence made her feel isolated and doubtful of her reality. Sharing her story lifted a weight she hadn't even realized she was carrying. For the first time, she felt the possibility of freedom, the faint light of a life beyond the confines of Scott's influence.

Shannon sat across from her friend Elly at a quiet café, fingers nervously tracing the rim of her cup.

"I just—sometimes I feel like I'm losing track of what's real," Shannon admitted, her voice barely above a whisper.

Elly looked at her, concern softening her features. "Is it because of Scott?"

Shannon nodded, eyes searching for Elly's for reassurance. "He makes me question everything. One minute he's attentive, the next he's cold and dismissive. It's like my feelings are always wrong, and they are the only ones that matter."

Elly reached out, squeezing Shannon's hand. "You're not alone, Shan. It sounds like he's twisting things to keep you dependent. That's not love or partnership."

A shaky breath escaped Shannon's lips. "For so long, I thought it was just me. Like I was being too sensitive, or maybe even imagining things. But after talking to you... I see that I'm not losing it. I'm not crazy."

"That's the power of sharing," Elly said gently. "You deserve to trust yourself. You deserve to feel safe."

The weight seemed to lift from Shannon's shoulders. "Thank you, Elly. I think... for the first time, I can see a life beyond him. I can see the possibility of freedom."

Elly smiled. "You're stronger than you know. This is just the beginning."

With each step forward, Shannon found herself questioning less and asserting more. She began to redefine what a healthy relationship looked like, one built on mutual respect, compassion, and emotional honesty, and qualities that Scott had consistently withheld. She realized that love was not about submission to another's control, but about partnership and growth.

Though the road ahead was uncertain, Shannon knew she was ready to carve her own path. Scott's shadow might remain, but it no longer dictated her choices. The power he had wielded over her was waning, replaced by the resilience she discovered within herself. Shannon realized that she needed to reclaim her own power through her worth and identity not his to define.

This realization was not a destination, but a beginning pathway to unearthing the strength she had long buried under the weight of Scott's dominance. Shannon started to explore her own aspirations and boundaries; things she had once suppressed to accommodate his needs. She began to reconnect with the friendships and hobbies that had faded during their relationship, rediscovering joys that made her feel whole and grounded.

Freedom for Shannon wasn't simply about escaping Scott's control; it was about rebuilding the foundation of her life with intention and clarity. She reflected on the emotional toll of their time together, not with bitterness, but with determination to learn from it. The journey was arduous, with doubt and vulnerability, but she learned to recognize her need for empowerment, authenticity, and mutual respect in relationships.

As Shannon asserted her independence, she also discovered how vital self-compassion is, realizing its profound importance. She acknowledged the courage it took to break free and recognized that healing was not linear but cyclical, often requiring revisiting past wounds to move forward.

Chapter 10
Body and Mind

Scott's physical condition began to show deterioration. He moved more slowly. Winced when sitting. His hands sometimes trembled when he thought she wasn't watching.

"You, okay?" she asked once.

His reply was swift. Cold. "Don't project your anxiety onto me."

He never spoke about his medical history again. Neither did I. Yet he continued to offer opinions about me. About my sleep. My emotions. My habits. It all comes across in very clinical language, almost like a mask of concern.

Scott seemed determined to maintain an illusion of strength and control, even as his body betrayed him in quiet, persistent ways. The tremors of his hands, the hesitation in his movements, and the wincing that betrayed discomfort told a story he refused to acknowledge. To admit vulnerability would have meant confronting a reality that he seemed desperate to avoid, a reality that might shatter the carefully constructed image of invulnerability he presented to the world and to Shannon.

His denial wasn't just about not knowing; it was a deliberate choice to reject what his declining health represented.

Weakness, he seemed to believe, was an opening for others to question his authority, his intellect, and the control he wielded so effortlessly over those around him. By cloaking his physical fragility in curt dismissals and sharp remarks, he maintained the narrative of invincibility, a narrative that allowed him to dominate, critique, and manipulate without resistance.

Scott would rationalize his perfect health conditions by downplaying Shannon's health and emotional state, and even her sleep patterns. It was a tactic that helped strengthen his position of influence in their relationship. If Shannon ever questioned his health, he would deflect or rebuke her, accusing her of projection or overreaction, as though her concern was a flaw rather than genuine care.

This denial was not only a defense mechanism but a calculated act of control. By refusing to admit his own struggles, Scott ensured that Shannon remained the one under scrutiny. By dissecting her vulnerabilities, he remained hidden behind a veil of stoicism. His failing physical condition became another tool in his arsenal, a secret tightly held. Scott's illusion of strength was not just about appearance; it was about preserving the power he had over Shannon and shielding himself from the terror of losing it.

Shannon's perspective was starting to change. She realized she didn't need to break down Scott's walls or try to change him anymore.

The more Shannon reflected, the more she understood the fragile foundation upon which Scott had built his strength. His reluctance to admit vulnerability was not a reflection of invulnerability, but of fear Shannon no longer shared. Where Scott clung to his perceived control, Shannon was learning to embrace her uncertainty. She was beginning to understand that the unknown was not a void to fear but a field of possibilities, waiting for her to take her first brave steps.

Scott's power seemed to wane as Shannon's clarity grew. His words, once sharp and stinging, began to lose their potency. His dismissal of her concerns no longer felt like a failure on her part but rather a failure on his to connect. Each curt remark, each cold rebuke, became less about her shortcomings and more about his refusal to confront the crumbling edges of his own facade.

Shannon began to reclaim the narrative of her own life. She didn't need Scott's acknowledgment to validate her worth or his approval to guide her path forward. Each day, she found herself letting go of the need for answers he refused to give, focusing instead on the truths she could create for herself. The weight of his control, once unbearable, now felt lighter with every step she took away from it.

It wasn't a dramatic break or a single moment of clarity that freed her, but in her quiet moments of self-realization. It was in the decision to call an old friend, the rediscovery of a forgotten passion, or the simple act of sitting with her own thoughts without the shadow of his judgment looming over her. Each of these moments was a small but significant act of defiance against the narrative Scott had tried so hard to script.

Shannon was no longer seeking closure from Scott. She no longer needed his explanations or apologies. She began to understand that closure wasn't something he could give her; it was something she had to create for herself. Once she reached that point, she was able to shape her own portrait of the woman she really wanted to be. Her own masterpiece, full of unfinished brushstrokes and vibrant, untamed colors ready to be revealed to the world.

Chapter 11
The Empty Promises

In the aftermath of Scott's final departure, Shannon found herself alone with a silence that rang louder than any argument they'd ever had. The echoes of his empty promises and calculated tenderness played over in her mind, scenes she desperately wished she could rewrite. The fantasy of who she believed he was, and the knowledge of his true personality as a true narcissist with mental health issues and the fine crafted façade he portrayed to others.

She realized she was holding on not because she missed what was lost in the relationship, but because she needed to untangle the ways he had skillfully misled her emotionally.

One evening, she sat alone at the kitchen table, with a thick journal and a pen laid out before her, inviting her to put her thoughts on paper.

Carefully, she began to write down every promise he'd ever made: the trips that never happened, the vacation home he talked about buying together, the family gatherings that always remained just an idea and the love sessions he was too tired to perform . She recorded the way he spoke in vague somedays.

Each one kept her suspended in hopes for a life that was always just out of reach.

With each recollection, Shannon felt the web of guilt and confusion begin to loosen. She could see now how Scott had wielded promises not as gifts, but as shackles; how his reassurances were not acts of love, but strategies for holding her at arm's length while demanding her devotion. Naming these truths, seeing them in black and white gave her the clarity he'd always denied her.

Shannon recognized the absence of genuine emotional openness and honesty, realizing that the early visions of a shared future remained empty promises.

But as Shannon stepped into this fragile new space, she realized that the echoes of Scott's empty assurances still remained just empty promises. The promises in the end became background noise to her growing sense of self.

She began to recognize that his assurances were never about partnership, but about maintaining the delicate architecture of his own image.

Gone were the nights when she clung to his words for comfort or waited for him to fulfill vows that dissolved with the morning light. Instead, she traced the patterns in his behavior: the way his commitments flickered with uncertainty, the way his attention shifted with the tides of his own anxieties. She saw the gulf between what he claimed to offer and what she received, and the ache of unmet expectation gave way to a new resolve.

Now, when Scott spoke in platitudes and half-promises, Shannon felt less disappointment and more distance. She let his words settle around her like mist, no longer absorbing them as truth. This gentle yet significant change marked the beginning of Scott's unraveling from the hold he once had.

In this newfound clarity, Shannon understood that her power did not depend on his promises or his presence. She found herself able to reshape her life, choosing to invest in what was genuine and lasting, even as Scott kept offering only the illusion of something more committed.

Scott embodied the qualities Shannon admired: intelligence, eloquence, and quiet sophistication; paired with an aura of control and respect.

He carried an aura of someone who had seen life from an elevated vantage point, yet his actions often betrayed his promises. He would pledge to spend time with her during the holidays but refused to commit to shared plans or support her ambitions, instead retreating behind vague excuses or dismissals.

One evening, Shannon sat alone at her kitchen table, the glow of her phone illuminating unanswered messages and broken plans.

She replayed their recent exchanges, searching for sincerity beneath the practiced cadence of his voice. It struck her then: this was not a partnership built on trust, but on the precarious balance of hope and uncertainty.

His reluctance to confront his health issues mirrored the emotional barriers in their relationship, turning promises of honesty and mutual care into hollow gestures.

The following dialogue was statements made by Scott to Shannon that she remembers as manipulative plays in their relationship interactions:

Shannon: "Scott, you've seemed tired lately. Are you sure you're, okay?"

Scott: "I'm perfectly fine. If anyone should be worried, it's you. You haven't been sleeping well."

Shannon: "I just want to make sure we're looking out for each other."

Scott: "You're always so anxious. You should relax a bit."

Shannon: "You promised we'd go to the vineyards this weekend. I've been looking forward to it."

Scott: "I know, but work came up. Why do you always focus on the negative?"

Shannon: "It just feels like your promises keep slipping away."

Scott: "You're overreacting. Can't you see how much I'm trying?"

Shannon came to see these patterns not as missteps but as calculated deflections, a way for Scott to maintain dominance while keeping her tethered to an illusion of connection and future possibilities. She realized that the more she tried to untangle his words, the further she drifted from her own sense of stability.

Each conversation, meant to bring them closer, seemed instead to leave her with more questions than answers. Questions that he ignored stayed in the silent spaces between his cool assurances and her persistent doubts.

The next time Scott brushed off her concerns with charm and distraction, Shannon simply chose not to fill the silence, letting it hang comfortably between them. Instead, she let it stretch between them, heavy with things unsaid, waiting to see if he would choose honesty over comfort. In that pause, she realized that her clarity was growing stronger than the illusion he so carefully maintained.

There was his unwillingness to provide the emotional truth and vulnerability Shannon sought from him, and the promise of a future he had made in the early, hopeful months of their relationship. This was a promise that once felt like a foundation but now seemed like a mirage. For Shannon, it became painfully clear that Scott's reluctance to share his inner world was not a temporary hesitation, but a deliberate choice, one he used to maintain the balance of power in their dynamic.

Scott's charm, his carefully curated sophistication, were tools he wielded with precision, drawing Shannon in just enough to keep her believing, and yet ensuring she always felt slightly off kilter, constantly questioning whether she was asking for too much. It wasn't about the emotional walls he had built; it was the way he turned those walls into mirrors, reflecting her own doubts and insecurities at her. Shannon was continuously seeking answers from a man who consistently avoided giving direct responses.

But the illusion was beginning to crack. The promises Scott made, coated in subtle eloquence, were losing their ability to soothe. Shannon's growing clarity allowed her to see the mechanisms at play. She now saw how his assurances were less about love and more about control, how his reluctance to be vulnerable wasn't strength, but fear masquerading as fortitude.

Shannon recalled conversations where the dialogue was riddled with broken promises and false excuses:

Shannon: "Scott, can we talk about last weekend? You said you'd be there for dinner, but you canceled again."

Scott: "Work ran late. You know how important this project is to me. Why do you always make it about you?"

Shannon: "I'm not making it about me. I just need to know when you make plans, you'll follow through."

Scott: "You're always on edge. It's exhausting sometimes. I said I'd make it up to you. Didn't I? You should try being more understanding."

Shannon: "It's not just this time. It feels like every time we get close to what you promised, something gets in the way. The vineyard trip, the dinner, moving in together…"

Scott: "So you're keeping score now? That's not fair. I'm trying, but nothing I do is ever enough for you."

Shannon: "That's not what I'm saying. I just want to know what you say means your word. Not empty promises."

Scott: "Look, someday we'll do all those things. We're just not ready yet. You always want to rush things."

Shannon: "I'm not trying to rush. I just want honesty, Scott. I want to know you mean what you say."

Scott: "You're overthinking this. If you keep pushing, you're going to ruin what we have."

Shannon: "I'm not trying to ruin anything. I just want to feel secure, to know you care."

Scott: "Of course I care. I wouldn't still be here if I didn't. Let's just not fight, okay? I'll make dinner reservations for next Friday. Happy?"

Shannon: "I'll believe it when I see it."

Scott: "Always doubting me… That's the real problem."

What stood out the most was how Scott reacted when he was confronted, showing his true character. He didn't crumble under pressure; instead, he doubled down, using deflection and condescension as shields and sometimes intimidation and threats. Shannon had started to recognize that these were not the signs of a man protecting his heart, but of someone terrified of exposing his flaws. And as she pieced together the truths he tried so hard to hide, she found herself not mourning the loss of what they could have had but questioning why she had ever believed it in the first place.

For Shannon, the realization marked a turning point and one defined not by explosive conflict, but by quiet resolve for herself. She began to focus less on Scott's failures to fulfill his promises and more on her own ability to break free from the hold those promises had on her. The future Scott had painted for them was no longer her anchor; it was a canvas she was ready to repaint, one brushstroke at a time. She realized this fairytale had no hold on her dreams.

His promises always seemed to drift away, laced with just enough earnestness to keep her hope flickering. He painted pictures of cozy nights together and reignited connections with the moments Shannon yearned for but never got from him.

Every so often, he revealed a trace of softness, hinting that he might finally let down the barriers between them. He spoke with conviction and longing, offering words that resonated with possibility, yet those words never truly became actions.

Each promise was a thread tied to a dream she could never quite reach, always flying before it became real. For Shannon, it seems the longer she was with him, the less he offered. Each time, her faith in his words diminished a little, as did her trust in him.

Shannon noticed the pattern. He provided assurances that addressed her concerns while maintaining the dynamics of their relationship. They were the tools Scott used to maintain the illusion that he cared deeply, even as his actions spoke of avoidance and withdrawal. For every promise he made, there was a moment that contradicted it: a missed dinner, a canceled plan, a conversation that ended before it began.

The emotional intimacy she craved from him seemed to be forever out of reach, replaced by a calculated sort of tenderness meant to keep her waiting, hoping, and believing. Shannon wondered if his actions were out of love or control. So, she was unable to look elsewhere for the connection he refused to make.

Scott's words were like delicate threads spun from moonlight, so beautiful in the moment, yet so fragile they disintegrated with the dawn of reality.

He spoke of trips they would take: a weekend getaway to the coast, a journey to the vineyards she had always dreamed about, a ski trip during the winter holiday, and a New Year's Eve stacation that never materialized.

Yet each plan dissolved into a haze of excuses: work commitments, family obligations, and bad timing. The promises remained in the air, just long enough to keep Shannon tethered, before vanishing without a trace.

There were moments when Scott gave her just enough to keep her tied to the idea of their future. A surprise dinner reservation, a rare evening where he was attentive and listening intently to her stories.

Those nights felt like the Scott she had fallen for in the beginning: warm, present and sincere. Shannon soon realized they weren't signs of change but carefully placed reprieves to keep her thirsting for more like a small oasis in the desert.

Even the way they spoke of "someday" was masterful.

"Someday, we'll move into a place together," he would say, or "Someday, we'll take that trip to Europe."

Someday became the beacon she chased, a destination that always shimmered just beyond the horizon. But with every passing month, it became clearer that Scott's "someday" was a mirage, a device to keep her anchored to a dream he never intended to fulfill.

And yet, the most heartbreaking of his promises was the one he never actually said out loud but somehow made her believe in: the promise of change.

Throughout every argument and tearful conversation, Scott would nod, seem to reflect, and gently offered her hope that things might change for the better. Yet, the pattern stayed firm and unchanging.

He wasn't offering her a path forward; instead, he was creating a maze of false hopes and endless detours.

Shannon began to recognize that his empty promises were not merely failures of follow-through. They were tools of manipulation, carefully calibrated to maintain his power and her dependency. Each promise was a subtle act of control and a way to dictate the terms of their relationship which kept her doubting her worth and her demands.

She finally felt a weight lift from her chest as she realized she'd been waiting so long for someone who never truly intended to keep his promises. Her heart was breaking with every broken promise, causing her emotional and physical pain that was so psychologically damaging to her. The weight of his empty words, once buoyed by hope, now felt suffocating. It was a burden she could no longer carry, and Shannon felt a quiet anger simmering beneath her sorrow.

For every unkept promise, Shannon decided to make a new one to herself. A promise to reclaim her time, her energy and her dreams. Scott's promises had been fleeting, but hers would be steadfast, a foundation upon which she could finally begin to build a life unshackled by his illusions.

Chapter 12
Broken Heart Syndrome

Shannon had been in an eight-month, on-and-off relationship with Scott. At first, he had dazzled her with charm, intellect, and a sense of authority that made her feel both seen and safe. But it did not take long for the pedestal to become a cage.

He was sarcastic when she was vulnerable, dismissive when she needed reassurance. He controlled the cadence of their relationship. He controlled when they saw each other and when they did not. He controlled when to pull her close or push her away. It was always on his terms, never Shannon's schedule.

Shannon had spent months trying to keep the peace, convincing herself that the problem was her sensitivity, her inability to "lighten up," as he often said with a smirk. But the emotional whiplash wore her down until the final breakup was delivered with clinical detachment, which sent a shock through her system that no amount of logic could buffer. Her body reacted before her mind could process it. What she thought was heartbreak was, quite literally, her heart breaking.

From outward appearances, Scott embodied everything Shannon believed she desired: Successful, eloquent, and perpetually in control. He carried himself with the ease of someone accustomed to commanding situations from a place of authority. Early on, his attention felt like a rare privilege and something Shannon believed he was lucky to receive.

Scott spoke in measured tones that made her feel calm, even when the words themselves sliced at her self-worth.

When she expressed concern or hurt, he would arch an eyebrow and say, "You're reading too much into things," or worse, "Don't be dramatic, Shannon."

At first, Shannon laughed it off. But over time, her laughter became more strained, and her joy turned to sadness. Every small disagreement turned into a subtle power play. He withheld affection when she set boundaries. He gave praise only when she validated his actions. Their relationship had become more complicated and less fun, and more troubling. Each day brought more rejection and disappointment, and less expressions of appreciation and more apologies for his actions. She began to question her instincts, reconsider her responses, and apologize for requesting basic decency and understanding.

Yet he never yelled. He never hit. And that made it harder. The damage was not visible. It was slow erosion. Emotional sleight of hand.

Shannon had embarked on her relationship with Dr. Scott under the belief that they were committed to each other in monogamy. He had often reassured her in his subtly condescending, but measured tone, "You are the only one, Shannon. I do not want distractions."

But his actions, as Shannon painfully discovered over time, told a vastly different story.

Scott had crafted an image of exclusivity. He painted Shannon into his life narrative as someone important, someone who grounded him amidst the chaos of his demanding schedule. "Golf weekends, consulting work, endless paperwork," he would often lament, sipping his wine with a weary sigh.

Shannon had held onto these moments, believing she was his respite, even if she only saw him once a week in fleeting encounters.

But beneath the surface of his polished, articulate persona lay a web of lies. The reality unraveled slowly, as Shannon noticed patterns that did not add up: his avoidance of deeper commitment, his refusal to stay the night, his carefully choreographed dinner dates and conversations that never veered beyond what he allowed.

The truth came crashing when Shannon stumbled upon his lap computer one evening, left carelessly unlocked while he showered. She had not intended to snoop, but a sudden unease compelled her to look at what she found confirmed her worst fears: countless female contacts, conversations dating back months.

There were pictures, selfies sent to other women, accompanied by captions that mirrored the charm he had used to win Shannon over. Each conversation revealed a different version of Scott, tailored to the preferences of the women he pursued. And Scott's name or presence? Nowhere in sight. He had been crafting other lives, other connections, all while letting Shannon believe in their exclusivity of their relationship.

In a moment of impulsive anger, she answered one of his messages with a flirtatious text to someone named Anne Marie. Shannon hit the keys on his phone, typing a single word: "Idiot."

She knew the consequences. Either Scott would discover the message and confront her, or Anne Marie would alert him to the strange reply. But Shannon no longer cared about the fallout. She needed to know if he would fight for her if he loved her enough to own up to his deceit. Deep down, she feared the answer.

When Shannon confronted him with the messages, Scott's response was as cold and calculated as she feared.

"I never said we were exclusive," he said, leaning back with an air of unbothered confidence. "You just assumed."

The coldness of his words cut her deeper than the betrayal itself. It was not just that he had been unfaithful; it was the way he had manipulated her trust, allowing her to believe in a monogamous relationship while he operated on his own terms.

Shannon felt a wave of emotions, from fury to heartbreak to utter disillusionment. He did not apologize. He did not even acknowledge her feelings. To him, it was nothing. To him, it seemed, she was just another piece in his carefully orchestrated life, a life he controlled and a narrative he dictated. In the aftermath, Shannon struggled to piece together her sense of self.

Scott's betrayal tore through Shannon's sense of reality. The monogamy he had promised was never real, and the love she thought she was building was little more than a facade carefully maintained to suit his needs. His actions left her questioning not only his integrity but her own instincts. How had she missed the signs? How had she let herself believe his words when his actions consistently contradicted them?

Shannon's story is a painful reminder of the damage caused by emotional manipulation and betrayal. It highlights the importance of trusting one's instincts and recognizing the red flags that often accompany relationships built on deceit.

For Shannon, the journey to healing would be long, but it began with the realization that she deserved honesty, respect, and love that was not conditional or fictional.

Shannon had clung to the idea that what they had was real, even if it often felt more like waiting than living. She saw Scott once a week, always just one evening a week. He said his schedule was full: golf on weekends with "colleagues who expected him to show face," medical consulting work he still dabbled in, and endless paperwork he described with an air of martyrdom. "You don't know what it's like, Shannon," he would say, sipping his wine. "Even in retirement age, people expect too much of me."

She believed in him at first. She told herself that good things were worth the wait. That mature relationship did not need constant contact.

But deep down, uneasiness began to creep in to her insecurities. He never spent the night at her home. He never introduced her to friends. Everything happened on his terms. He made the choices of restaurants, chose the conversations that he carefully stayed at surface-level and those mysteries trips by himself that seemed to happen more frequently.

Later that day, after the betrayal. The following dialogue transpired between the two only to cause the final argument that ended the relationship.

Scott texted Shannon: "You texted Ann Marie from my phone?" His tone was condescending and accusatory. "Who does something as crazy as that?"

Shannon texted: "I needed to know the truth. That you have been lying to be about exclusivity in our relationship. That there are other women. That this, whatever this is, has not been real."

Scott texted: "What are you nuts?"

"This is my life you are messing with?"

"So, you go through my phone? Text people like some jealous teenager? Do you have any idea how invasive that is?"

Shannon texted: "Do you have any idea how cruel it is to pretend to love someone while you're grooming half the internet?"

That stopped him. For a moment, he said nothing. Then he texted back to her, "You do not get to make accusations when you violate my privacy. If you are that insecure, this is not going to work."

That was it. No apology. No confession. Just the same cold deflection he always used to make *her* the problem. Making *her* the one to blame.

Shannon stood slowly, her legs numb beneath her. She texted back, "I was hoping you would at least try to fight for me. For us. Admit what you have done. But you are not even capable of that."

Then he texted, "We are over."

This time, she did not cry. Not yet at least.

She finally accepted the truth that she had months but had been too afraid to name: He never loved her. And he never would. He was emotionally unavailable to her.

For the first time, Shannon allowed herself to sit with the magnitude of her emotions, no longer brushing them aside to stay strong or composed. She felt the sharp sting of betrayal, the hollow ache of loneliness, and the bittersweet relief of finally naming the truth.

As the minutes stretched into an hour, her mind began drifting to a deeper place. One that wasn't about Scott, but about herself. She thought every time she had silenced her instincts to make him comfortable and every moment she had traded her own well-being for a fleeting sense of approval. She realized that those actions fractured her own autonomy. Over months of abuse by this man, she had diminished to the point where she could no longer recognize herself in the mirror.

Tears began to sting her eyes, but this time, they weren't for him. They were for herself. Shannon realized she had been chasing an illusion. All smoke and mirrors, nothing real.

She remembered how often she had diminished herself to fit into his unappreciative life. The tears flowed more freely now, but they carried with them a strange sense of release, finally letting go of the months she had clung to hope, to illusion and to a version of love that demanded sacrifice without reciprocity.

A quiet determination began to rise in her, threading through the pain like a fragile, but unyielding thread of steel. Shannon was raw, yes, and wounded, but she was also awake. Awake to her worth. Awake to the lies she had told herself to stay in a relationship that slowly unraveled her from the inside out. Afraid to ask for what she needed; she allowed him to manipulate her. She was too afraid of making a second mistake in loving Scott that she lost his respect and interest in their relationship.

Scott was no better than Dennis. They both were abusive and manipulative. More importantly, both were controlling and cared about their own needs and validation.

For the first time in what felt like forever, she allowed herself to imagine a different future. One that was defined not by his approval or his absence. She envisioned days filled with her own laughter, evenings spent with friends who lifted her spirit rather than drained it, and quiet nights where solitude didn't feel like a punishment but a gift. She saw herself as whole person. Not as an individual seeking fulfillment from another, but as a person who is already whole and sufficient.

Tomorrow would not be easy, she knew that. There would be moments of doubt, waves of regret, even nights where loneliness would feel unbearable. She now had a fragile yet undeniable belief that she deserved more than the scraps she had received. That she could build a life, brick by brick, in which her happiness was not contingent on anyone else's capacity to love her.

For now, that was enough. And for the first time in months, she allowed herself to believe that enough could grow into everything.

Her heart felt like it was folding in on itself, not in sadness alone, but in exhaustion. The woman she had fought to be, through love and pain, was still there. She just needed to find her way back to herself.

The reality of the breakup hit her hard. Scott had never loved her, nor had her husband. Neither of these men knew what real love meant. Maybe not even a version of unconditional love. What they had loved, if you could call it, was her admiration, her patience and most importantly to them was her ability to play the part they had written for her. She had mistaken crumbs for a feast and misread control for care. And now, stripped of the fantasy, she could finally see it for what it had always been a performance. A script she couldn't edit. Both men were illusions of what she hoped they could be, not who they truly were in a relationship with her. They both wore masks to cover who they were deep inside, and slowly, through months and sometimes years, like Dennis, the masks came off, and the ugly, broken parts of their personalities became visible.

She remembered every time they both dismissed her needs as "too much," every deflection when she asked for more time, more honesty, more clarity, how they had made her feel demanding for wanting simple things, like commitment or truth. She remembered the pauses in conversation when she questioned them, the change in their eyes and the way affection turned cold in an instant when she disappointed them. She had always walked on eggshells and now she finally understood why answer. Both men never had any intention of giving her solid ground. Narcissists never do.

She had sought out the same bad traits that Dennis had in Scott. Never realizing that the mask of charm and sophistication was a play on her emotions to win her over and entrap her.

Tears of sorrow came slowly, not in a wave but in small, steady drops. Not even for what she had shared with each of these men. But for the version of herself, she had abandoned. She had spent years and months with two different men trying to earn the love of a man who never offered it freely.

Shannon realized that love should not require pleading, justification, or validation through suffering. What Scott and Dennis had given her was not love, but smoke and mirrors.

It was control dressed as companionship. Loneliness disguised as attention. She stopped calling it by any other name but narcissistic abuse.

The next morning, Shannon tried to return to a routine. She brewed coffee, but she could not drink it. She stared at emails that she could not process. Her mind would go blank, and her emotions would prevent her from completing simple activities. Her body moved as if on autopilot, but her mind

floated elsewhere, replaying the moments of these relationships.

By mid-morning, a strange pressure began to form in her
chest. Not sharp, not stabbing just heavy. Like something
was sitting on her ribcage and refusing to move. She told
herself it was stress or anxiety and she dismissed the warning
sign. She took deep breaths. She paced. But the pressure
grew. It was not like any panic attack she had before. This
was sharper and more persistent.

And then came the pain radiating across her chest, into
her jaw and down her left arm. Her legs gave out in the
kitchen and she collapsed to the floor while the phone was
still in her hand. She managed to dial 911. An ambulance
came within 10 minutes to her home.

Shannon sat in the ambulance, her pulse echoing in her
ears, as the medics worked swiftly around her. The siren
wailed faintly in the background, a dissonant reminder of
how fragile everything had become. Her thoughts drifted,
fragmented and unsteady, to moments she wished she could
forget but knew she never would. Scott's indifference and
his cold detachment. She remembered each moment vividly
and more clearly than the discomfort in her chest.

She thought of the ways she had made herself small for
him and the sacrifices that had felt monumental to her but
invisible to him. Now, as her body betrayed her, she realized

there was no rewind button, no safety net and no eraser for the scars these men had left on her spirit and on her heart.

Her grip tightened momentarily on the stretcher's edge as the ambulance swerved turning a corner heading for the trauma hospital. She could see the city lights blurring into streaks of color outside the window as she wondered if she was go to die. She wondered whether this was what people meant by heartbreak, truly meant. Not a metaphor, not a figure of speech but a physical rupture of something vital. Something, so fragile that she had fought to hold together for far too long and now it may be too late for her to find that love.

Yet even in the chaos, a quiet determination began to stir within her. She needed answers, not just about her health. But about herself.

What had led her here, to this moment of collapse? What did it mean to rebuild when her sense of self felt unstable?

As the ambulance came to a halt and the hospital loomed into view, Shannon whispered to herself, "I will learn to stand again. I will."

At the hospital, everything moved in blurs and fragments for her. First came the oxygen mask, EKGs, panicked voices asking about family history, blood pressure measurements and questions on medications. Shannon heard the word *heart attack* more than once. She lay there stunned, unable to connect what was happening in her body and to her own grief still radiating through her.

It was not until hours later, when the tests came back, that the cardiologist entered her room with a gentler tone. "It's not a heart attack," he said. "But it is something very real. The condition is known as Takotsubo cardiomyopathy. We sometimes call it broken heart syndrome."

Shannon blinked, unable to speak. The doctor continued, his voice measured but compassionate. "It's a condition we see more often in women than men, particularly after intense emotional distress. Your heart mimics the symptoms of a heart attack, pain, and shortness of breath, but blocked arteries do not cause it. Instead, it's your body's reaction to extreme stress. The left ventricle of your heart temporarily weakens and can't pump blood as effectively."

In this condition, profound emotional stress mimics the symptoms of a heart attack and leaves the heart physically weakened.

Shannon listened, each word landing with a peculiar weight. She was relieved to learn that the condition was not life-threatening. However, she understood that her emotional state had begun to affect her physical health. Her body had carried what her mind had tried to suppress for so long.

"This is reversible," the doctor reassured her. "With rest, care, and paying attention to your mental health, you can recover fully. But it's important to recognize the role your emotional well-being plays in your overall health. This didn't come out of nowhere."

As the doctor spoke, Shannon's mind drifted back to the weight she had carried for months: Scott's neglect, the invisible erosion of her sense of self, and the small compromises she had made until they no longer felt small. Her heart had finally forced her to confront these truths. There was no escaping them now.

After the doctor left, she laid in the hospital bed next to the faint beeping of monitors punctuating the silence. She felt something shift inside her. It was quiet, but resolute strength, she could feel growing. This was not just a wake-up call about her physical health. It was a reckoning, a moment to redefine how she wanted to live and who she wanted to be. It was her heart telling her to wake up and make changes in her life and live life for herself, no one else.

The first time Shannon felt her heart break, it was not metaphoric. It was real and her body listened and responded to the emotional pain that Shannon for months had not recognized. She needed to do something to change her life for the better and for herself. She mattered and her life mattered.

At the hospital, doctors delivered an unexpected diagnosis: takotsubo cardiomyopathy, better known as broken heart syndrome. As Shannon lay in the sterile hospital room, she realized her grief had not just changed her life; it had changed her physically. Shannon never imagined that heartbreak could be fatal. It might lead you into a dark room for a while, but fatal… she didn't see that coming.

Her heart, fragile but resilient, had given her a message she could no longer ignore. It was time to heal, not just from this condition, but from everything that had led her here. It was time to stop shrinking herself for someone else's convenience, to stop dismissing her own pain as inconsequential. She needed to share her story with others and help others get through the pain she had experience and grow from it.

For the first time in what felt like years, Shannon allowed herself to believe that she could rebuild, not just mend, the fractures left behind by both Scott and Dennis. Shannon could learn from her mistakes in love and create a life that was truly her own and a life where her heart could beat freely, unburdened by the weight of someone else's indifference.

Tears welled up in her eyes, not from fear but from the terrifying validation that her pain was real. Tangible. Measurable. Her heart had cried out louder than she had allowed herself to believe. She was hurting and damaged.

She was not crazy. She was not overreacting. Her heart had broken in a way no one could ignore.

As the doctor stepped out, Shannon lay back against the pillow, machines softly beeping around her. For the first time since Scott, she felt seen, not by him, but by her own body. Her heart, weary and wounded, had told the truth she had tried for months to swallow. Her heart had mimic her feelings of despair and emotional pain.

Shannon had to decide what she would do with it. This clarity that had settled over her was sharp, unyielding, and oddly empowering. Shannon realized she couldn't value herself based on someone who didn't appreciate her. Scott's indifference had been a mirror, reflecting not her inadequacy, but his own inability to care.

The days of excuses were over. She wouldn't waste her recovery or her chance to rebuild her life trying to extract meaning from his silence or attempting to bridge a gap he had never wanted to close. For the first time in years, she felt the faint, but unmistakable stirrings of freedom.

Shannon began to sketch out a vision for her life: not what it had been with Scott, but what it could be without him. She thought about taking up yoga again, a practice she had abandoned in the throes of their relationship. She imagined weekends spent exploring art galleries, reading novels she'd set aside, and reconnecting with old friends, she'd unintentionally left behind while trying to fit into his world.

Her heart, both in the physical and emotional sense, deserved this fresh start. It was time for her heart to beat for her own dreams and joys, not just to keep pace with the emptiness of someone else's neglect. The sunlight spilling through the window reminded her that there was still so much life left to explore, to feel, and to claim as her own.

Scott wasn't her story anymore. Dennis was her past. Both men were characters who had ended. Shannon turned her gaze from the past to the possibilities ahead and made a silent promise to herself. She would heal, she would grow, and she would finally embrace the life she had always been meant to live. It was that moment of clarity that her podcast idea began

Word got to Scott through a mutual acquaintance, a retired nurse Shannon had once met at a charity event he brought her to months ago, back when he was still pretending to care.

Shannon never expected him to come rushing to her side. She was not even sure she wanted him. But a part of her, still bruised, still human, wondered if the news would stir something in him, guilt, or concern. *Anything.* Instead, he did exactly what Scott always did: he distanced, deflected, and diminished.

When asked if he had reached out, Scott shrugged and said, "She is dramatic. Always has been. Just another anxiety episode she is making a big deal out of to get attention." And that was that no concern. No text. No call. Not even a polite inquiry.

Shannon found out days later, what Scott had said to the nurse. Afterwards, Shannon felt that familiar heat rise in her chest which signaled the shame, disbelief and the quiet ache of not being worth even a moment of real care from the man she had once loved. How could she have loved someone so self-absorbed and unfeeling? How many other women experienced what she had gone through and recognized the pain?

But this time, the pain did not bury her. It clarified her. Because now she understood he had not failed to show up for her in a moment of crisis. He had simply remained true to who he was, cold and guarded, incapable of genuine empathy. It had just taken something this severe for her to see it without the fog of hope. She did not cry.

Shannon just nodded, thanked the nurse, and turned her gaze to the window where late afternoon light spilled across her blanket. The world outside still turned. And so would she. Scott's silence was not a mystery. It was an answer. A brutal one. But the answer is all the same.

Shannon left the hospital the next day. She texted Scott that she wanted to see him that weekend and pick up some things she had left at his house. He did not reply that day, but Shannon decided that she would stop by the restaurant they frequented.

Shannon had not meant to go there. She was driving aimlessly, trying to clear her head after another long day of recovery appointments, when she passed by *Il Fornaio*. In this upscale Italian restaurant, Scott would take her, always on weekends and to the same patio table overlooking the city.

A strange pull made her turn into the parking lot. Probably nostalgia for memories of past. Maybe it was the need to reclaim something that had once felt special. She told herself she would just walk by and take a look. But as she approached the window, she froze. There he was engaged in conversation with someone else. Scott laughing and enjoying his time with a young lady.

He leaned forward, wine glass in hand, eyes performing as she once thought they were just for her. Across from him a blonde lady, much younger woman than Shannon. Late thirties. Long legs crossed, a low laugh and hand brushing his arm like it was already hers.

Shannon's heart did not break again; it did not have to. This time, it just settled into something steel-hard and clear.

She walked inside before she could stop herself. Scott saw her approaching, and for the briefest second, his expression faltered. But then he recovered.

"Can I help you?" he said, coolly, as if she were a stranger.

Shannon stood tall. "You're seriously going to pretend you don't know me?"

He gave a forced chuckle. "Shannon. I did not recognize you at first."

The young woman glanced between them, confused but intrigued.

"I ended up in the *hospital,* Scott. So why did you not even bother to call or try to see me?" Shannon said, her voice calm and measured. "My heart failed. You did not even check on me. You told people I was dramatic. That I had issues."

Scott leaned back in his chair, clearly uncomfortable now with his hands shaking as he held a glass of wine. "I tried calling," he lied. "But… You have always had these emotional spirals. It is not fair to expect me to fix that."

Shannon took a deep breath. "Do you love me?" she asked, steady. "Or her?"

The woman's eyebrows lifted slightly, but Scott did not flinch. He did not even hesitate.

"I love her," he said, flatly.

"Remember this, Scott," Shannon said, her voice cutting through the room like a blade, each word heavy with unyielding conviction. "When your heart fails you, when the weight of your lies crushes what little remains of your soul, no one will be there. Not her. Not anybody. Because you've spent your life driving away the people who cared."

She turned on her heel, head high and unshaken, the embodiment of quiet fury and self-respect. She didn't look back, didn't falter, not even once. The sound of her high heels on the floor marked her departure, each step signifying that she had concluded seeking affection from someone unable to reciprocate. Just the quiet power of a woman who had finally stopped begging for love from someone who only knew how to take it from others.

For Shannon, the clarity of her decision was liberating. She had spent months trying to hold on to the hope that Scott might one day become the person she needed and the person who might love her without conditions or cruelty. But now, the scales had fallen from her eyes, and she saw him clearly not as a partner, not even as an adversary, but as a hollow shell of someone she had once trusted.

The night before had been a catharsis. It was not just about Scott; it was about reclaiming her voice against anyone who dared to undermine her existence. She hadn't acted out of rage but out of a deeper need to affirm her worth and something she had spent too long doubting.

As she poured herself a coffee that morning, her thoughts wandered to the message she had received earlier. Scott's threat, hollow as it was, seemed almost comical now. The realization hit her fully: she wasn't scared of him anymore. She wasn't afraid of his lies, his manipulations, or his attempts to paint her in the wrong. The person she had become was steadier, stronger, and far beyond his reach.

There was no need to retaliate and no desire to respond. His words had no power. For the first time in months, Shannon felt the freedom of stepping away from his shadow. She wasn't looking back only forward, into the light of a life untethered by his toxicity. And that life was hers to reclaim, one empowering step at a time.

The next morning, Shannon's phone buzzed with a message from an unfamiliar number. But she knew the tone. She knew the arrogance woven through every syllable before she even finished reading it.

Shannon,

Just so you are aware, I have filed a police report after your outburst last night. I have made it clear to the police department that you are not coming near me or to my property again. This is the last time I will warn you. Scott.

No greetings. No acknowledgment of her pain. No reflection on his part in any of it. Just a legal threat, manufactured to scare her into silence.

For a moment, she felt her breath catch. Had she gone too far? Had confronting him in public really warranted this? But then something steadier than fear settled in her chest; suspicion of his motives. This sounded exactly like Scott, bully, deflect, and a lie to control the narrative.

So, she picked up the phone and called the local police department.

The woman on the other end was kind and efficient. After a brief search of their records, she came back with a definitive answer.

"No report has been filed against you, Ms. Sullivan. We have no record of any Scott Brannigan making a statement. You would have received direct communication regarding any issues, particularly those pertaining to a no-contact order. This sounds… suspicious."

Shannon thanked her and hung up, her hands no longer shaking.

Scott had not changed. Even now, he could not own his actions. Could not confront her without hiding behind lies and intimidation.

His message was not about safety. It was about power. This time, it did not work. She did not text back. She did not explain herself.

She simply saved the message. Blocked him. Documented the lie and moved on with her life.

In that quiet act, Shannon began reclaiming something Scott had tried for months to steal: her voice, her reality, and her right to truth. No one would silence her again. It was the building blocks that helped contribute to the growth of an idea she had wanted to try. A podcast for people who had been abused. She had the time and now the incentive to create a podcast that would offer something more valuable than counseling centers could offer. A community of like-minded listeners who would reveal their trauma and share their healing with others,

And so, Shannon leaned into the quiet triumph of moving forward. She started small, simplifying her surroundings. She reorganized her closet, donating clothes she no longer wore and clearing the physical clutter that echoed the emotional chaos she had endured. She set up a large desk in her bedroom in the corner near the window for a podcast center.

As the space around her grew more open, so did her mind. She spent evenings researching abuse articles and mental health issues. In her spare time she sketched and read novels that made her heart ache in all the right ways.

Shannon filled her home with music that spoke of hope and resilience and melodies that reminded her of the strength she had within her all along. Each day felt like a step toward herself, not the person Scott had tried to shape, but the person she had always been.

One afternoon, as she wandered through the bookstore downtown, she discovered a journal with a soft leather-bound cover and pages lined with faint blue ink. She bought it immediately, feeling an urgency she hadn't felt in years. That night, under the glow of her bedside lamp, Shannon opened the journal and began to write. Her scattered thoughts soon formed a coherent story. She wrote not just about the pain, but about the moments of joy that had sustained her, the people who had stood by her, and the dreams she was now daring to dream.

The journal became a companion, a witness to her healing. And with each page, Shannon found herself imagining a future she never thought possible, a future filled with courage, purpose, and peace. She was no longer just surviving; she was beginning to live.

She started to set gentle goals for herself, piece by piece, rebuilding the parts of her life, Scott had tried to dismantle.

One morning, sunlight streamed through her kitchen window as she sipped her coffee, and for the first time in ages, she felt anticipation for the day ahead rather than dread.

Shannon began reaching out to old friends, rekindling connections that had faded in the shadows of her past relationship. She attended a painting class at the local community center, where laughter came easily and mistakes were simply part of the process. Each experience, every new or rediscovered joy, added a brushstroke to the portrait of the life she was creating.

Gradually, hope replaced hesitation. The weight on her chest grew lighter, making room for new dreams. In the quiet hours of the evening, journal in hand, Shannon discovered that healing was not a single moment of transformation but a collection of ordinary days, steadily stitched together by her own patience and resolve. And though she knew there would be challenging moments still to come, she faced the future with a resilience that could not be erased.

Weeks passed, but Shannon did not spiral. She did not isolate. She did not beg for closure from a man who had proven again that he had nothing to give her. Instead, she walked through the glass doors of the small counseling center nestled in the basement of her church. Some church acquaintances had told Shannon about the counseling services and about a counselor named Denise.

It had taken courage just to call and make an appointment. She had sat with the number for three days before pressing *send*. Now, as she sat in the softly lit room across from the counselor, she felt her shoulders loosen for the first time in months.

The counselor's name was Denise. She was a middle-aged woman, her eyes reflecting sincerity, and she spoke with a directness that Shannon found unfamiliar. Shannon was a little shy at the first meeting with Denise. This counselor didn't rush or push her; she simply listened. Shannon continues to open up about Scott, the manipulation, the gaslighting, and the denial of reality that nearly shattered her. Denise remained steady and unflinching by what she heard. She listened to every word. Shannon opened, revealing all the shame, disappointment, anger, hurt, and pain she experienced with Scott.

"You were in a coercive, emotionally abusive relationship," Denise said, plainly. "You did not imagine it. You survived it."

Denise's words settled into silence, their simplicity giving them weight. Shannon sat still, absorbing the truth like a thread woven into her understanding. She hadn't imagined it. She hadn't exaggerated it. For so long, she had questioned herself, doubted her perceptions, and even apologized for things she shouldn't have. But now, someone else had named it. Denise saw her, believed her, and validated her reality.

"You survived it," Denise repeated, her gaze steady and unyielding, yet kind. "That's significant. It takes strength to come out of something like that and still be willing to seek out healing. Shannon, you're stronger than you believe. Let yourself grieve and heal and move on."

The words sparked something deep within Shannon, not fiery defiance, but a quiet recognition of the resilience that had carried her through the storm. She hadn't labeled herself as strong; in fact, she had often felt weak, broken, and adrift. Yet here she was, sitting in this softly lit room, daring to confront the scars she had hidden for so long. Shannon hesitated before speaking.

"I've spent so much time trying to figure out what I did wrong," she murmured. "What I could have done differently to make things better or to stop it from happening in the first place."

Denise leaned forward slightly, her tone gentle but firm. "That's the trap many survivors fall into. You didn't cause him to behave that way. You didn't deserve the manipulation or the gaslighting. People like him create their own distorted realities and try to impose them on others. It's not about what you did or didn't do. It's about who he chose to be. He was beyond repair. Not your job to save him."

For Shannon, the clarity in Denise's explanation felt like light pouring into a room long shuttered and dark. The counselor's words dissolved the fog of self-blame that had clouded her perspective for months, even years, going back to childhood trauma. Slowly, Shannon began to see the situation as it had been. A toxic environment designed to erode her sense of self and not a reflection of her worth or choices.

Her voice softened. "It's hard to stop asking those questions, though. It feels like... if I don't, I'm somehow letting it happen again."

Denise nodded, understanding etched onto her face. "Healing isn't about forgetting or pretending the pain didn't exist. It's about facing it, understanding it, and learning from it. Your experiences don't define your worth. You're more than the wounds he left."

Shannon felt the sting of tears rise, but this time, she didn't fight them. She let them fall, each drop carrying the weight of the shame and guilt she had held for so long. In their place, she began to feel something new, a tentative but undeniable sense of release. The truth was not just a balm; it was a compass, pointing her toward the person she was meant to reclaim.

There, in that quiet room, Shannon took the first real step toward accepting the truth; she had survived, and surviving was just the beginning.

The words felt like oxygen. Shannon breathed them in, then cried harder than she had in weeks, not from pain, but from release. Denise's words felt like a soothing balm; gently easing wounds, Shannon had barely dared to confront.

For the first time, she began to view her journey not as a collection of shattered fragments but as a beautiful mosaic coming together not despite its cracks, but because of them.

She began to appreciate the strength she had garnered, not despite her struggles but because of them.

The cracks in her heart were no longer blemishes; they were reminders of her ability to endure. Each fragment of her story became a shimmering tile of resilience, pieced together into a mosaic that reflected the beauty of a life rebuilt with intention.

Through quiet moments of reflection and deliberate acts of self-care, Shannon found ways to honor her journey. She started lighting a candle each morning as a symbol of hope, watching the flame flicker and thinking of the light she was slowly reclaiming within herself. She practiced gratitude for the insignificant things, the warmth of her morning tea, the softness of her favorite blanket, and the way the sunlight danced in the room. These rituals, though simple, brought a sense of grounding to her days.

Her newfound courage extended beyond introspection. Shannon began reconnecting with old friends she had lost touch with during her time with Scott. Tentative phone calls turned into heartfelt conversations, and soon, coffee dates and laughter filled the spaces that had once felt lonely. She realized that the relationships that weathered absence and silence were the ones worth nurturing, and she embraced the joy of rediscovery.

As the weeks passed, Shannon ventured further into uncharted territories of self-expression and creativity. She dusted off her guitar, an instrument that had sat unused for years, and began strumming melodies that mirrored the ebb and flow of her emotions. Her music became a diary, filled with notes of sorrow, joy, and healing, a testament to her journey back to herself.

In these moments, Shannon understood healing is neither linear nor a destination. It was a continuous process of rediscovery, of learning to carry your past not as a burden but as a part of the story that shapes who you are. Even in the quiet moments when doubt crept in, Shannon reminded herself that she was building something new: a life not dictated by fear or shame, but by the quiet strength within her.

One evening, as she gazed at the stars from her small balcony, Shannon whispered to herself, "I survived, and I'm still surviving."

The words no longer felt like a plea for reassurance. They were a declaration, a promise to honor her resilience every step of the way.

The weeks that followed were transformative. Shannon found herself drawn to spontaneous acts of courage; stopping to speak with strangers who offered kind smiles, volunteering at the shelter near her home, and joining a local poetry club where she shared verses that had once lived only in her head. Each act, however small, was a reclamation for Shannon. A way of saying, "I am here. I matter."

When she wasn't busy reclaiming her space in the world, Shannon rediscovered her love for nature. She marveled at the changing colors of the trees, the crispness of autumn mornings, and the sound of leaves crunching under her boots. These moments became reminders of impermanence that seasons change, and so do people. Each walk through the hills behind her home felt less like an escape and more like communion and a chance to embrace the quiet solitude she had once feared.

Her journal grew thicker with pages, the faint blue lines now brimming with reflections, affirmations, and dreams for the future. She wrote letters to herself, letters of forgiveness, hope, and fierce self-love. As she wrote those words, Shannon felt an undeniable transformation. She wasn't healing for anyone else, not for Scott, nor for those who had witnessed her struggles, but for herself. For the woman, she had always been and the one she was still becoming.

It wasn't always easy. There were nights when the memories crept back, unbidden, and sharp. But Shannon no longer fought them. She acknowledged the pain; then calmly let it pass like clouds drifting across the sky. She had learned that healing wasn't about erasing the past but about learning to carry it differently and less as a weight, more as a story.

One day, as she stood on a hilltop gazing out at the expanse of fields below, Shannon felt an unfamiliar but welcome sensation: *peace.* It wasn't the dramatic kind that swept away all sorrow, but a quiet, steady presence, an assurance that she was exactly where she needed to be in her life. For the first time in years, Shannon smiled, not out of habit or politeness, but because she felt it. She felt her authentic self-reborn from the ashes of hurt and despair.

The center became her anchor. She joined a small group for survivors of narcissistic and emotional abuse. At first, she barely spoke. But as the weeks unfolded, she listened to story after story that mirrored her own: the charm that turned cold, the love that walked a tightrope, the way reality was slowly rewritten until they no longer recognized themselves. In those women, Shannon began to see something beautiful: *resilience.*

Little by little, Shannon began to find her voice in the group. At first, it was just a few hesitant words. A brief acknowledgment that she understood the pain they were describing. But as the days turned into weeks, her confidence grew. Sharing her story wasn't just cathartic; it was empowering. Each time she spoke, it felt like she was reclaiming a part of herself, peeling back the layers of doubt and fear to reveal the quiet strength that had always been there.

One afternoon, the group facilitator invited Shannon to lead a conversation about the steps she'd taken to rebuild her life. As she faced the circle, her heart pounded, but she steadied herself with a deep breath. She spoke candidly about lighting the morning candle, about walking through the hills, about the music that had become her diary. She shared how she had learned to embrace the impermanence of life, to accept the seasons and changes, both within and outside of herself. She spoke about her experiences with broken heart syndrome and how she wanted to help heal others. The room listened, not just with their ears, but with their hearts, and Shannon realized she was no longer just surviving. She was helping others to thrive.

After the meeting, a woman named Carla approached Shannon with tears in her eyes. "You don't know how much I needed to hear that today," she said, her voice trembling. "I've been afraid to take even the smallest step forward, but you've shown me that it's possible." Shannon smiled warmly, realizing the ripple effect of her actions. By sharing her journey, she was creating space for others to find their own paths. Carla told Shannon she should share her journey with others like in a podcast so that other women can share and get healed. Just think, Shannon how many lives can be healed or even saved from shame and guilt and from those ugly secrets. They in turn could share their stories and reveal their pain and journey and those secrets that families kept in the closet for so many years can be shared for healing purposes. I would be willing to share my story on your podcast. Think about it and get back to me. Other women in the group that day also share their ideas and thoughts for a podcast with Shannon.

The connections she forged in the group gave her a new sense of purpose. She began volunteering to organize events, helping to bring in speakers, planning workshops, and even designing thoughtful activities to encourage healing through creativity.

One day, she suggested a vision board session, where everyone could express their hopes and dreams visually, and a gentle reminder that even in the darkest moments, the future was still something to look forward to in living your life to the fullest.

Outside of the group, Shannon continued to carve out moments of joy and growth. She started a blog to document her reflections, her progress, and her experiences with healing. The blog quickly gained traction, with readers reaching out to thank her for her honesty and vulnerability. Shannon realized she was not alone in her struggles; there was an entire community of people seeking solace and strength in her words.

Her guitar became more than just an instrument; it became a tool for expression. She began writing songs based on her experiences, pouring her emotions into the lyrics and melodies.

One evening, she mustered the courage to perform at an open night mic at the local café. As she played the chords and sang the journal's words, the room resonated with her notes. Applause filled the air, but what mattered most was the sense of liberation Shannon felt was as if she had turned her pain into something beautiful and something transformative.

The journey wasn't without its challenges. There were moments of self-doubt, nights when memories threatened to pull her back into darkness. But Shannon had learned to face those moments with grace, to remind herself that healing wasn't about perfection; it was about persistence. She carried her past not as a weight, but as a badge of resilience, a testament to everything she had overcome.

It was the beginning of a chapter in which she was no longer held captive by the shadows of her past. Shannon instead was empowered to welcome all the possibilities her future could hold. It meant she was prepared to face life with open arms, to seek out joy and meaning without the fear or hesitation that had once held her back. It was a vow to allow herself to love deeply, whether through relationships, passions, or simply in the way she moved through each day.

Moreover, her promise to never stop growing reflected her understanding that healing is not a finite process but an evolving journey. Shannon had learned that growth often comes from facing challenges head-on and that each step forward brings her closer to becoming the person she was meant to be.

This moment on the hilltop encapsulated Shannon's triumph over her struggles. It was a celebration of her resilience and courage and a quiet yet monumental step in claiming the life she deserved. In that instant, Shannon wasn't just surviving; she was thriving, ready to embrace every new day as an opportunity to create something beautiful out of her experiences.

So, she started walking again. Around her neighborhood. Then through the park. Then, longer, deeper hikes into the hills behind the church, where the quiet no longer felt threatening, but felt holy.

She changed her phone number. She deleted old emails. She even stopped looking at the photos of her and Scott together. Those images had once kept her tethered to a fantasy. She no longer needed to decode the past. She was too busy making space for the future.

One afternoon, after the group, she stayed behind with Denise.

"I feel like I'm waking up," Shannon said quietly. "Like I finally remembered who I was before him."

Denise smiled. "You're not going back to who you were," she said. "You are becoming someone even stronger.

Someone who knows her worth, not because someone gave it to her, but because she claimed it herself."

Denise watched the flicker of understanding brighten in Shannon's eyes, a sight that always made her heart swell. She knew the road Shannon was traveling. It was familiar territory for her, too. She had once stood at the precipice of rebuilding herself, by piecing together the shards of her life after years of emotional warfare. It was hard-earned wisdom and she felt compelled to share it.

"People think resilience is about never breaking," Denise added softly, her voice steady and warm. "But it's not. It's about how we rise after the fall. It's the grace we give our-selves to start again, even when the world says we should crumble. You don't owe anyone your story, Shannon. But you owe it to yourself to live the ending you deserve.

She could see Shannon fighting back tears, her lips trem-bling as she searched for words. Denise didn't press; she knew the value of silence, of allowing someone to feel their way through the moment.

"I haven't told you this," Denise continued after a pause, her gaze soft but unwavering, "but I see so much of myself in you. That's why I wanted to help. I remember the nights of doubt, the mornings when it felt impossible to smile. But those days passed, just like they're passing for you. The joy that followed was brighter than anything I'd had before. Be-cause it was mine, and no one could take it away."

Denise leaned back in her chair; her hands folded neatly in her lap. "You're already making peace with your past, Shannon. That voice inside you? It's not just getting louder; it's becoming the person you were meant to be all along."

She smiled steadily and encouragingly, hoping Shannon could feel the truth of her words echoing in the quiet air between them.

Shannon nodded, wiping her eyes. She believed it. Maybe not fully. Not yet. But it was getting louder inside her each day, that voice of her own.

The silence between them stretched, but it wasn't heavy. It was alive, a shared understanding blooming in the quiet. Shannon's shoulders relaxed slightly, as though some invisible weight had shifted. Denise watched her, knowing the moment was delicate and sacred, and a significant step on the long journey of healing.

"I've been so scared," Shannon admitted, her voice barely a whisper. "Scared of losing myself again. Scared of trusting... of feeling."

Denise leaned forward, her elbows resting lightly on her knees. "Fear is part of the process," she said softly. "It's your mind trying to protect you, but it doesn't mean you have to obey it. Sometimes, stepping into the unknown is the bravest thing we can do."

Shannon looked down at her hands, fingers twisting a tissue into threads. "What if I fail?"

"You won't," Denise said firmly, her voice carrying a quiet strength. "But even if you stumble, that's not failure. Learning, growing, and trying again, that's the real courage. And every time you do, you'll get closer to the life you deserve."

Shannon nodded slowly, Denise's words sinking in like rain on parched soil. "I want that," she said, her voice trembling but resolute. "I want to feel whole again."

"You will," Denise assured her, a smile spreading across her face. "And when you do, it won't be because someone saved you. It'll be because you found your way back to yourself."

Shannon briefly imagined a life free from her past, where she could breathe easily and laugh openly. It felt distant, but for the first time, possible.

"Thank you," Shannon said, her voice thick with emotion. "For believing in me when I couldn't."

Denise reached out, placing a hand over Shannon's. "You don't have to thank me. Just promise me you'll keep believing, even on hard days. Especially on the hard days."

Shannon met Denise gaze, her eyes steady despite the shimmer of tears. "I promise, you Denise."

The two women sat there, hand in hand, as the sun dipped lower in the sky. Outside the window, the world carried on as usual, but inside, something had shifted. It was a quiet yet profound moment of connection, hope, and a future to reclaim.

From one trial to the next, each step grounds her in the present and urges her toward the future. She discovered new corners of her world with hidden paths that wound through blooming gardens, and tree-lined avenues that rustled with life.

The rhythm of her footsteps became a meditation and a quiet reminder of her progress.

Shannon noticed details she had long overlooked. The laughter of children in the distance, the fragrance of jasmine wafting through the air, and the sparkle of sunlight on a pond's surface were all small moments of beauty. Each walk became a celebration of her growing courage, and a declaration that she was reclaiming her place in life.

As days turned into weeks, Shannon expanded her horizons. She joined a local hiking group, finding solace in shared experiences and camaraderie. She learned to appreciate the challenge of scaling steep terrain, the exhilaration of reaching a summit, and the quiet awe of standing amid sweeping landscapes. She began to see nature not just as an escape, but as a mirror reflecting her inner journey and its strength, resilience, and boundless capacity to evolve.

With each mile she traveled, her promise to herself grew stronger. She was no longer merely pushing against the weight of her past; she was moving toward a future rich with possibilities. The act of walking became an emblem of her healing and a way to honor the progress she had made and the joy she was determined to find.

And when Shannon returned to that hilltop, standing once more where she had made her promise, it was not with hesitation or fear but with a heart full of gratitude. She gazed out at the horizon, where the sky stretched endlessly, and whispered, "I'm ready." The words spoken not as a question but as a statement felt like a key unlocking a door to everything that lay ahead.

Shannon's recovery is attributed to her engagement with nature and her commitment to personal development through diverse experiences. Both avenues serve as catalysts for rediscovering her inner strength and reclaiming her sense of self. Shannon finds solace in the simplicity and beauty of the natural world. Her walks become more than just physical activity; they transform into a meditative practice that grounds her in the present moment.

Nature mirrors Shannon's inner journey. The strength and resilience of landscapes reflect her determination to grow, while the boundless beauty of the outdoors inspires hope. By joining a local hiking group, she not only challenges herself physically but also fosters connections with others who share her desire for exploration. The act of reaching summits and standing amidst sweeping vistas becomes symbolic of her progress, both in conquering steep terrain and overcoming personal struggles.

In addition to her connection with nature, Shannon reinvents her life by seeking opportunities for personal development and community involvement. Her decision to join the hiking group highlights her willingness to engage in shared experiences and form camaraderie with others. Through these interactions, she begins to rebuild her social life, allowing herself to be vulnerable and open to new friendships.

Her appreciation for life's challenges grows as she learns to scale steep trails and celebrate the exhilaration of achievement. Each milestone she reaches becomes a metaphor for the emotional and psychological hurdles she has faced. These achievements symbolize her resilience and her ability to transform adversity into empowerment.

Shannon's promise to keep moving forward, even on the hardest days, becomes the cornerstone of her healing journey. Whether through her meditative walks or her interactions with a like-minded community, she makes a vow to never stop growing. This understanding that healing is a continuous process allows Shannon to approach life with gratitude and purpose.

Shannon's healing journey is a testament to the power of nature and personal growth. By immersing herself in the beauty of the world and seeking new avenues of connection, she unlocks the strength within her to move forward. Her story is a celebration of resilience and a reminder that even in the face of hardship, there is a path toward hope and renewal.

For Shannon, saying "I'm ready" was an affirmation of her readiness to live fully. It meant she was prepared to face life with open arms, to seek out joy and meaning without the fear or hesitation that had once held her back. It was a vow to allow herself to love deeply, whether through relationships, passions, or simply in the way she moved through each day.

Moreover, her promise to never stop growing reflected her understanding that healing is not a finite process but an evolving journey. Shannon had learned that growth often comes from facing challenges head-on and that each step forward brings her closer to becoming the person she was meant to be.

Chapter 13
Begin of the Podcast Journey

Shannon's Journey from Healing to Hosting

Shannon never imagined that the quiet sanctuary of the counseling center would become the birthplace of her boldest adventure yet. For months, the center's pale green walls and sunlit windows had witnessed her transformation from a woman cloaked in self-doubt and old wounds to someone quietly radiant, her scars now softened by understanding and acceptance.

It began as a soft whisper. During her final group session, Shannon found herself listening more intently to the stories of those around her, their triumphs, setbacks, and the shared ache of vulnerability.

She realized there was power in these confessions, a kind of unspoken permission that rippled through the circle each time someone dared to tell the unvarnished truth.

Walking home one brisk evening, Shannon's mind tumbled with memories: the trust she'd built, the comfort of shared silences, the courage that seemed to bloom only when secrets were spoken aloud. She wondered how many others, outside the counseling center's walls, were still waiting for that permission to be honest, with themselves and with the world.

The idea struck her on a rainy Thursday, as she sat journaling at her kitchen table. *What if those honest voices could travel beyond these walls? What if healing could be contagious?*

Driven by a sense of purpose, Shannon spent weeks researching, jotting down ideas, and mapping out what a safe, supportive, and empowering space might look like outside the center. She wanted to create something that wasn't about advice or answers, but about connection, a place where people could unmask, step by step, and discover they were not alone in their struggles or their victories.

She christened her new project **"Unmask."**

The name felt right: simple, evocative, and accurate.

It spoke to the act of peeling back layers. It was not in pursuit of perfection. It was to reveal the raw, resilient self beneath.

With a modest budget and a heart brimming with hope, Shannon purchased a microphone and a set of headphones. She watched late-night tutorials on audio editing.

The first episode was an act of courage: her voice trembled as she recounted her own journey, but by the end, she felt lighter, free, almost.

It didn't take too long for "Unmask" to find its audience. Listeners wrote in from across the country, sharing their own stories of *unmasking*, of healing, heartbreak, and hope.

Shannon guests: Old friends from the counseling center, experts in mental health, and everyday people with extraordinary resilience. The podcast became a gathering place, a digital hilltop where honesty blossomed and healing echoed.

Each week, as she sat before the microphone, Shannon remembered the promise she made to herself on that first day at the counseling center: to never stop growing, to never stop reaching out. "Unmask" was no longer just her story; it was the story of everyone who dared to be seen.

And with every episode, Shannon's heart, which was once scarred and guarded, opened wider, reminding her and her listeners that the bravest thing we can do is to tell the truth, not just to others, but to ourselves.

A week after the podcast aired, Shannon sat at her kitchen table, scrolling through a flood of emails and messages. The episode had gone viral not in a sensational way, but in the kind that broke something open. Something sacred. Something long buried. It felt like people were longing for this. She no longer felt alone in all of this.

The subject lines were raw, unfiltered:

- *"That was me."*

- *"I finally told my therapist."*

- *"Can I be on the next show?"*

- *"My daughter listened with me — she finally told me the truth."*

One message stood out. It was brief, almost hesitant, but its weight stayed:

"Hi, I'm Maria. I called in last week. I need to talk again. Something happened."

Shannon remembered Maria, the woman who had drawn a painful thread between her abusive mother and her choice in men.

That Friday, Maria returned to the show this time, in the studio. She was taller than Shannon expected, with intense eyes that had both defiance and exhaustion buried in them.

As the recording started, Shannon gave her the floor.

"I was afraid to come back," Maria began, her voice trembling. "But after the podcast, I broke up with my boyfriend. I finally saw what I was trying to heal, and it wasn't him. It was me."

Listeners across the country held their breath as Maria recounted the aftermath. The fear. The guilt. The loneliness. And then, the clarity. So many people felt the same way. They felt seen and valid.

"I started therapy. Not to 'fix' me, but to understand me. I learned that I've been living in survival mode for so long, I thought fear was love. But it's not."

Shannon nodded slowly, eyes damp. This was more than an update. This was a transformation in real time.

Later that night, during the open lines segment, a new voice came through.

"I'm Jada. I didn't call last time because I was ashamed. But I listened. And it unlocked something. My brother abused me. He died three years ago, and I still feel like it's my fault."

Shannon leaned in, a gentle steadiness in her voice as she adjusted her headphones and softened her gaze toward the glowing studio mic.

"I'm here, Jada," she said quietly, inviting the silence to open. "Jada, it's not your fault. And you're not alone. Take your time. We're all listening.

There was a pause, and then Jada said something that would stay with Shannon for days: "You all permitted me to feel again. I thought, I had gone numb. But hearing Maria tonight realized: survival isn't the same as living."

By the end of the night, Shannon knew something was shifting. The podcast was no longer just a platform. It was becoming a movement. A closed Facebook group started that week for survivors of childhood trauma. Within three days, it had over 12,000 members. Women were sharing photographs of themselves showing various emotions, from smiling to crying, and holding hands with their daughters, while speaking about experiences they had previously kept private. The podcast had done more than start a conversation. It had started a revolution of healing. A movement that allowed survivors of abuse to reveal their shame and share their experience for healing purposes.

The inbox was bursting. Shannon had stopped trying to keep up with every message, and her producer, Melanie, had to hire two volunteers just to manage the incoming calls and vet the ones that could go live.

A positive charge seemed to cause a buzz in the air; this was no longer just a podcast, but a living pulse, drawing women to the edge of their own honesty and courage. Each episode, created a new wave of truth that was unleashed carrying voices once silenced into the open world. Stories spilled into the inbox, into the Facebook group and into late-night text chains between strangers who felt seen for the first time.

Shannon realized with awe and humility that what had started as a simple recording in a quiet studio had become a safe harbor for so many. The microphone was now a lifeline; connecting survivors across miles and generations. They weren't just sharing stories; they were reclaiming them.

It was in this fervent atmosphere of vulnerability that Melanie's voice broke through Shannon's reverie. "Shannon, there's someone on the line," Melanie's voice murmured through the headset, "She says her story is heavy. She's frightened. Wants to remain anonymous."

Shannon inhaled gently and nodded. "Let her speak."

The line crackled. Then a hollow, shaky voice filled the room.

"You can call me Elle. My stepfather trafficked me. He started when I was nine. My mother knew. She told me it was my duty. Said I owed him for putting food on our table."

The silence in the studio felt like a scream held in stasis.

"I ran away at sixteen. I've had four different names. I've never told anyone this. But when I heard Maria and Jada, I knew it was time."

Shannon's voice trembled.

"Elle, thank you for your bravery. I know this story just saved someone's life."

That night, the episode received 1.3 million downloads in 24 hours. But it didn't stop there. Two days later, a woman named Soraya called in. Her voice was low, controlled, but her words cut like broken glass, "I'm a school principal. I'm also a survivor of incest. I've built a perfect life. I have a perfect husband, two children, and a great career. But I've never told anyone. Not even my therapist."

Shannon glanced at Melanie, eyes wide. The air in the studio quivered with anticipation, as if the walls themselves were listening. For a moment, no one dared to breathe.

Soraya's words hung between them, raw and heavy. Then, Shannon steadied her voice, careful and soft. "Soraya, you don't have to carry this alone anymore. You have us now. You have everyone listening."

A hush lingered before Soraya replied. "Thank you. I… I'm terrified, but I think, I just took my first breath in years."

Melanie squeezed Shannon's hand under the table, a silent pact, a promise: every story would be heard, and every silence broken.

"What made you decide to speak now?" Shannon asked.

A pause. "Because my daughter's ten. The age it started for me. And every time I tuck her in, I break inside. I keep seeing *me*. I don't want to pass this silence on to her."

That episode sparked a national debate. The podcast was trending on every platform. Survivors began coming forward from every lifestyle, including therapists, pastors, mothers, CEOs, cashiers, and women in prison. The stories poured out like a tidal wave.

Tina called, but she didn't wait for the line to clear. She burst in during a live recording session. Her voice exhibited signs of intense agitation and distress.

"Shannon, I'm sorry, I couldn't wait. I'm in danger. He found out I was going to tell my husband. He locked me in the bathroom with my phone. I don't know how long I have."

Melanie's hand flew to her mouth. Shannon's heart pounded.

For a heartbeat, silence thundered across the studio, everyone paralyzed, breaths held in collective fear. Shannon gripped the edge of her chair, forcing her voice to steady. "Tina, listen to me. You're not alone. We hear you. Help is coming."

"Tina, are you safe right now? Can you tell me where you are?"

"He's gone to get drunk. He always comes back angry. Please, I don't want to die tonight."

Without hesitation, Shannon signaled to her team. They muted the broadcast and called local police based on the signal trace. The show resumed ten minutes later with a blanket message:

"To any woman listening who thinks she must suffer in silence, you don't. If you're in danger tonight, please call for help. You're not alone. If you are experiencing any kind of abuse, like you have heard on my podcast, then contact us or your local police. No woman deserves to be abused in any way. Good night, everyone. This is Shannon, and we are Unmasked, signing off for the night. Thank you, listeners, for your support."

Shannon's podcast had become a lifeline, but it was also becoming something heavier and darker. More urgent… The trauma was real. The danger was real. She stared at the monitor, then at the tiny red "ON AIR" light above her studio booth every night. She listened and she soothed people in distress with her empathetic, caring response.

"We're not just telling stories," She whispered. "We're stopping cycles. We're catching women in mid-fall life threatening positions."

Shannon's podcast had grown into more than a show. It was a lifeline for many listeners, a beacon reaching into the shadows. Each night, as she sat in the studio, the little red "ON AIR" light seemed to pulse with the urgency of every story shared. The trauma was no longer just spoken; it echoed in her heart and in the trembling voices that reached out through the static.

"We're not just broadcasting stories," she whispered to herself. "We're breaking chains. We're catching women before they hit the ground."

Yet with each call, the weight grew heavier. The studio's walls felt thinner, as if the pain and courage of so many were pressing in, demanding justice, demanding action. Shannon knew this was no longer just about giving voice, it was about defiance, about hope, about refusing to let silence win.

And somewhere deep inside her, a resolve tightened.

This isn't just a podcast anymore. This is a war against silence.

1. Call from "Carol" — The Locked Closet

"I was eight when my mother started locking me in the hallway closet. She said it was punishment for 'stealing her air.' I would sit in total darkness for hours. Sometimes days. She'd only open the door to slide in cold leftovers. I learned not to cry. If I cried, she'd pour bleach under the door to 'clean the sin out.' Now, at 37, decades later, I still can't sleep with the door closed. My husband doesn't know. I told him I'm claustrophobic. But the truth is that I have never felt safe in this world. Not even once."

The line went silent. Listeners reported sobbing in their cars, pulling over to cry. That episode was shared over 250,000 times in a single day.

1. Call from "Nina" — The Baptism of Silence

"I was raised in a strict religious cult. At 12, I was forced to 'confess' I had tempted a church elder. I didn't even know what that meant. He'd cornered me, touched me. But I was blamed. They baptized me in freezing water and held me under until I passed out. Upon waking, my mother remarked, "Now you are pure once more." Though I have not attended church in 23 years, each time it rains, I continue to experience a profound sense of being overwhelmed.

The phone line shook with her cries. Shannon said nothing for a full minute. Just breathing with her. Letting her feel heard for the first time.

2. Call from "Amber": The Bruise That Won a Pageant

"I was crowned Little Miss Florida at age nine with a bruise the shape of a belt buckle under my sequined dress. My mother beat me for missing a pirouette the night before. The judges called me 'poised beyond my years.' I'm 42 now. I haven't danced since I was twelve. My daughter wanted to take ballet, and I signed her up… then pulled her out. I was afraid she'd be *too good*. That she'd end up like me, polished and broken."

Amber's voice cracked. Her daughter was listening to the show in the next room.

3. Call from "Desiree" — The Sound of a Lighter

"He used to light matches. Not to burn me. Just to make me watch. He'd snap a lighter again next to my bed. Told me that if I ever told him, he'd burn my whole family alive. I was ten. I still can't hear the click of a lighter without vomiting. My boyfriend smokes. I pretend I'm allergic to cigarettes. But the truth is, I'm afraid he might become him."

Shannon was stunned. The sound of a lighter was played on the air, followed by a trigger warning, and women flooded the lines, saying they *knew that sound*. It haunted them, too.

4. Call from "Rosa" When the Babysitter Became the Predator

"I was six. My babysitter was thirteen. A girl. She touched me and told me it was a secret game. I never told anyone because I didn't think girls could do that to each other. I'm married to a woman now. And I still feel guilty when she kisses me like I'm doing something wrong, even though I know it's love this time. I hate that my first lesson in touch came from confusion and silence."

Rosa's story opened conversations on female-perpetrated abuse, a subject rarely discussed. It sparked hundreds of other women writing in to say, *"That happened to me, too."*

5. Call from "Leila" Her Mother's Mirror

"My mother sold me. The first time, I was eleven. She said, 'We need the rent." Be a good girl.' I thought good girls helped their moms. Now I have a daughter. She's ten. Looks just like me. And every morning I brush her hair; I stare at her face and wonder: how did my mother look at mine and still give me away?"

Shannon barely breathed. That evening, Leila's story aired on *Good Morning America*, sparking a national investigation into human trafficking survivors.

It started with a trickle. A few brave voices, trembling over the phone lines, releasing decades of pain. But now, the podcast had become a floodgate of agony and truth.

Listeners were spellbound. Some had pulled their cars over. Others sat in the dark, clutching tissues or their own children.

By the end of her call, the studio's email was exploding. Women were sending in messages titled *"That was me."* Shannon's assistant, Melanie, had to shut down the live feed chat because of the overwhelming flood of echoes of trauma.

That night's episode, *"Polished and Broken,"* hit two million downloads in 36 hours. A national helpline mentioned in the episode saw a 700% spike in calls.

Survivors of childhood trauma flooded social media with a single phrase: *"I was silent too."*

In the comments under the podcast, one message stood out:

"This isn't just a show. It's a mirror. And for the first time, I'm seeing myself clearly."

Shannon closed her laptop that night, hands trembling, heart sore.

6. Call from "Carla"

"I was eight the first time my mother called me a parasite. I had just spilled orange juice on her white rug. She slapped the cup out of my hand and said, 'You don't deserve nice things." You suck the life out of me."

Surprisingly, unlike others, Carla's voice was steady; in fact, it was too steady. Like someone who'd learned to dissociate from pain.

"She used to wake me up at 2 a.m. to clean the kitchen. Said it was 'training for life.' If I missed a crumb, she'd dump the trash on the floor and make me start over. I was in second grade. I'd go to school with purple bags under my eyes and no lunch. I told my teacher I was doing a science experiment on fasting."

Shannon's chest tightened. Melanie, in the control booth, slowly took off her headphones. The silence in the studio was dense.

"She didn't hit me much. That would've been easier. Instead, she made me question my sanity. She'd move my toys, then punish me for lying when I said they were gone. She told me I was dramatic. Too sensitive. That I was always looking for attention, one time, she threw away my birthday cake because I blew out the candles before she said I could."

Shannon softly asked, "Did anyone else in your life see it?"

"No one dared to. She was *charming.* The PTA president. The mom always baked the cupcakes. Everyone said I was 'so lucky.' And you know what the worst part was? Sometimes I believed them. Sometimes I thought: 'Maybe I *am* the problem.'"

Then came the quiet part. The part that landed like a slow knife in every listener's heart.

"I'm 37 now. I haven't talked to her in 12 years. But I still flinch when someone praises me. Compliments feel like traps. Love feels like an exam I'm going to fail."

Shannon says, "Carla, you were never the problem. You were a child trying to survive a warzone no one could see. Emotional abuse doesn't leave bruises; it leaves echoes. And I hear them in your voice."

Listener Reaction (within the story)

Carla's call went viral on social media faster than any before. Listeners would comment:

"Carla just told *my* story."

"This is the kind of abuse you can't show in court... but it kills you anyway."

This makes her trauma even more chilling and intimate for the listener and reveals how a child trapped in emotional torment can survive without ever physically escaping.

Carla (Expanded: The Dissociation Years)

Carla's second call came two weeks after her first. Her voice had changed. Slower. Deeper. As if another version of her had taken the phone.

"I need to tell the part I didn't say before. The part I used to pretend wasn't mine..."

Shannon felt the weight immediately.

"When I was little, I used to pretend I was a ghost. Not dead, just invisible. I would sit in my closet and imagine floating above my body, watching everything happen like it was a movie. My mother would scream, break plates, call me 'a mistake with legs,' and I would just… *leave.* Float up to the ceiling and count the cracks in the paint. I didn't even cry. I couldn't. Crying made her angrier. So, I made a rule: *Carla cries. Carla survives.* That was the first time I split. I didn't know what I was doing. But I needed someone to hold the pain… so I created her."

Shannon felt her stomach tighten. The silence that followed wasn't dead air. It was sacred.

"Carla was the soft one. The one who wanted to hug people, who loved singing in the car. Carla… she was the protector. She did the chores. She got the grades. She took the blame. But overtime, even Carla started to break. So, I made a third."

Her voice dropped to a whisper.

"Her name was 'Nobody.' Nobody felt it. She didn't speak. She didn't *exist.* When things got bad, nobody would take over. She'd stare at the wall while my mother screamed or threw hot coffee. One time, she cut my hair off while I was sleeping. Said I looked too much like my father. Nobody flinched. When I turned ten, she stopped using the closet. She said I was too old. So, she made me stand in front of the mirror. For hours. She'd sit behind me and list everything that was wrong with me. My nose. My posture. My smile. When I looked away, she slapped the back of my head and started over. She told me my father left because I was *too ugly to love.* That I had 'a garbage soul.' She said I was broken. That if anyone touched me, they'd be cursed." Carla's voice didn't break; *it cracked like dry porcelain.* No tears. Just shrapnel.

"Eventually, I stopped hearing her voice. I only listened to the buzzing. I'd stare at the corner of the mirror until it melted. I'd whisper to myself, *'Carla sleeps, nobody forgets.'* It became a mantra. In high school, teachers thought I was gifted. I never talked in class. But I aced every test. That wasn't me, that was Carla, the machine. *Nobody* dated a boy in college. I let him do things I didn't understand because I thought pain meant love. When he hit me, I apologized because I wasn't there. I've spent years in therapy. I still sleep with the closet light on. I still flinch when I hear a vacuum, she used to run it outside the door to drown out my crying. I don't have kids. I'm terrified of them. Terrified I'll become her. Or worse… that they'll see through me and realize I'm not real. Just fragments in a trench coat."

Shannon finally asked, her voice shaking, "When did it change? When did you begin to *return to yourself?*"

"A therapist once said to me: *'What if the voices in your head aren't crazy — what if they're just children trying to tell their stories?'* That broke me. Or it made me whole."

"Now, when I walk past a closet, I open it. I whisper, *'You can come out now.'* Sometimes, *Carla* answers."

After a slight pause, Carla continued: "I'm 37 now, and I still dissociate. I'll be at work, typing an email, and suddenly I'm eight again, scrubbing the floor with a toothbrush while she screams. My body's here, but I'm *gone.* Gone too far to get back. My therapist tells me I have Complex PTSD. I laugh because I thought I was crazy. Turns out, I'm *well-adapted to hell.*"

Toward the end of the call, Carla's voice trembled as she said, "No one ever hit me. That's the part that kills me. People look at me and say, 'But your mom seemed so nice.' And I want to scream, *she didn't need to hit me. She taught me how to hate myself so well, I took over for her.*"

Shannon broke down. The episode ended with just ambient music and Carla's final words playing on repeat:

"I wasn't crazy. I was surviving the only way I knew how."

Listener Reaction

This episode, titled "The Girl Who Became Three," became the most downloaded in the podcast's history.

- Survivors wrote in saying, *"I had a Carla too."*

- Therapists began referencing the episode in sessions.

- A mental health nonprofit reached out to create a healing guide based on the show. One viral tweet read:

"I never got hit. But Carla made me realize — I still got wounded."

7. Lena's Podcast Episode: "The Children in the Closet"

Shannon returned to the mic. Her voice was quieter than usual reverent.

"Tonight's call is different. It's not just one woman. It's four children. One of whom lived to tell the story. We warn you: what you're about to hear is deeply disturbing."

A woman named Lena called in. Her voice was flat. Hollow.

"I was the oldest. Four and a half. I say half because I counted every day. I didn't want to be forgotten. What happened can't be forgotten. My siblings were three, two, and ten months old. All of us lived in a two-bedroom apartment in rural Nevada. But we didn't live in the rooms. We lived in the *closet*."

Shannon sat back in stunned silence. Lena kept going.

"My mom was a waitress. Worked nights. Sleeping during the day. Said we made too much noise. So, she put us in there.
She gave us a pot to pee in. One time, she forgot to empty it for three days. It spilled."

The Conditions of Confinement

"There were no windows. No light. She'd throw a towel over the crack at the bottom of the door to block the sound. The baby cried all night. So, she stopped feeding her after 8 p.m. Said she needed to learn to sleep. I used to scratch tally marks on the inside wall with my fingernail. I lost count around sixty."

Shannon could barely breathe.

"We weren't allowed out unless she bathed us or we had a 'visit' from a social worker then she'd clean us up, give us a cookie, and make us say 'thank you.' I learned to lie early. I made my siblings practice smiling."

"The worst week… she left us in there while she went out of town with her boyfriend. Said we had 'enough food.' A neighbor said she heard screaming."

Child Protective Services Gets Involved

"We were in there for five days. No food. Just half a bottle of juice and three crackers. I fed the baby the juice cap by cap. We all got sick. The neighbor finally called the police. They broke down the door. I remember the flashlight in my eyes. The voice saying, *'My God, they're all still alive.'*"

Shannon had to pause the show. A soft piano played briefly before she returned.

"What happened after that?"

"We were taken. Foster care. My brother never talked again. The baby had seizures. I… told them she was just hungry. But really, deep within me, I knew something inside her was broken."

Lena's Adult Life

"I'm 30 now. I work in early childhood development. I have cameras in my home. I panic if I can't see my daughter for more than 30 seconds. Sometimes, when it's dark, I still flinch if I hear breathing that isn't mine. But I go to therapy. I parent my inner child like I parent my daughter. I told her, *'You are safe. You will never be left again. '*"

Final Words

Shannon asked, "If you could speak to your mother now, what would you say?"

Lena's voice quivered. "I'd say… *You didn't deserve us. But we deserved to live. And we did despite you.*"

The line went quiet.

Then Shannon said something she hadn't done before. "To anyone listening who suspects abuse: call. Don't hesitate. Don't think twice. One neighbor saved four lives."

Listener Reactions

- Therapists flooded the hotline, offering free sessions to survivors.

- Thousands of people lit candles and posted pictures of open closets tagged #NeverAgain.

- A nonprofit started a Closet Fund to support trauma survivors from domestic captivity cases.

8. Elena's Podcast Episode: *"Behind the White Coat"*

Shannon's voice softened into a tone of disbelief as she introduced the next call.

"Our next story comes from a listener who's lived a Luxury masking nightmare. It's a story about silence, power, and control behind closed doors."

A woman named Elena called in, her voice steady but laced with pain.

The Perfect Family, The Perfect Mask

"My father was a renowned surgeon. Everyone in town admired him. The kind of man who wore white coats like armor. But inside our house, he was a tyrant. We had five children. Two older brothers in college, two little kids under eight, and me, the teenager, stuck in the middle. I was supposed to watch them. But the responsibility was a trap. Dad controlled everything. What we ate, said, wore, even though. If you stepped out of line, the punishments were invisible but devastating."

Psychological Abuse and Control

"He didn't hit us much. No bruises, no broken bones. His weapons were words, cold, surgical cuts. 'You are worthless,' he'd say. 'A failure. Your mother married beneath you.' 'Don't look me in the eyes unless spoken to.' We were ghosts in the house. Silent, obedient, terrified to breathe wrong. I learned early to dissociate to float outside myself when he raged. Because the rage came suddenly and lasted for hours."

The Teenager's Dark Role

"Dad made me the 'enforcer' for the younger kids. If they cried or misbehaved, I had to 'correct' them."

Her voice cracked. "I hated it. But if I didn't, the punishments came back to me, harder. Sometimes, my little sister would hide under the table. Dad would drag her out by the hair, screaming at me for 'letting her get away.' One night, I caught myself doing the same things to them. That's when I knew the abuse was breaking me."

The Cycle of Abuse

"I was fifteen when I started running away. I'd sneak out and stay at friends' houses, terrified to go home. One night, Dad found me. He didn't scream. He just said, 'You'll never leave. This family owns you.' He controlled the money. The phone. The car. I was trapped. And worse, my brothers in college? They knew. They saw the bruises on the kids. But they didn't speak. They stayed silent to protect Dad's reputation."

Elena's Breaking Point

"It wasn't until my younger brother was hospitalized with dehydration and exhaustion from being locked in a room for days that CPS was finally called. But even then, the system moved slowly. Dad hired the best lawyers. Manipulated therapists. Made us say everything was fine." I'm the only one who spoke out."

Elena Today

"Now I'm 22. I'm in therapy. Studying psychology. I want to break the cycle. The hardest part? Learning to trust. To speak my truth without fear."

Elena's story takes a darker turn. What she reveals now is almost unimaginable, the twisted abuse inflicted by a man trained to heal but broken inside."

The Doctor's Dark Side

Elena's voice was low, almost mechanical.

"Dad was brilliant. But he was unwell. Diagnosed with bipolar disorder, though no one knew the full extent. He was self-medicated with pills, alcohol, and sometimes worse. When his mood flipped, so did the house."

Shocking Physical and Medical Abuse

"Dad would use his medical tools on us, not for healing, but to punish. He kept a small kit: needles, scalpels, and clamps. Once, after my little brother spilled juice on the couch, Dad forced him to sit still while he pricked his finger repeatedly with a syringe, telling him, 'You will learn pain, so you remember your place.' He gave us 'medication' that weren't prescribed pills that made us dizzy, nauseous, or worse, completely numb. If we cried, he'd put a cold cloth soaked in rubbing alcohol on our faces until we gasped."

Bizarre and Terrifying Rituals

"Dad believed he could 'cleanse' our spirits. He'd lock us in the bathroom for hours with bright lights and harsh chemicals. He made us stand in freezing water, his version of 'therapy', while lecturing us on 'obedience and pain.' Sometimes, he'd perform bizarre 'examinations,' forcing us to repeat medical terms like 'hypoglycemia' or 'tachycardia' while he watched with a twisted smile. He recorded some of these sessions on his phone, calling them 'evidence' to show how 'broken' we were."

Mental Illness and Abuse Collide

"His bipolar swings were terrifying. When manic, he'd talk to himself, argue with invisible doctors, and threaten us with horrific punishments. When depressed, he was silent but cold, neglecting us for days, sometimes forgetting to feed us. He told us we were 'experiments' that his abuse was 'for our own good.'"

The Teen's Burden

"As the oldest at home, I had to keep the children quiet during Dad's episodes. I learned to read his signs, the twitch in his eye, the pacing footsteps, and shield the younger ones. But I was terrified he'd turn on me next."

Aftermath

"Even after CPS intervention, Dad fought to keep control. His medical reputation gave him power in court. I'm haunted by nightmares, the cold steel, the silent screams, the smell of antiseptics.

Podcast Scene: *"The Reckoning"*

"After years of silence, Elena found the strength to face her father, a man who wielded power not only in the family but in the community."

Confrontation

Elena stood at the threshold of her childhood home, the place that had haunted her dreams for so long. The front door swung open.

"You're here," Dad said, voice cold but laced with disbelief.

"I'm here to speak the truth," Elena said, her voice steady but trembling inside.

"You ruined my childhood," she continued, "and the lives of my siblings."

His eyes darkened, "You have no proof."

"I have my memories, my scars, and I'm not alone anymore."

The Tense Exchange

"You think you can destroy me?" he hissed. "I'm a doctor, respected in this town. You're just a rebellious child."

Elena's hands clenched.

"I'm no child. And your reputation doesn't erase your crimes. You abused us with your knowledge, your tools... You treated us like experiments. People will listen now. The CPS reports, the medical evaluations, the testimonies."

Elena's Closure

"It's not about revenge," Elena said softly, "It's about truth, justice, and healing. I want my siblings to be safe. I want other families to know abuse hides behind all masks, even the white coat."

Shannon's voice cracked. "Elena, thank you for your bravery. You are a beacon of hope for so many."

Consequences Begin

Shortly after Elena's courageous confrontation, an anonymous letter arrived at the hospital administration. It detailed chilling allegations not only of abuse at home but of the doctor's unstable mental state and dangerous behavior behind the scenes.

The letter described how he was bipolar, self-medicating with a cocktail of prescription drugs and alcohol. Worse, it accused him of illegally prescribing medications not just for himself, but for family members, including unapproved sedatives and painkillers for the children.

The hospital launched an urgent internal investigation. Medical boards reviewed his patient files, pharmacy records, and communications. Interviews with colleagues revealed whispers of erratic behavior, unexplained absences, and signs of deep personal struggles.

He was placed on leave during the investigation. The medical licensing board formally sanctioned him, opening a disciplinary hearing that could revoke his license permanently.

Meanwhile, authorities reviewed the prescriptions he'd written. Evidence of forged signatures and illegal distribution to his family surfaced, exposing a dangerous breach of medical ethics and laws.

This anonymous whistleblower, perhaps a colleague or a deeply concerned nurse, became a key catalyst in bringing the truth to light, showing how courage can come from unexpected places.

Elena's testimony, combined with this new evidence, built a powerful case that shattered his facade and forced justice to move forward.

The hospital suspended him immediately. His medical license was under review. Legal proceedings started, with prosecutors building a case. Elena's brothers finally broke their silence, providing crucial testimony. Neighbors who once admired him spoke out, revealing years of rumors and whispers.

Trial Proceedings: "A Father on the Stand"

The courtroom was in use. Doctors from the hospital sat quietly in the back row, their faces pale with discomfort. News crews lined the hallways outside. The once-revered surgeon now sat at the defendant's table, shackled by the very system he had once manipulated.

Elena, now composed and determined, sat across from him, and the survivor turned into an accuser.

The Prosecution's Case

The prosecutor opened with a chilling statement:

"This is not just a case of child abuse, this is the deliberate exploitation of medical power. A man who took an oath not to harm used his skills to inflict it."

Exhibits were presented:

- Photographs of bruises and injuries hidden for years.

- CPS reports that it documented repeated emotional neglect and coercion.

- Prescription records showing illegal self-prescribing of opioids, benzodiazepines, and anti-psychotics to both him and his underage children.

- Hospital records showing altered documents and forged signatures.

The prosecution brought in medical experts, including a psychiatrist who testified:

"In my professional opinion, the defendant exhibited traits of narcissistic personality disorder, with comorbid unmanaged bipolar disorder. He knowingly used his license to shield his actions a textbook case of a doctor who weaponized medicine."

Elena's Testimony

When Elena took the stand, the courtroom fell silent.

"He used needles when we cried. He locked my brother in a utility closet for two days with no food and called it 'punishment therapy.' He made us take pills we didn't understand and said we were 'defective.' And I kept the secret because I thought I'd die if I didn't." As she spoke, the jurors wiped away tears.

The judge looked visibly shaken. One alternate juror requested to be dismissed, emotionally unable to continue.

The Defense Crumbles

The defense tried to paint the doctor as overwhelmed, a man battling mental illness who "lost his way."

But emails, recordings, and journal entries revealed a different truth, calculated, repeated cruelty masked by a public persona. He refused a plea deal, insisting on his own brilliance until the end.

His eldest son testified in the prosecution.

"We were all scared to do something. I left for college and blocked it out, but I knew. We all knew. I should've said something. I'm sorry I didn't protect them."

The Verdict

After only six hours of deliberation, the jury returned.

"We find the defendant guilty on all counts."

- Child endangerment

- Intentional infliction of emotional distress

- Illegal prescription and drug distribution

- Medical malpractice and criminal abuse of power

The judge sentenced him to 35 years in prison, with eligibility for parole in twenty. His medical license was permanently revoked.

Shannon's Closing Words

"Elena didn't just survive she changed the course of justice. This story reminds us that the truth, once spoken, can topple even the most untouchable abusers. "To those still silenced: You are not alone. And to those listening: Believe the quietest voices. They often carry the deepest truth and personal healing journey as well as the podcast's evolution from a storytelling platform to a national movement for change."

Shannon's Reckoning — From Echoes to Action

The courtroom verdict echoed through Shannon like a bell ringing deep in her soul. Elena's bravery, both raw, unwavering, had stirred something long buried. When the cameras turned off and the headlines faded, the stories didn't. They stayed with her. And so did the pain.

A Wave of National Support

In the weeks after Elena's trial aired on the podcast, Shannon's inbox overflowed.

- Emails from survivors: "You helped me break my silence after 30 years."

- Letters from therapists offering free counseling to podcast guests.

- Support from advocacy groups like RAINN and Child Help, who pledged resources and partnership.

One message stood out.

"Shannon, I'm a pediatric nurse. We've been listening. Your podcast saved a child in my care. I saw the signs. I intervened. Thank you."

Shannon held the letter to her chest and sobbed.

A New Mission

The podcast had started as a lifeline for Shannon's healing. Now, it had become a platform for change.

She formed a nonprofit organization, *Haven House*, with three goals:

1. Provide trauma-informed therapy to survivors of childhood abuse.

2. Train professionals to recognize and intervene in emotional abuse cases.

3. Give survivors a voice, with storytelling workshops and podcast guest support.

A Closet Full of Silence – Shannon's Reflection

It was during a quiet moment after one of the podcast's most harrowing episodes, the one where a caller described being locked in a closet for days, that Shannon felt her breath catch in her throat.

She ended the recording and just sat there, the silence in the studio pressing against her like a wall.

And then it came back.

Unlike a memory. More like a *flash flood* overwhelming, unstoppable.

Under the Dirty Laundry

She was six.

Her baby brother was barely two.

The closet was small and dark, the air thick with dust and the sour smell of old laundry. She remembered pressing her body flat against the wooden floor, trying to pull her brother into the pile of clothes with her, muffling his cries against her chest.

"Shhh, baby... we're hiding. Daddy's mad again..."

Outside the door, the sounds were unmistakable.

A crash.

Her mother's scream.

The belt.

The thud of a body hitting the floor.

Her father's voice slurred and full of hate.

"You made me do this!"

Shannon covered her ears. But no matter how hard she tried, she could still hear her mother sobbing.

The Little Girl Who Waited

She remembered counting.

Counting the seconds between screams. Counting the bruises on her mother's arms the next morning. Counting the times her father said, *I love you,* like it made up for everything.

She would hold her brother's tiny hand and whisper promises she didn't understand.

"When I grow up, I'll take care of you. I'll take us away." However, they did not depart at that time. They went to school with secrets under their skin, smiling through bruises no one ever asked about.

Shannon Speaks the Truth

Now, decades later, in the wake of Elena's trial and the tidal wave of stories from survivors… Shannon finally let her own story breathe. She shared it live on the podcast, her voice trembling but resolute.

"I used to hide in the closet, too. With my baby brother. While our father beat the hell out of our mother. I remember the rage in his voice more than I remember the sound of my own because I stopped speaking back then. I went quiet so quiet, I thought I had disappeared."

A long pause. A breath.

"But I'm not hiding anymore."

Transformation Through Memory

That memory became the moment Shannon realized: *she was still protecting that little girl. Still blaming herself. Still carrying the silence like a second skin.* But not anymore.

Elena's bravery. The other survivors. The anonymous letters. The children were rescued. The trials, the letters, the tears, they permitted Shannon to finally say:

"What happened to me was not my fault. And it wasn't love. It was survival."

Chapter 14
Honoring Family Shame

"Today's episode is… different. It's personal in a way I never imagined I'd be ready for. A family member, someone who loved my brothers, who grew up around the very home where my pain began, is joining me. His name is Jimmy. He's, my cousin. A Naval Officer. A leader. A man of honor. And someone who knew… something. Not everything. But enough."

[Call-In Begins]

Jimmy's voice came through the mic: steady, deep, but laced with something raw and vulnerable.

"Hey, Shannon.

I've been listening to your episodes. I cried more than I ever have in my life. It was time."

Jimmy's Confession

"I loved your dad, Shannon. He was larger than life to me as a kid, charming, funny and generous in public. He used to flip me quarters and wink like we were buddies. But I always knew something wasn't right. My mom, your aunt, would whisper things when she thought I was asleep. She'd say, *'He's got demons. He's got rage. I feel sorry for those kids.'* she feared him. We all were, in a way. When I got older, I saw bruises on your mom once at a barbecue. And I remember your little brother, just four or five, clinging to me like he didn't want to go home."

Jimmy paused.

"I didn't say anything. I told myself, *'It's not my business.'*
I told myself, *'He's a good man going through a hard time.'* But I knew. Deep down, I knew all along."

The Family Code of Silence

Jimmy's voice grew more intense.

"In our family, there was this unspoken rule: **'Don't talk about what happens behind closed doors.'** Your dad was mentally ill, but no one dared say the word. Bipolar? Rage disorder? It didn't matter what mattered was keeping the family name intact. We went to church on Sundays, smiled for family photos. But the women were terrified. And the kids… the kids were ghosts."

Guilt and Grief

"I served in the Navy for 20 years. I've seen war. But nothing has haunted me like knowing I didn't speak up when I could've. I'm sorry. I was too afraid to break the illusion."

His voice cracked.

"Shannon… I'm sorry. I failed you. I failed all of you."

Shannon spoke, "You didn't fail me, Jimmy. You were a child, too. You were in a system, in a family that taught you to stay silent. But you're speaking now. That's what matters now."

The Ripple Effect

After Jimmy's call, the podcast was flooded with more family members and listeners writing in. A few cousins sent messages:

"I remember things now I tried to forget."

"I saw bruises, too."

"Your bravery helped us remember our own truth."

Jimmy's confession cracked open the wider family secret: a generational culture of suppressed trauma, normalized abuse, and patriarchal silence.

Shannon's Closing Words

Truth can be revealed after many years and may not always become known immediately. But when it comes, it liberates everyone it touches. Jimmy, thank you for being the man who stood up, even if it took a lifetime. To everyone listening: If your family told you to stay silent, I'm telling you something different: *Speak. Break the cycle. Say it aloud.*

Withholding information within the family does not ensure protection; in fact, it may have detrimental consequences.

The Older Brother: Dismantled From Within

Shannon's older brother, Mark, had once been the golden child. Intelligent, athletic, protective of Shannon when they were young. But their father had a special kind of cruelty reserved for Mark, the boy who dared to stand up to him.

"You'll never be anything," their father would snarl. "You think you're a man? You're weak. Just like your mother."

When Mark hit puberty, the psychological games intensified. Their father undermined him constantly, mocking his appearance, sabotaging his confidence, and later shaming him for being emotional or vulnerable.

Shannon remembered overhearing fights between them.

"You're too soft. Toughen up. Real men don't cry."

By seventeen, Mark was drinking. By twenty, he was experimenting with harder drugs. He spent the next decade in and out of rehab, a cycle of addiction, shame, and relapse, all while desperately seeking the approval of a father who would never give it.

"I'm trying, Dad," Mark once said after a year of sobriety. "Trying what?" his father barked. "To be a failure?"

Mark eventually severed ties, but the damage was done. His addiction wasn't about partying; it was about numbing pain and burying the voice of the man who lived in his head.

The Baby Brother: The One Who Hid with Her

Shannon's baby brother, Danny, the one she used to cradle under dirty laundry in the closet, had grown up into a gentle, brilliant man.

He went to law school, clerked for a respected judge, and became a defender of children's rights.

But inside, he was haunted.

He never talked much about the past, but Shannon knew the truth: Danny was plagued with chronic depression, intrusive memories, and suicidal thoughts that refused to be silenced.

He had told her once, in a rare, vulnerable moment: "I don't remember everything. But I remember the screaming. And the fear. And how I used to watch you, thinking you were the only reason I survived."

Despite a prestigious career, Danny struggled with intimacy, trust, and deep emotional wounds that therapy never fully healed.

The Tragedy

On a quiet morning, just two weeks after Danny's 40th birthday, Shannon received the call. He had been found dead in the basement of their family home, crushed under a barbell during a solo workout. The coroner called it an accidental death.

But Shannon knew better. There were no drugs in his system. No heart condition. No plausible explanation except one.

"The weight of our father finally crushed him," she whispered into the microphone weeks later. "It just… took 40 years."

Shannon's Grief and Reckoning

Shannon grieved Danny with a rage she didn't know she had.

"He got out. He became everything our father was not. And still the trauma hunted him down and dragged him under."

She began speaking openly about intergenerational trauma and how abuse rewires the brain and body, how the scars might not always show, but they shape every thought, decision, and relationship.

Podcast Episode: *"The Ones Who Didn't Make It"*

In a special tribute episode, Shannon shared her brothers' stories not as tragedies, but as testimonies.

"Mark was not a failure. He was a boy broken by a man who couldn't live without violence. Danny was not weak. He was a survivor who gave everything he had to make the world safer for kids like us."

Shannon ended the episode with a solemn vow: "If you're listening to this… And you're carrying your childhood like an anvil strapped to your soul… Please. Don't carry it alone. Get help. Break the silence."

Chapter 15
What the Cousins Remember

The Phone Call That Changed Everything

After Daniel's death, a storm of grief and curiosity stirred within Shannon.

She began calling the cousins she had grown up with, the ones who came to holiday dinners, backyard parties, and family reunions.

She hadn't spoken to many of them in years. But something in her had shifted.

"Do you… remember anything?" she asked her cousin Lisa one night.

Lisa paused. Then she began to cry. "I do. God, I do."

Lisa's Memory: The Boy Who Made Rhymes About Pain

Lisa told Shannon a story she'd buried for decades.

One summer, when they were all around 9 or 10, the kids were playing in the basement of their grandparents' house. Mark, just a few years older, sat on the stairs, his arms folded, bruises visible on his upper arms, "Your dad hit you again," he said in a flat, matter-of-fact tone.

Then, with a strange glimmer of defiance, he began to chant:

"He punches my back, He slaps my face, I run and hide, He gives me a chase. He pulls my ear, he makes me crawl, He says I'm nothing at all. But one day soon, I'll fly away. And I won't come back. No matter what they say."

The cousins went silent. Some laughed nervously, thinking it was a weird joke.

But Mark didn't smile.

He stared at the floor.

"I remember that day so clearly now," Lisa whispered. "But back then? We just thought that was… Mark. Being weird. No one stopped to ask why a kid that age would know how to rhyme his own abuse."

Other Cousins Chime In

As word spread through the family that Shannon was *telling the truth*, more cousins began calling her. Some hesitantly. Others urgently.

"I remember Mark limping once and saying it was from football. But I saw your dad yelling at him in the garage the night before."

"Your mom's black eyes. We never asked."

"We were told not to talk about it. That your dad was 'strict.' But strict doesn't make kids draft poems about being nothing."

The Family Mirror

Shannon was stunned by how much the family had seen — and ignored. It wasn't that they didn't care. It was that they had been conditioned to look away.

To protect our reputation.

To preserve the illusion.

To keep the peace.

But now, the illusion was shattered. And in its place was something real: honesty, mourning, and slowly, a chance to heal.

Shannon's Reflection on the Podcast

"My brother Mark was telling us all along. He was writing his trauma in rhymes. He was sending distress signals in a language only a child could understand. And none of us, not one, heard it the way he needed us to."

She paused.

"But we hear it now, Mark. And I promise you… your words weren't wasted. They'll help break the silence for thousands.

The Wake After Danny's Death

Danny's funeral was subdued and sterile, as if no one knew quite how to mourn him.

The family gathered in black suits and stiff hugs, pretending everything was fine. But Shannon saw it. The unspoken tension clung to the room like thick smoke.

"He was always such a bright boy," an aunt whispered to her.
Shannon stared at her. "Then why didn't anyone protect him?" That question was simple and seismic, set off a chain reaction in the weeks that followed.

Shannon, shaken by her brother's fates and the flood of memories of her cousins, decided: no more secrets. She organized a family meeting. Not everyone came, —but enough did to stir the pot.

There were cousins, a few aunts, uncles, and even her mother's surviving sister. Shannon stood before them with trembling hands and an unwavering voice.

"We all saw it. We all *knew*. And we all stayed quiet."

Murmurs. Shifts in chairs. A thick silence.

Then her cousin Jimmy, a former Navy officer, stoic, respected, spoke up, "I saw the bruises on Mark. I heard him crying through the vent. And I did nothing."

His voice cracked.

"We were raised to think men like your dad were 'just strict.'
But he was cruel. And we let it happen."

Tensions Ignite

Not everyone agreed.

One uncle stood up, red-faced and angry.

"This is disrespectful to the dead! He was a good man. He provided! He kept that family fed!"

Shannon's voice was ice.

"He fed us dinner, yes. Right before dragging our mother by her hair and slamming Mark into the wall."

The room fractured.

Some relatives stormed out, muttering about loyalty and keeping the past in the past. Others stayed — finally sobbing, talking, and sharing. It was messy. Raw. Necessary.

Generational Trauma Exposed

As stories poured out, patterns emerged.

One cousin admitted their own father, Shannon's uncle, had been verbally abusive for years.

Another revealed her husband's alcoholism, rooted in his own abusive upbringing.

"It's like a disease," someone said. "Passed from father to son like a cursed inheritance."

Shannon nodded.

"But we don't have to pass it on. We get to be the ones who break the chain."

Shifts in Relationship

Some relatives grew closer to Shannon after the meeting, thanking her for her bravery.

Others distanced themselves, accusing her of "digging up dirt" and "disrespecting the family name."

But Shannon had made peace with that.

"You don't owe your loyalty to a lie. You owe it to the children who didn't survive, and the ones still trying.

Chapter 16
Courtroom and the Cover-Up

The courtroom was colder than she expected. Shannon sat on the hard wooden bench, her fingers curled tightly around the edge of her purse as she stared ahead, unblinking. The judge's bench loomed at the front like a throne meant to intimidate. To silence.

Beside her sat Elly, chin high, jaw tight, dressed in muted navy.

They were character witnesses in a hearing against Dr. Allen Whiteman, a beloved local physician with decades of accolades and glowing community praise, and a sealed history of complaints. Complaints that no one wanted to acknowledge. Not the hospital board. Not the state medical licensing board. And indeed not the network of lawyers that orbited him like flies to rotting fruit.

But Cassandra had come forward. Her voice shaking, she had finally filed the report after years of denial, manipulation, and gaslighting. She had been one of his interns, just twenty-four at the time when the grooming began. First, it was special attention. Then it was favors. Then it was touching. Then silence. Always the silence. How did we get to this point?

"To the hospital's Human Resources department," Cassandra replied, her voice steady yet laced with a quiet frustration. "I told them everything. His words, his actions, and how they made me feel unsafe. They told me they'd investigate it. But weeks passed, and nothing changed. When I followed up, they claimed I must have misunderstood his intentions. That I was reading too much into his mentorship."

Shannon felt her throat tighten as the defense attorney leaned against the lectern, his expression dripping with calculated skepticism. "Do you have proof of this communication with HR? What about correspondence, documentation, anything to corroborate your claims?"

Cassandra hesitated briefly, "I have emails," she said firmly. "I kept notes, dates, times, his exact words."

There was a shuffle in the gallery, a murmur of low voices that the judge silenced with a sharp rap of their gavel. The defense attorney straightened, unfazed. "Ms. Bryant, you were an intern at the time, correct? Young, inexperienced. Is it possible you misinterpreted a mentor's gestures of support? Dr. Whiteman has mentored dozens, if not hundreds, of young professionals. Not one has made claims remotely like yours."

Cassandra's chin dipped slightly, her focus shifting to the tabletop in front of her. Shannon clenched her fists. She wanted to shout, —to scream at the absurdity of the question, the deliberate twisting of events into something palatable for an audience eager to disbelieve.

But she couldn't. Not yet. Cassandra raised her gaze, her fingers visibly trembling as they gripped the edges of the witness stand. "I know what I experienced," she said quietly. "If no one else has come forward, it's because they're afraid. They are too afraid of what might happen if they speak out against someone like him. I was afraid too. But fear doesn't erase the truth."

Her words lingered in the air, heavy with unspoken histories. Shannon felt the weight of it pressing down on her, urging her forward. Beside her, Elly shifted, her hands tightening around her folder, the faintest flicker of resolve crossing her features. Shannon knew she'd have to speak soon; her voice would be next.

The judge finally broke the silence, their tone measured and inscrutable. "Ms. Bryant," they said, "please submit any documentation you have to the court for review. Until then, let us proceed."

As Cassandra stepped down from the stand, her shoulders rigid, but her steps were deliberate, Shannon braced herself. Cassandra had planted the first seed, exposed the cracks to Dr. Whiteman's carefully curated facade. But the battle was far from over. Shannon only hoped her voice would be enough to widen those cracks.

A public hearing was supposed to be neutral and fair. It was none of those things.

The moment Shannon entered the courtroom, she saw it in the faces of the men lining the gallery, defense attorneys, hospital administrators, and legal "advisors." They weren't here for the truth. They were here for the show. They were here to win.

Cassandra took the stand first. Her voice was stronger than Shannon had expected. Her spine was straight.

But when she described the first time Dr. Whiteman called her into his office, closed the door, and brushed her hand as she passed him her notes, Shannon saw the tremble in her fingers.

"He said I was special. That I reminded him of his daughter," Cassandra said, blinking hard. "Then he kissed my forehead. And later, my lips. He said he was testing my boundaries. That it was part of the mentorship process."

"So, if it was this bad, why did you continue working for him? You continued working under Dr. Whiteman, despite your concerns about his behavior?" the defense attorney pressed, their voice calculated, their tone sharp but controlled.

Shannon wanted to laugh. Not because it was funny, but because of the absurdity.

"Yes," Cassandra replied, her voice steady despite the tension in her clenched hands. "I did. Not because I wanted to, but because I had no other option. The hierarchy within the institution left me powerless to refuse."

The defense attorney's smile widened fractionally, a predator sensing weakness. "Ms. Bryant, were you aware of Dr. Whiteman's esteemed reputation at the time? His accomplishments in research? His dedication to advancing the careers of his mentees?"

Cassandra's smile didn't waver. "I was aware, but reputation doesn't absolve someone of wrongdoing. It doesn't erase what happened."

The gallery rustled again, a murmur swelling like distant thunder. The judge's gavel struck once, silencing the room.

The defense attorney leaned forward. "Yet, you continued to seek mentorship opportunities with Dr. Whiteman. You continued to rely on his guidance. Is that correct?"

Cassandra hesitated, her lips parting as if to speak, but no words came immediately. Shannon held her breath, feeling every ounce of tension in the room. Then Cassandra's voice emerged, quiet but resolute: "I relied on him because I didn't have the privilege of choice. Staying silent was survival, not consent."

The defense attorney began to respond, but the judge interrupted. "Ms. Bryant has answered the question. Let's move forward."

A brief silence draped the room like a heavy curtain. Each moment stretched, vibrating with the weight of Cassandra's words. Shannon knew her own testimony would need to match this clarity, this courage. She felt her pulse quicken. Soon, it would be her turn to face the defense's calculated dance of questions.

The judge cleared their throat, turning to the defense. "Proceed."

The defense attorney nodded slightly, adjusting their posture. "Ms. Bryant," they began again, careful to maintain an air of professionalism, "do you have any documented evidence to support these claims? Correspondence, emails, or written reports?"

Cassandra's expression faltered for the briefest of moments, her jaw tightening. "I submitted documentation to my supervisor at the time. Whether it remains intact in institutional records, I cannot say."

"And you have no personal copies of these records?"

"Correct."

The defense attorney paused, their silence speaking volumes. With a practiced glance toward the gallery, they took a step back. "No further questions, Your Honor."

As Cassandra stepped down from the stand, her gaze swept the courtroom. Her expression conveyed defiance and vulnerability. Shannon's chest tightened. The cracks had begun to show in Dr. Whiteman's defense.

Now it was her turn to pry them wider. Someone in the gallery scoffed. The judge didn't bat an eye.

Then it was Shannon's turn.

She took the stand slowly, deliberately. Her heels clicked against the polished floor like the ticking of a clock. The prosecution had requested her as a character witness, not for Cassandra, but for the culture that created men like Whiteman.

She was ready.

The defense team smiled thinly. "And did you report this alleged behavior at the time?"

"I did."

"To whom?"

"My attending supervisor."

"And what was the outcome?"

"They said it was a misunderstanding. That I was flattered and confused."

"And you continued working under Dr. Whiteman?"

Shannon met the defense attorney's gaze with a calm steadiness that seemed to still the room. "You're right."

The jury remained focused, and Shannon saw their interest piqued. Her words had shifted the atmosphere in the room, planting seeds of doubt where the defense had tried to sow confidence.

"I run a podcast called *Unmasked,*" she began. "We give voice to women who have been silenced. Some of them are by partners. Some by employers. And some by doctors just like the one on trial today."

"You're not a doctor, are you, Ms. Sullivan?" the defense attorney asked, his tone slick.

"No."

"Nor a lawyer?"

"No." She said. "I'm neither a doctor nor a lawyer. But what qualifies me is the testimony of hundreds of women who've shared their experiences on my podcast. Many women have faced systemic failures, dismissals, and harm under the guise of professional care. My role here is to ensure their voices don't go unheard."

The defense attorney smirked, clearly unimpressed. "So, you're here to offer anecdotes rather than evidence?"

Shannon tilted her head slightly, her tone steady but pointed. "I'm here to provide context, Mr. Staley. Context for a long-overlooked pattern. You can call it anecdotal if you like, but every case starts with a story. And sometimes those stories reveal uncomfortable truths."

The attorney took a step closer, his voice dripping with skepticism. "Tell me, Ms. Sullivan, would you agree that painting an air of profession with a brush of a few bad actors is... reductive?"

"Absolutely," Shannon replied, her voice unwavering. "Just as it's reductive to dismiss victims because their testimonies challenge an image of professionalism that's too often taken at face value."

The courtroom held its breath; the air charged with an almost tangible tension. Every creak of a chair, every faint rustle of paper felt amplified, as though the room itself was waiting for something to break the oppressive stillness. The jury's eyes flickered between Shannon and the defense attorney, caught in the tug-of-war between her fiery conviction and his calculated detachment.

The defense attorney finally broke the charged silence, his voice smooth but cutting. "Ms. Sullivan, your passion is admirable, but passion does not equate to proof. This court operates on facts, not feelings."

Shannon turned her head sharply, her gaze piercing as if to slice through the calm facade he wore. "You're right," she said, her voice low but unyielding. "This court operates on facts. Why aren't women's facts considered important? Why is it that the system demands perfection from victims and nothing from the accused?"

The attorney opened his mouth to reply, but the sudden murmur from the gallery drowned him out. People were leaning forward in their seats now, their whispers like dry leaves rustling in a rising wind. The judge banged their gavel once, twice, calling for order.

"Ms. Sullivan," the judge said, their tone a thin line between irritation and sternness, "this is your final warning. Keep your statements grounded in evidence and relevant to this case."

Shannon's throat burned with unsaid retorts, but she nodded, her composure collected like armor. "Understood, Your Honor."

She glanced briefly at Cassandra, who sat at the plaintiff's table with her hands clenched in her lap. Shannon understood that it was up to them to fight.

The defense attorney adjusted his stance; his smirk tempered with the faintest hint of frustration. "Ms. Sullivan, you claim a pattern exists, but the burden of proof demands much more than anecdotes and collective outrage. Can you provide documented evidence beyond hearsay?"

Shannon inhaled deeply, feeling the weight of the room pressing down on her. Her response had to strike with precision, not just to hold her ground but to make her words impossible to dismiss. "I'd like to submit Exhibit E-2," she said, her voice steady. The courtroom stilled as she gestured toward a manila folder on the plaintiff's table. "Your honor, these documents are from the hospital archive and include schedules, emails, and internal memos that have inexplicably been altered or disappeared over the years." They paint a picture of a system that bends over backward to shield predators like Dr. Whiteman.

The defense attorney's smirk faltered for a fraction of a second before returning. "Convenient, isn't it, that these so-called alterations conveniently align with your narrative?"

"Convenient?" Shannon shot back, her tone sharp enough to make the air in the room quiver. "No, Mr. Adler. What's convenient is a system designed to erase the evidence that women need to be believed. What's convenient is the effortless dismissal of survivors who dare to challenge the status quo."

The judge's gavel struck again, a stark interruption that set the tense atmosphere crackling like static. "Ms. Sullivan, that's enough. Let's proceed with examining the evidence."

Shannon stepped back, a faint tremor in her hands, as adrenaline coursed through her. She had done what she came to do, planted a seed of doubt, a crack in the polished veneer of the defense's argument. Now it was up to the jury to decide whether they would let that seed grow or smother it beneath the weight of tradition.

As the proceedings continued, Shannon caught Cassandra's gaze once more. This time, there was no question in her eyes, only fierce determination. Whatever the verdict, they had made their voices heard, and that, at least, was a start.

For Shannon, this wasn't about Cassandra; it was about every story shared on her podcast, every woman who had dared to speak despite the risks. Her voice carried the weight of their collective anger and exhaustion, and she refused to let it falter. She met the faces in the jury box, daring them to see humanity in her argument.

"Ms. Sullivan," the judge's voice broke the spell, measured yet firm, "we appreciate your passion, but remember that this court demands evidence, not conjecture."

Shannon's lips pressed together, a deep breath steadying her resolve. Fine, if they needed specifics, she would deliver. She saw the reports had been altered, and files were missing. This wasn't conjecture; it was a pattern, each story a thread weaving into an undeniable truth.

As she spoke, her words carved fissures into the courtroom's veneer of indifference. But Shannon knew the scars of systemic injustice ran deep, and she wasn't naive enough to believe a single testimony could undo decades of complacency.

When she finally stepped down from the stand, her heart pounding, Shannon cast a glance at Cassandra. The younger woman's expression was unreadable, but her clenched fists told her everything she needed to know. If nothing else,

Shannon had given her a voice; whether the court would listen was another matter entirely.

The defense attorney recovered quickly, his lips curling into a practiced smirk. "Ms. Sullivan, are you suggesting that this court should base its decision on anecdotes and sensationalism rather than documented facts?"

Shannon's gaze didn't falter. "I'm suggesting that this court should stop ignoring the patterns that are as plain as day. Dr. Whiteman's actions weren't a one-time lapse. These issues reflect a longstanding systemic problem. Why else would so many women of different ages, backgrounds, and professions all have eerily related stories?"

"Yet, Ms. Sullivan," the attorney pressed, "the burden of proof remains unmet. Unless you can provide concrete evidence rather than conjecture, your claims are worth no more than the paper they're written on."

Shannon leaned forward, her voice sharpening as she addressed the jury directly. "The burden of proof? That has always been the convenient escape hatch for men like Whiteman. They rely on the fact that victims often do not report incidents, that evidence may be compromised or destroyed, and that the system can sometimes offer protection to them. So, yes, there's no smoking gun because the system made sure there wouldn't be. But that doesn't make the truth any less damning."

The judge intervened before the attorney could respond, their tone even but firm. "Ms. Sullivan, kindly keep your remarks focused on the case at hand."

Shannon nodded, though she knew her point had landed squarely where it needed to. She continued, her voice steadier now, recounting specific instances she had heard during her podcast interviews, including Cassandra's story. She explained that victims' medical records were frequently ignored, altered, or removed.

When the court broke for recess, Shannon walked outside into the chilled hallway, her heart racing. Elly followed, her face pale.

"They're not going to find him guilty," Elly said flatly.

Shannon blinked. "What?"

"They're going to dismiss it. No disciplinary action. No license suspension. I saw the clerk's note on the judge's desk before he turned it over."

Shannon's stomach dropped.

"They already made up their minds before today." Elly nodded. "This isn't a hearing. It's a performance." They returned to the courtroom just in time for the judge's decision.

The judge opens the verdict in his hand, "In the matter of Dr. Allen Whiteman, this panel finds insufficient evidence of professional misconduct. Courts will not take further action. The hearing is over.

Cassandra gasped beside her attorney. Elly let out a low, bitter laugh. Shannon just sat, paralyzed, as her blood turned ice-cold. It wasn't that they had lost. It was that the system had never been theirs to win in the first place.

As they left the courthouse, Shannon spotted Dr. Whiteman near the steps, smiling, shaking hands with a board member.

"You're still a hero, Allen," the man said. "Don't let these accusations slow you down."

Shannon turned to Elly. "He's going to do it again." Elly replied, "He never stopped."

As Shannon stood there, watching Dr. Whiteman's smug smile glint under the late afternoon sun, a thought struck her with the force of a gale. "Elly," she said quietly, her voice trembling not from fear but from the burgeoning storm of resolve within her. "What if... we don't wait?" Elly's brow furrowed. "Wait for what?"

"For justice. For the system to work," Shannon hissed, her words sharp as broken glass. "It won't. It never will. You said it yourself. This is all a performance. But we're not the audience. We're the ones in the wings, holding the curtain strings. What if we tear it down?"

Elly's lips parted in surprise, but before she could respond, Cassandra appeared at Shannon's side, her face pale yet fierce.

"You're thinking it, aren't you?" Cassandra whispered. "Exposing him. Every single one of them connected to him."

Shannon met Cassandra's gaze, the unspoken alliance forming like the snap of magnets. "Not just him," she said. "The whole network."

Elly scoffed, a bitter chuckle escaping her throat. "You're talking about dismantling a fortress, Shannon. These people have money, power, and connections we can't even fathom."

"And what do they have to fear from us?" Shannon asked, her tone sharpening. "We're the ones underestimated. They see us as victims, not as threats."

Elly's silence spoke volumes. Shannon could see the calculations playing out behind her piercing gaze. Finally, Elly nodded, her lips curling into a slow, predatory smile. "Alright, then. Let's flip the script."

Later that evening, back in Daniel's old office, Shannon stared at the glowing screen of her laptop, her fingers poised above the keys. The names on the list glared back at her like taunts. Her mind churned, replaying the laughter of Dr. Whiteman and the dismissive gaze of the judge who had already sealed their fate before the hearing had even begun.

Shannon clenched her jaw and typed out an email. She addressed a whistleblower journalist she had once worked with and a connection she hadn't used in years. The subject line read: "You Need to See This: A Story That Will Burn Their House Down."

As she hit the send, her phone buzzed on the desk.

It was a message from Cassandra. The text read: "Meet me tomorrow. I found something on Scott. It's bigger than we thought."

Shannon's heart raced. She didn't need to ask; she knew what Cassandra meant. Scott wasn't just a name on Daniel's list. He was a thread, one that, if pulled, might unravel the entire rotten tapestry.

The next day, they gathered at Haven House, where Cassandra revealed a stack of old financial records she had uncovered. "It's a shell corporation," Cassandra explained, her voice trembling with adrenaline. "Scott was moving money for them. All of them, including Whiteman and others. Do you know what this means? This isn't about him preying on patients. It's trafficking, Shannon. They're buying and selling lives. They're selling body organs."

Shannon's breath hitched, and Elly, who stood by the window, turned sharply. "We're not just fighting a predator," Elly said, her voice low and dangerous. "We're stepping into a war zone."

That night, Shannon didn't sleep.

She sat in Daniel's old office at Haven House, staring at his favorite worn law book. Her hand drifted toward the podcast mic, but she didn't turn it on.

Instead, she pulled out her laptop and opened a folder Daniel had once titled: *"The Ones Who Got Away."*

Inside, there were five names. One of them was Dr. Allen Whiteman, and the other was Scott Brannigan.

Written below those names, in bold:

"To expose the network, follow the money, not the victims. They already buried them."

The rage built slowly, then all at once. Her breath caught in her throat. It wasn't just a bad apple. It was a whole orchard. How do we attach them and uncover the truth?

Shannon's fingers hovered over the keys as her mind spun through the implications of what lay before her. She thought back to Daniel's relentless pursuit of truth. A quest that had cost him everything. The folder he had left behind wasn't just a collection of names; it was a map of connections stretching back years. These weren't isolated incidents. They were threads in a web of corruption that was far larger than Shannon had dared to imagine.

"Follow the money," she whispered to herself, the words etched in Daniel's handwriting burning into her thoughts. Her eyes scanned the list again, noting patterns she had previously missed.

Whiteman, Brannigan, and the others weren't just names. They were gatekeepers, intermediaries in a systematic exploitation network.

In the center was Scott Brannigan, whom Cassandra had unearthed as a key player in moving funds for the shadowy entities behind it all.

A faint memory stirred, one Shannon had buried deep. Years ago, before Haven House had become the sanctuary it is today, Daniel had confided his fears about certain legal cases he couldn't crack. "Sometimes, the law's hands are tied," he had said bitterly. "The ones pulling the strings are hidden behind layers of bureaucracy that keep them untouchable."

At the time, Shannon hadn't understood the full weight of his words, but now she felt the truth like a vice around her chest.

She scrolled through the financial documents Cassandra had provided. Shell corporations. Offshore accounts. The trail was elaborate and hidden in a weave of deception. If Scott was a thread, then Whiteman was a knot, central figure around whom much of the operation revolved. The scale was staggering, but Shannon knew the key wasn't simply exposing the network; it was making people care.

The victims, buried and forgotten by the system, deserved more than cold facts. They deserved voices, names, and faces.

Elly's words echoed in her head: *"We're stepping into a war zone."*

It wasn't hyperbole; it was a warning Shannon could no longer ignore. She thought of Cassandra's trembling hands as she laid out the records, of Elly's sharp gaze scanning the room for threats, of the whistleblower journalist who hadn't replied to her email yet. Each person was a piece of the puzzle, and the stakes had never been higher.

She stood, pacing the room. The walls felt closer now, suffocating in their silence. The world outside the Haven House was asleep, but Shannon could feel the weight of the battle ahead pressing down on her. She was dismantling decades-old barriers and exposing corruption. And she knew the beasts lurking behind them wouldn't go quietly.

Her laptop pinged with a new message. It was from a nurse who had worked with Whiteman years ago. The email was short, hesitant, but it revealed something Shannon hadn't known: an address tied to one of the shell corporations.

Her heart hammered as she typed a reply, thanking them and urging them to send anything else they could remember. The floodgates were opening.

Before the night ended, Shannon called Cassandra and Elly back to Haven House. The three huddled around the desk, tracing lines between names, corporations, and institutions. Elly's sharp intellect pieced together connections Shannon would have missed, while Cassandra's gut instincts filled in the blanks. Shannon now had the framework for her podcast's first episode on whitecoat corruption, but there was more work to do. They weren't just chasing leads; they were preparing for battle.

"This isn't just about exposing them," Shannon said, her voice steady despite the exhaustion creeping in. "It's about making sure they can't bury this again."

Cassandra nodded, determination blazing in her eyes. Elly crossed her arms, her expression resolute. "Then let's make them listen. Let's make them afraid."

Shannon clicked open her podcast software. Her hands didn't tremble this time. Her voice didn't falter. The truth was coming, and she wouldn't stop until the world heard it.

It was a rotted orchard protected by white coats and blind-folded justice.

She clicked open her podcast software. Her voice was steel. "This isn't about one doctor. This is a machine. And if the courtroom won't give us justice, then we'll make sure the world knows their names. Tomorrow, I'll begin a special three-part investigation, starting with Dr. Whiteman. I will give you evidence that leads to the one who tried to kill Daniel Robertson. If you have proof or want to help me uncover the injustice here, please feel free to contact me by email or on this podcast in the next three-part series. This is Shannon Sullivan, and we are here to uncover the truth as always."

She stared into the dark. Let them come. She decided to stop being polite.

Chapter 17
Shadows in White Coats

By the time the sun rose, Shannon had already recorded the entire first episode of her three-part exposé on *Unmasked*. She had not slept. She hadn't even changed out of the black suit she wore to the courtroom. Her voice was raw, but her message was clear:

"This is not just about Dr. Whiteman. It's about every institution that protected him. The hospitals. The licensing boards. Men with diplomas on their walls sit behind desks, while women like Cassandra rebuild their lives quietly.

Within hours, the episode exploded. Over 200,000 downloads. Thousands of comments. Former patients, nurses, and interns began flooding Shannon's inbox.

Many had never spoken out before.

Some were still afraid to use their names.

But others? They were ready to burn it all down.

Shannon's phone buzzed incessantly, a relentless stream of notifications lighting up her screen. Messages poured in, some uplifting, filled with gratitude and encouragement, while others dripped with veiled threats and ominous warnings. Each thing felt like a spark, igniting her resolve further. She wasn't just making noise; she was making an impact.

By mid-morning, a package arrived at the Haven House. It was small, wrapped in plain brown paper with no return address. Shannon hesitated as she reached for it, her instincts tugging at her like a warning bell. Elly, standing nearby, caught her eye.

"Careful," Elly said softly.

Shannon nodded and carefully unwrapped the package, revealing a single, crisp photograph. It was a picture of her walking out of the courthouse the previous day, her face determined, a crowd in the background. Scrawled across the photo in red marker were the words: ***"You're next."***

You're next.

Elly gasped. "They're escalating."

Her hands trembled, but she forced them to steady. Elly leaned closer, her wide eyes reflecting both fear and determination. Shannon's breath caught as her resolve sharpened. Taking the photograph in hand, she marched down the hallway to her office, Elly trailing behind her. The fluttering of papers, ringing phones, and muffled conversations seemed to blur as she closed the door behind them.

"I'm not waiting for them to take the next step," Shannon said, her voice steely. She grabbed her phone and dialed the local police station. The call connected after a few rings.

"This is Officer Daniels. How can I help you?"

Shannon steadied her voice, though her hands betrayed her tension, gripping the photograph tightly. "My name is Shannon Sullivan. I am reporting threats against myself and my organization, Haven House."

"Are you in immediate danger?" The officer's tone shifted, cautious but professional.

Shannon hesitated, glancing at Elly, then at the photograph on her desk. "Someone sent me this photograph," she described the photograph, and the chilling words scrawled across it. "We've also received warning notes and noticed suspicious activity, like a vehicle parked outside for hours."

The officer asked for details, prompting Shannon to recount everything: the SUV parked outside, the typed notes, and the escalating hostility surrounding her podcast's latest episode. Elly nodded along, silently urging Shannon to keep pushing through.

"We'll send an officer to investigate," Daniels assured her. "In the meantime, stay vigilant. If you notice anything further, don't hesitate to call."

As Shannon ended the call, she sat back, the tension in her shoulders easing slightly. Yet, her mind churned. Reporting it was only the first step, and she knew the system's shortcomings all too well.

"They'll look into it," Shannon said to Elly, though her tone carried a skepticism that Officer Daniels might not be able to break through. "But we need to be ready for any-thing."

Elly nodded, a determined look rising in her expression. "We'll stay alert, and we'll protect Haven House."

Shannon felt the weight of the moment. Haven House was no longer just a refuge; it had become the frontline. But if the threats were meant to silence her, they had miscalculated. She would meet them head-on, and the battle for truth was only beginning.

Tuesday Morning – Haven House

The reception desk received many phone calls and deliveries. Some were from survivors sending flowers. Some notes were typed, unsigned, or extracted from newspapers. They include the following messages and warnings: "You've gone too far."

"Stay in your lane, podcast lady."

"People like you disappear."

Shannon read them in silence and dropped them into the shredder, one by one.

But her staff noticed.

Haven House was no longer a sanctuary. It was becoming a battleground. They were worried about their safety and the reputation of Haven House.

Elly approached Shannon quietly. "They're watching us."

Shannon didn't need to ask who *they* were. She motioned toward the window. "I know. A silver SUV was observed parked across the street starting from 7:00 a.m. Same one from the courthouse."

Elly frowned. "Should we report it?"

"To whom?" Shannon asked.

"The police? You saw how well the system protected Cassandra."

That afternoon, Lena Ford arrived.

The former detective-turned PI. She moved like a soldier, crisp, alert, no wasted words. She previously managed domestic abuse cases until her dismissal following the exposure of a corrupt police captain.

Shannon handed her Daniel's *"Ones Who Got Away"* file.

"These are the men he was investigating before the crash. The ones tied to Whiteman and even to Scott Brannigan."

Lena scanned the file. "This goes deep. Medical board members, judges, politicians, and clergy members. At least several hospitals with buried misconduct complaints. None of them ever made it to public record." She looked up. "You understand the risk?"

Shannon's eyes flared. "They already killed Daniel. They don't get to scare me into silence now."

Later That Week — A New Email

It arrived through a burner account, masked behind several proxy servers. The subject line simply read:

"You're Not the First."

The attached file contained internal memos from the State Medical Review Board. One email thread from five years ago made Shannon's blood run cold:

"Re: Dr. S. Whiteman

Recommend suppression of patient complaints. Risk of litigation. Per Chairman's orders, scrub from disciplinary records.

MB"

Another file was a patient's formal complaint. Never fail. Access has been restricted.

And in the lower left corner of the PDF was a code: SWH: St. Whiteman Hospital.

CASE#R37 — the same case number Daniel had scribbled into the margin of his last journal before the crash. She stared at it for a long time. He hadn't just been exposed to them. He had known exactly who they were.

Shannon's mind raced as she pieced together the implications. Daniel hadn't stumbled upon a random puzzle; he had uncovered a deliberate web of deceit. One that spanned years and ruined countless lives. The crash wasn't an accident. It was a warning, or worse, a method of silence.

Her fingers hovered over the keyboard, the cursor blinking impatiently.

She typed "SWH.104-D/CASE#R37" into the search bar on a private server.

The results were sparse, fragmented.

A few anonymous forums mentioned St. Whiteman Hospital in hushed, cryptic tones. Keywords popped out at her: whistleblower. Cover-up. Missing records.

Her heart thudded as she clicked on a link titled "The Vanishing Cases."

A blog post by "Nightshade" alleged that complaints were addressed, doctors' misconduct concealed, and staff reprimanded or dismissed.

But it wasn't just the doctors and administrators, it included law enforcement and other organizations. The threads tied back to law enforcement, legal systems, and even funding from a prominent pharmaceutical company. The rabbit hole went deeper than she ever anticipated.

Suddenly, a loud knock on the door shattered her thoughts. Shannon froze; her breath caught in her throat. It was late, and she wasn't expecting anyone.

"Who's there?" she called out, her voice steadier than she felt.

No answer. Just another knock, louder this time. She grabbed her phone, inching toward the door. Through the peephole, she saw a figure cloaked in shadow, a baseball cap pulled low.

Her pulse quickened as she hesitated. Whoever was out there knew she was inside.

She typed a quick message to her closest friend, Mia: "Someone's at my door. If I stop responding, call the police."

Sending it, she gripped the handle tightly, her hand trembling as she unlocked it.

The door creaked open just wide enough to see the shadowed figure standing a few feet away. The dim hallway light cast an eerie glow on the stranger's face. It was a man she didn't recognize. His cap shadowed his features, but his stance exuded an unnerving confidence.

"Shannon, right?" His voice was low, calm, but the edge in his tone sent chills down her spine.

"Who are you? What do you want?" she demanded, voice firm despite the fear clawing at her chest.

He stepped closer, his hands raised in a placating gesture. "I'm not here to hurt you. But you're digging into something dangerous. You don't know how far this goes."

Her grip tightened on the door frame, her instincts screaming at her to slam it shut. "If you're here to threaten me, you can save yourself the effort. I'm not scared of you or anyone else."

The man let out a bitter laugh. "Brave words. You think you're uncovering the truth, but the truth isn't what you think it is. Daniel didn't crash by chance. He was silent with intent, not the outcome." He leaned in, his voice now a whisper. "And if you keep pushing, you'll end up just like him."

Shannon's heart thundered in her chest, but she refused to let him see her falter. "Get out."

He didn't move. Instead, he placed a folded piece of paper on the floor at her feet. "This will explain everything. But it's your choice. Dig deeper or walk away."

She stared at the paper, her mind racing. Before she could respond, he turned and walked down the hallway, disappearing into the shadows.

Shannon slammed the door and locked it, her hands shaking. Slowly, she unfolded the paper.

Inside was a single cryptic line: "Project R37 isn't what it seems."

Beneath it were coordinates.

She stared at the page, her head spinning. Daniel's was the code, the hospital. It all swirled together in a whirlwind of unanswered questions.

But one thing was clear.

She had stepped into something far greater than she ever imagined. And now, there was no turning back.

That Night – Podcast Recording Room

Shannon hit a record. Her voice trembled at first, but then steadied as fury took hold.

"Tonight, I'm naming names. Not just the perpetrators, but the protectors. The enablers. The white coats who hide behind credibility while they destroy lives."

"Dr. Allen Whiteman was just the beginning."

"Next: Dr. Russell Kane. Three nurses accused a well-known pediatric surgeon of inappropriate touching. All complaints were dismissed within 48 hours by hospital counsel. Then Judge Vernon Shawman, who presided over fifteen abuse cases, all ruled in favor of the male defendants, despite hard evidence. And finally, Board Chairman Matthew Brand, the man who personally oversaw the suppression of internal investigations, including the one connected to Daniel's crash."

Her voice grew sharper, cutting through the silence like a blade. "Matthew Brand has shielded predators and silenced victims for over a decade. He's the linchpin of this entire

system, and it's time to reveal his name.

She paused, her voice trembling.

"They thought they buried the truth. But I'm still digging."

The Fallout

The backlash was immediate.

Three sponsors dropped *Unmasked* within 24 hours.

Local news ran hit pieces questioning Shannon's credibility.

Online trolls called her unstable, a "grieving widow gone off the rails."

But none of it mattered because the women kept coming. Messages, voicemails, handwritten letters.

Several short messages, emails: "I thought I was alone. I'm not. Thank you."

Messages that shook her: "He delivered my baby. He molested me while I was still numb from anesthesia. He said *no one would believe me*. He was right until now."

One, unsigned: "I know who killed Daniel. I can prove it. But I won't speak unless I know I'll live through it."

Shannon stared at the unsigned note, her hands trembling slightly as she reread its ominous message. The weight of its implications pressed down on her, but beneath fear, a spark of determination flared. Daniel deserved justice, and no threat would stop her from finding the truth.

She placed the letter carefully on the desk and looked at Lena, who was scanning through the latest batch of reports.

"We need to find out who sent this," Shannon said, her voice steady but laced with urgency.

Lena and Shannon sat across from one another in Daniel's office, now converted into an operations war room. Spread across the room were files, names, maps, timelines; they were building a bigger case than they had imagined, and this was just the beginning.

Lena circled a name in red marker. The following names include Dr A. Whiteman and Dr. Scott Brannigan. Shannon stared at it, her breath hitching. "You really think he's part of this?"

Lena nodded. "Not just part of it. He's tied to three of these names. And the accident? It wasn't random." A cold silence stretched between them. Then Shannon whispered, "He's not going to get away with it." Lena leaned into Shannon. "Then we'd better move fast.

Shannon's mind raced as she looked at the name circled in red. Dr. Whiteman. The name felt heavy with unspoken truths, like the echo of footsteps in a darkened hallway. Lena leaned forward, her expression a mix of conviction and hesitation. "His name keeps coming up in connection with Daniel. Witness accounts, financial records, even whispers from people too scared to go on record."

Shannon's voice dropped to a near whisper, her focus sharp. "If he's involved, he's not working alone. Someone is shielding him. We need to figure out who and why."

Lena nodded, pulling out a folder marked with a single word: "Whiteman."

Inside were pages of meticulously compiled notes, photographs, and phone logs. The evidence was still circumstantial, but it painted a picture rife with suspicion. Shannon scanned the pages, her determination hardening with every connection that seemed to weave itself tighter around the name.

Shannon's fingers tightened around the edge of the desk as she leaned forward, her eyes fixed on the damning folder. "We need more than this. Something concrete that no one can bury," she said, her voice cutting through the tension.

Lena hesitated for just a moment before sliding another sheet of paper across the desk. "There's a warehouse registered under a shell company. It's tied to Whiteman, but he's hidden it well. If there's anything solid, it'll be there."

Shannon's gaze darted to the paper, absorbing the address scrawled in neat handwriting. "Then that's where we go."

Lena frowned. "It's dangerous. If Whiteman knows we're closing in, he'll have eyes everywhere. We can't just walk in—"

"We won't," Shannon interrupted, her tone resolute. "But we can't wait either. If he's already watching us, we can use that to our advantage."

Lena tilted her head, her skepticism evident. "What are you suggesting?"

Shannon stood, her mind racing with a plan that seemed reckless but necessary. "A diversion. We make him look one way while we're going another. He thinks he's in control, but we're the ones pulling the strings."

For a moment, Lena said nothing, studying Shannon's determined expression. Then she nodded slowly. "If we're doing this, we need to move tonight. He won't see it coming."

The room seemed to shrink around them as the gravity of their decision sank in. Shannon reached for her coat, glancing back at the circled name on the board. "It ends here. One way or another."

Outside, the cool night air wrapped around them as they stepped into the shadows. Somewhere out there, Whiteman's network of secrets was unraveling, and they intended to be the ones to pull the final thread.

The distant hum of traffic was the only sound that accompanied their footsteps as they made their way toward the car waiting in the alley. Shannon glanced at Lena, her jaw set in determination, but her thoughts clouded with the weight of what lay ahead.

Chapter 18
Quiet Before the Storm

How Daniel and Shannon Met

The ballroom was all crystal and gold, filled with tuxedos, pearls, and carefully rehearsed smiles. But Shannon felt like she was standing on a stage without a script. This was the annual *Phoenix Gala for Hope*, a high-profile event raising money for domestic violence shelters. She was invited to discuss *Unmasked*, but the evening felt off. It was all too polished.

The ballroom shimmered with soft golden light, string quartets playing quietly beneath the low hum of conversation. Shannon adjusted the edge of her black wrap dress, feeling awkward and overdressed despite the formal crowd. The Phoenix Gala for Hope, an annual fundraiser for shelters supporting survivors of domestic violence, was far outside her comfort zone.

However, after a year of sharing her soul on her podcast, *Unmasked*, one of the board members had invited her to speak.

The Phoenix Gala for Hope represented more than just an event on Shannon's calendar; it was a milestone in her journey of healing and advocacy. After years of enduring the unseen scars of abuse, this gala offered her an opportunity to step into a spotlight she had once shunned, to use her voice for those who felt voiceless.

For Shannon, the evening stood as a testament to resilience, not just her own but also that of countless survivors whose stories she had chronicled on her podcast, *Unmasked.*

Each photograph displayed at the gala showed a remarkable story of someone rising above their past to reclaim their future. Seeing the smiling face of the young woman standing before her reminded Shannon of her own journey, of the nights when hope seemed like a distant dream.

The gala focused on highlighting courage, fostering understanding, and showing survivors they're not alone. For Shannon, it was a chance to honor the strength it takes to rebuild, piece by fragile piece, and to show others that even in the darkest moments, a glimmer of hope could shine through. It was an evening that transformed pain into purpose, making every shaky step she took to the microphone worth it.

Shannon had learned the hard way that abuse is more than bruises. It's the erosion of self-worth, the invisible chains of fear, and the silent wounds that linger long after the physical scars fade.

Her podcast, *Unmasked*, had become a lifeline, a way to unravel the complexities of survival and give voice to those whose pain had remained unseen. The gala tonight wasn't just an event; it was a testament to the power of resilience, a chance to honor the stories of those who dared to rebuild their lives piece by fragile peace. Standing there, surrounded by people she barely knew, she reminded herself why she had come: to share the truth, to show others that hope, however distant, was always within reach.

Her fingers tightened briefly around the microphone as the last words of her speech echoed in her mind. Shannon stepped off the stage to a smattering of applause, the weight of her vulnerability still pressing against her ribs. She scanned the room for a familiar face, but the sea of strangers reminded her just how out of place she felt.

She made her way to the refreshment table, seeking solace in a glass of sparkling water. As she sipped, the faint clink of glasses and laughter swirled around her, but she was too lost in her thoughts to join in. She caught fragments of conversation, words like "brave" and "powerful" drifting past her ears. *Were they talking about her?* She wasn't sure if she wanted them to be that way.

Out of the corner of her eye, Shannon noticed a man leaning against the far wall, watching her with a quiet intensity. His slightly disheveled appearance set him apart from the rest of the evening's polished elegance. They shared a quick glance, but she quickly looked away, wondering if it was just curiosity or maybe a lucky coincidence.

His warm gaze lingered, steady and unassuming, framed by the soft lines that hinted at a life filled with both trials and compassion. The faint smile that graced his lips carried an air of reassurance, as if he understood the weight of her vulnerability and sought to lighten it. He wasn't in the center of the room. He didn't hold court with donors.

He stood near the back, quietly watching her with a gentle presence, unlike the way men used to, who felt like they claimed ownership of her story. His gaze was calm, warm, and deep, conveying a sense of genuine admiration and kindness.

Shannon glanced back at the man, her curiosity piqued despite her reluctance to engage. He seemed unaffected by the gala's glimmering facade; his focus fixed solely on her. Something was grounding about his presence. He had an understated calm that stood in stark contrast to the whirlwind of emotions she had been navigating all evening. His slight smile, almost imperceptible, carried no trace of pity, just an openness that made her feel seen rather than scrutinized.

He took a step closer, his movements unhurried, as if giving her the space to decide whether to acknowledge him or retreat. Shannon had grown accustomed to the fleeting glances of admiration and the shallow praise that often followed her speeches, but his gaze held a depth that uniquely unsettled her. It wasn't just admiration; it was a kind of quiet understanding, an unspoken connection that she couldn't quite place.

Her fingers tightened around her glass as she debated whether to turn away or confront the silent pull between them. Before she could decide, the man adjusted his tie absentmindedly, his eyes never leaving her. It was as though the crowd had melted away, leaving just the two of them in an unspoken moment suspended between curiosity and recognition.

For a second, Shannon wondered if he had heard her podcast, if he knew her story beyond the fragments she had shared tonight. He seemed more interested in her as a person than in her story. There was no sense of pity or performative empathy in his expression, just genuine intrigue, as if he wanted to know her beyond the words she had spoken, beyond the applause that followed.

As Shannon turned slightly toward the photographs, pretending to study them again, she felt the heat of his gaze linger on her. It wasn't invasive, just persistent, as though he was waiting for her to recognize something he already saw, a quiet strength that even she sometimes doubted.

Determined to shake off her nerves, Shannon moved toward a corner of the room where a small group of people surrounded a large display of photographs. Photos of survivors showing hope and resilience included quotes about rebuilding their lives.

One image caught her attention: a young woman, no older than twenty, smiling in front of a new apartment door. Beneath it, the words: *"For the first time, I am safe."*

Shannon felt a lump rise in her throat. She had been that woman once, years ago. Vulnerable, lost, and seeking freedom. Speaking tonight might have stirred old wounds, but seeing this reminder of why she had started her podcast gave her a small sense of peace.

Speaking tonight might have stirred old wounds, but seeing this reminder of why she had started her podcast gave her a small sense of peace. The image tugged at her heartstrings, grounding her amid the swirling emotions that had followed her speech. Shannon felt quiet pride in the impact her work had had, but also a lingering vulnerability.

She didn't hear the footsteps behind her until the voice broke through her reverie: "Excuse me."

Her words had stripped away a layer of armor she didn't realize she was still wearing.

When she stepped off the stage, flushed and slightly breathless after her vulnerable speech, he approached slowly, offering her a glass of water instead of a compliment.

"Your voice didn't shake once," he said softly.

She blinked, thrown. "I practiced."

"No," he said. "You lived it. That's what makes it matter."

His voice was low, his tone quiet but confident. Not flirty, *genuine.*

She stared at him a beat too long before finally offering her hand.

"Shannon Sullivan"

"Daniel Robinson."

Their handshake lingered.

Startled, Shannon turned slightly, clutching the edges of her cardigan as though seeking stability. The man who stood before her seemed to carry the weight of the room's decorum lightly, his casual yet sincere demeanor an anomaly amidst the gala's polished crowd.

His tie hung loosely, like an afterthought, and his suit bore the gentle wear of stories untold. Despite the imperfections, his presence was grounding, his steady gaze urging her to let go of the defensive walls she habitually built.

"Your speech," he continued, the words tentative but deliberate, "it felt like... like you were speaking directly to me."

Shannon blinked, unsure of how to respond. She had stood on that stage, her voice trembling as she unearthed fragments of vulnerability for strangers to witness.

For her, sharing her story was both an act of purpose and a paradoxical surrender, a way to empower others while revisiting wounds that had never fully healed. And yet, hearing him say those words felt unexpectedly validating, as if her truth had bridged an invisible gap between herself and this stranger.

"I don't usually connect with crowds," Shannon said softly, finally finding her voice. "But tonight... I thought someone might understand."

The man's nod was slow, measured. "You'd be surprised how many people see themselves in what you shared. It's rare to hear someone speak with that kind of honesty."

Before she could reply, the hum of the gala swelled and ebbed around them, but Shannon felt as though they were standing apart from the chaos, cocooned in a moment of quiet recognition. She gestured toward the photographs lining the room's walls, the images of survivors and hopeful beginnings that had inspired her podcast and her message tonight.

Before she could reply, the hum of the gala swelled and ebbed around them, but Shannon felt as though they were standing apart from the chaos, cocooned in a moment of quiet recognition. She gestured toward the photographs lining the room's walls, the images of survivors and hopeful beginnings that had inspired her podcast and her message tonight.

"You know," the man spoke again, his tone warm but edged with thoughtfulness, "I didn't think I'd find myself at a gala like this, staring at photographs that could so easily be my own past. But then your voice cut through. It was like...

I don't know, like someone had finally put words to things I've never been brave enough to say."

Shannon tilted her head slightly, studying him anew. There was a shadow in his expression, a vulnerability he seemed to navigate with care, and it stirred her curiosity.

"What brought you here tonight?" she asked softly, her voice inviting but unintrusive.

He hesitated, as though weighing how much he wanted to share. "A friend dragged me along, said it would do me some good. I thought I'd slip in and out unnoticed, but... well, here we are."

A small laugh escaped her before she could contain it. "So, my speech kept you from your stealthy escape plan?"

"Something like that," he admitted, a faint smile tugging at his lips. His gaze drifted back to the photographs. "But I'm glad I stayed. This... all of this," he gestured toward the displays and then to her, "it's important. You're giving people something real, something they can hold on to. That's rare."

Her cheeks warmed under the sincerity of his words, though she quickly turned her attention back to the photographs to steady herself. "I think we all need to feel like we're not alone," she said, her voice quieter now. "That's why I started this. To remind people and myself, too, that there's hope, even after everything we've been through."

He nodded, his expression softening. "You've done more than that. You've created something that connects people. That's no small thing."

Something about his words, the way he spoke to them with such quiet conviction, made Shannon want to know more about him. Not just about what he saw in her work. "It sounds like you've got your own story to tell," she ventured, her curiosity beginning to outweigh her usual caution.

He met her gaze, his green eyes thoughtful but unguarded. "Maybe I do," he said, his voice low, almost teasing. "But only if you promise to tell me more about yours."

For the first time that evening, Shannon felt the weight of her vulnerability lift slightly, replaced by something lighter and warmer.

This was a tentative connection she hadn't expected to find amidst the polished crowd. "I think I can do that," she replied, a small, genuine smile breaking through.

"I started this work because I wanted people to feel seen," Shannon admitted, her voice trembling slightly. "Like they weren't just stories tucked away in statistics."

"And you have," he said gently. "You've given me that, and I suspect you've given it to many others."

Shannon felt her lips curve into a tentative smile, gratitude mingling with the ache of vulnerability. She glanced again at the display, her gaze lingering on the photograph of the young woman, the words beneath it resonating deeply within her: "For the first time, I am safe."

In that instant, Shannon felt the weight of her purpose settle around her like a second skin, reminding her why she chose this path. And in the man's presence, she found a strange solace, a quiet understanding that she wasn't as alone in her journey as she had once feared.

Shannon stood rooted for a moment, the weight of his words settling over her like a blanket on a frosty night. The photographs seemed almost alive now, their silent stories kept company by his steady presence. She didn't know why, but she found herself wanting to linger in this moment, this fragile space where her vulnerability wasn't just hers to bear, but something shared.

"I don't usually meet people who understand," she said finally, her voice wavering but steady enough to carry the truth. "Most just see the display as art or activism. Few see the humanity behind it."

Daniel glanced at one of the photographs, a young boy's solemn eyes staring back at them, and nodded. "It's hard not to see the humanity when it's staring you in the face. You made that impossible to ignore."

Their conversation quieted for a moment, filled only by the hum of the crowd and the faint rustle of nearby movements. Shannon didn't feel the need to fill the silence; she was surprised by how comfortable it was.

"I get the sense you're used to being the one who listens," she said, watching him as he studied the images.

Daniel chuckled softly, a sound that felt warm despite its brevity. "I suppose you're right. Listening comes easier than talking for me."

"Is that why you came tonight? To listen?" she asked, her curiosity piqued.

He hesitated, his gaze lingering on the photograph of the young woman, the one who had spoken so deeply to Shannon, and then turned back to her. "I came because someone told me your work mattered... and because I thought I needed to see it for myself."

Shannon wasn't sure how to respond to that. Her work had always been about others, their stories, their truths. But hearing that someone had felt its impact made her chest tighten with an unfamiliar mix of gratitude and uncertainty.

She opened her mouth to reply, but before she could, Daniel nodded toward the stage where the microphone still stood, silent now. "That speech of yours... It wasn't just honest. It was brave."

Shannon blinked, taken aback by the simple sincerity of his words. Praise wasn't something she expected, especially not from strangers.

"Brave?" she echoed, unable to mask the surprise in her tone. "I don't feel brave, standing up there."

"That's usually how bravery works," he said, his lips curving in a slight smile. "You don't feel it, but it's there. Sometimes it's seen more clearly by others."

The weight of his gaze was steady but gentle, and Shannon felt something unspoken pass between them. It was a thread of connection she hadn't realized she'd been searching for. She studied him for a moment longer, then glanced back at the crowd, where faces blurred into one another under the dimming lights.

"I suppose bravery doesn't come from feeling safe, does it?" she murmured to herself.

"No," he replied softly. "It comes from moving forward, even when you don't."

His voice had a resonance influenced by his experiences. Shannon wanted to ask him more, to peel back the layers that lay beneath his calm surface. But before she could, a voice called her name from across the room, pulling her attention away.

She turned toward the source, catching sight of a colleague gesturing for her to join them. Shannon sighed lightly, the pull of obligation breaking the fragile bubble of intimacy.

When she looked back at Daniel, she offered him a small, apologetic smile.

Shannon forced herself to step away from the moment, her fingers slipped from his as she moved toward her colleague. But Daniel's presence lingered behind her, a quiet gravity pulling at the edges of her thoughts. She glanced back once, catching his gaze, and for a fleeting second, she thought she saw something there, a question or an unspoken invitation.

The hum of conversation swelled around her as she joined the group, their chatter filling the space between her and the strange clarity that Daniel's words had left behind. While her colleague discussed the event's planning with animated gestures, Shannon found her thoughts drifting to the man in the navy suit. His tie was slightly askew, yet his eyes remained steady and sincere, free from any pretense.

"Shannon," her colleague prompted, drawing her attention back. "Are you alright?"

"Yes," she managed, offering a smile that felt just shy of reality. "Just... thinking."

Her colleague nodded, diving back into their stream of words, but Shannon's heart wasn't here. It still echoed with Daniel's soft, convincing voice. She felt that he'd seen something in her she hadn't yet recognized in herself. His presence was both captivating and alluring to her and, yet comforting at the same time.

Later, as the room began to empty and the lights dimmed further, Shannon found herself drifting toward the spot where she'd last seen him. The crowd had thinned, and the faint murmur of conversations had softened into echoes, leaving the air charged with a kind of stillness. She scanned the room, searching for the uneven lines of his suit, the green steadiness of his gaze.

And then, there he was, standing near the far wall, hands in his pockets, watching her. Not with intent or expectation, but with a quiet patience that made her steps falter.

His presence was magnetic, pulling her toward him with an invisible force she couldn't resist. Shannon's steps, hesitant at first, grew steadier as she closed the space between them.

"Do you always wait for people like this?" she asked, her voice tinged with curiosity and vulnerability.

Daniel chuckled lightly, the sound warm and unassuming. "Only when I think it's worth it."

Her brow furrowed slightly, a trace of skepticism crossing her lips. "And how do you decide that?"

He tilted his head, studying her with an intensity that made her breath catch. "It's not a decision, Shannon. It's a feeling."

For once, words failed her. She didn't know how to respond, nor did she want to at this time. Because the way he spoke, the way he looked at her, made her feel like she was discovering something she hadn't even known she was missing.

They quietly stretched between them again, comfortably but charged, like the moments before a summer storm. Shannon, unused to such raw intimacy, swallowed hard and shifted her weight.

"I didn't mean to interrupt your evening," she said softly, apologetically.

"You didn't," Daniel replied, his tone resolute. "I was hoping for it."

Her cheeks warmed, a blush creeping onto her skin unbidden. She glanced down, her fingers brushing the seam of her dress as if searching for grounding. "That's bold."

He shrugged, the faint smile returning to his lips. "Sometimes boldness is necessary to find what truly matters."

Shannon couldn't deny the pull of his words, nor the pull of his presence. It was as though the moment had unraveled her carefully constructed hesitations, leaving her bare and uncertain, but not afraid.

"Maybe you're right," she whispered, her gaze lifting to meet his steady one. "But I'm still not sure what you want."

His smile softened, his voice lowering. "I want to know you, beyond fleeting conversations and half-shared moments."

It was an invitation, simple yet profound, and Shannon found herself wavering. Yet, beneath the surface, she realized she wanted the same. She wanted to know him, too, the man who seemed to see past the walls she'd built.

The hum of the dimmed room faded further into the backdrop as Shannon nodded, her lips curving into the faintest of smiles. "Alright, Daniel. Let's see where this goes."

Shannon could feel the attraction and the fragile beginnings of something clean start to unfold. She had confidence and determination. But the question in her mind was, could she open her heart to trusting someone again?

She approached slowly, her pulse quickening despite herself. "You waited," she said, her voice barely above a whisper. "I did," he replied simply, his lips curving into that same slight smile. "I thought you might want to finish what we started."

Shannon wasn't sure how to answer. Words felt insufficient, too fragile to hold the weight of what was building between them. But as she stood there, the distance closing, she realized she didn't need them. She only needed this moment, its quiet promise, and the spark of something entirely unexpected.

Daniel eased a little closer, moving gently as if he was being careful with the delicate moment they were sharing. The soft light highlighted the gentle smile still lingering on his lips. His eyes stayed focused and intent, radiating a seriousness that Shannon couldn't help but notice.

"You don't have to decide anything," he said softly, his voice both an anchor and a breath of air. "Not tonight. Not tomorrow. But I hope you'll let me stay in your world, even if just for a while.

Her heart stuttered at the simplicity of the offer, and yet it felt monumental. Trust didn't come easily to her anymore, not after the crack's life had carved into her. But here he was, not prying or demanding, just offering a quiet place where she could be herself, raw, imperfect, and unguarded.

"I don't know what it would look like," she admitted, her voice trembling slightly as she met his gaze. "To let someone in again."

His expression softened, and for a moment, he looked almost vulnerable to himself. "Then we'll figure it out together."

The words settled over her like a bomb, and for the first time in a long while, Shannon felt the faintest flicker of relief. She wasn't sure where this would lead, but it didn't matter. The act of opening the door, even just a crack, was enough for now.

She exhaled slowly, letting the tension in her shoulders fall. "Alright," she said, her lips curving ever so slightly. "Let's figure it out."

Daniel's smile grew, warm and genuine, and for the first time, Shannon felt the walls around her begin to shift, not crumble, but shift, making space for something she hadn't realized she was ready for.

"I should go…"

Daniel tilted his head slightly, his gaze unwavering but kind. "You don't have to, you know," he said, his tone gentle. "Not yet anyway."

Shannon blinked, unsure if she'd heard him right. "I don't have to go?" she asked, her voice barely louder than a murmur.

He nodded, his hand still faintly outstretched between them. "Sometimes, the hardest thing is letting yourself stay in a moment when all your instincts are telling you to leave."

She looked at him for a long moment, her mind searching for a response. The room seemed quieter now, as though the world had shrunk to just the two of them. "And what happens if I stay?" she asked finally, her voice carrying a quiet vulnerability she hadn't intended to reveal.

Daniel's lips curved into a small, reassuring smile. "Then we see where that moment takes us. Together."

Shannon tilted her head slightly, her eyes searching his face as though trying to decipher a hidden meaning. "You make it sound easy," she said, the faintest hint of a smile tugging at her lips.

Daniel chuckled softly, the sound filling the quiet space between them. "Not easy, just worth it." His words hung in the air, steady and sincere, grounding her in a way she hadn't expected.

Shannon's lips parted slightly as she considered his words. They carried a weight she wasn't sure she could entirely bear, but for the first time, she wanted to try. "Worth it," she echoed, her voice soft but resolute, as though testing the idea.

Daniel's gaze didn't waver, his expression calm yet inviting. "Sometimes, taking the first step is all you need. Let the rest unfold as it will."

She tilted her head, her eyes narrowing faintly in thought. "And what if I stumble?"

His smile warmed. "Then I'll be there to help you back up. That's the beauty of stepping forward, there's always someone willing to walk beside you."

Shannon's fear turned into cautious yearning. "Alright," she said slowly, the word rolling off her tongue like an uncertain promise.

Daniel grinned, his hand still outstretched, steady as though anchoring her. "Alright," he repeated gently. "Let's walk together."

As they began to walk, the rhythm of their footsteps seemed to synchronize naturally, filling the quiet space between them. The cool evening air carried with it a faint scent of jasmine, and the distant hum of the city softened their surroundings. Shannon glanced sideways at Daniel, noting the calm steadiness in his gaze as he looked ahead.

"So, where are we going?" she asked, her voice tentative but carrying the slightest hint of curiosity.

Daniel smiled, his hands slipping casually into his pockets. "That depends. Sometimes a destination isn't as important as the journey itself. Wouldn't you agree?"

Shannon tilted her head, her brows furrowing lightly as she considered his words. "Maybe. But it's hard to keep walking when you don't know where you'll end up."

He turned his head slightly, meeting her gaze with a quiet intensity that made her chest tighten. "True, but sometimes the best surprises are the ones waiting at the end of uncertain paths."

His response lingered in the air, resonating with something deep within her. Shannon looked down at the pavement, her shoes brushing against the loose leaves scattered by the wind. For the first time in a long while, she felt the edges of her guarded heart soften, just a little.

"Are you always this philosophical?" she teased lightly, the corners of her mouth tugging into a faint smile.

Daniel laughed, the sound warm and unguarded. "Not always. But you bring it out of me, I think."

Shannon shook her head softly, her lips pressing together to suppress the odd flutter in her chest. "Well, don't get used to it," she said playfully, though her tone lacked the usual edge she hid behind.

They walked in companionable silence for a while after that, the only sound between them was the rustle of trees and the occasional distant chatter of passersby.

For Shannon, the stillness was comforting, allowing her the space she often craved yet rarely found. And as she stole another glance at Daniel, she couldn't help but think that per-haps—just perhaps—this moment they shared was worth holding onto.

For a moment, Shannon felt the weight of her doubts shifting, not disappearing entirely, but making room for something else. "Together, then," she repeated, as if testing how the word felt coming from her, shaping it carefully.

Daniel's gaze softened further, and he nodded, as though acknowledging her courage. "Together," he echoed.

Her chest tightened, not with fear, but with the unfamiliar sensation of hope. Against the odds, she didn't step away. Instead, she placed her hand in his, feeling the warmth and steadiness of it. "Alright," she said softly. "I'll stay."

His smile deepened, but he didn't say anything else. He didn't need to. The silence that followed was heavy with un-spoken promises, and for the first time in a long while, Shan-non let herself believe that it might be okay to trust again.

He was tall, slightly unshaven, in a well-worn navy suit that didn't quite match the Polished crowd. His tie was loose, and his eyes, green and steady, held no hint of ego, just presence.

We should go back inside the building to the tables and get our seats for the rest of the evening. Daniel nodded, and they walked out of the moonlight on the grounds into the ballroom where the tables and activity surrounded them.

Daniel had donated $100,000 to the shelter the year before. But he didn't want his name on a plaque. He preferred to work behind the scenes, connecting shelters to mental health resources, creating scholarship programs for survivors, and funding legal aid for women trying to escape their abusers.

He didn't talk about it much.

But he asked about her.

"How did you find your way into podcasting?" he asked gently over dessert.

Shannon hesitated. "It started as therapy. Then it became something more. A way to survive. A way to give other women a voice when no one believed them."

Daniel nodded slowly, eyes never leaving hers. "My mother used to say silence was the second kind of abuse, the one that lets the first kind keep happening."

That made her pause. "Your mother?"

He took a breath. "She was married to a man with power, money, and influence. My father. On paper, she was one of the 'lucky ones.' In private... she wasn't safe. I watched her flinch every time he raised his hand, not to hit her, but to adjust his cufflinks."

Shannon's chest tightened.

"She left when I was ten," Daniel continued. "And I left with her. We lived in a studio apartment and survived canned beans and stolen moments of peace. That's why I do this work. Not because I want to be a savior. Because I remember what it's like to be a kid hiding in a closet listening to someone scream."

The gala faded into the background. They talked for hours about trauma, healing, justice, and trust. But mostly about the quiet things. Moments they regretted.

Survival didn't always mean moving on; sometimes it just meant standing still without falling apart.

The dinner crowd buzzed with conversation and empty praise, but Shannon couldn't focus.

When the music started, something soft and jazzy, Daniel reached over for her hand at the table and said, "Could I have this dance?"

They stepped out onto the terrace, the noise fading behind them. The air was cooler, wrapped in moonlight and soft echoes of music from inside.

But outside, under the stars, the two survivors stood still, both wrapped in something that felt dangerously close and personal. Shannon didn't know it yet, but this man would change everything.

Daniel reached out, slowly, and tucked a strand of her hair behind her ear.

"I don't know what your story is, Shannon. But I see you. You have not been visible or present for an extended period of time.

Three Months Later

Shannon and Daniel's relationship was like two rivers merging, their currents complementing rather than clashing, creating a powerful and harmonious flow. From the outset, their compatibility was undeniable, evident in both their shared passions and subtle gestures that spoke volumes about their connection.

Shannon still wasn't sure when friendship turned into something deeper. It wasn't like Scott, all grand gestures and emotional intensity. It was slow, respectful, and warm. Daniel would bring her coffee just the way she liked it. He'd walk her to her car, not because she needed protection but because it gave them more time.

He never touched her without permission. Never flooded her inbox with apologies or turned cold if she pulled away. He simply stayed.

One evening, outside her apartment, he looked at her like she was made of glass and said, "You don't have to say anything. But if you ever want to trust someone again. I'll be here."

She kissed him. For the first time in a long time, it didn't feel like a risk. It felt safe and natural, like the air she breathed.

Their compatibility wasn't about shared interests; it was about the way they complemented each other's souls. Daniel's steadiness balanced Shannon's fire, and her passion reignited his sense of purpose. Together, they were creating something new, something comfortable and easy. Daniel made Shannon feel at home. Not like what Scott had made her always feel on edge, like walking on eggshells. Daniel was so easy-going and had such a gentle nature. He provided a partnership that celebrated their individual strengths while embracing their shared dreams about helping abused women.

Something was developing in her like a sanctuary for her emotions and thoughts.

Daniel stands in front of the unfinished building that would soon become Haven House. Shannon joins him, holding blueprints. Together, they had been working on the blueprints for several months. Their dreams suddenly became a reality in this moment and a shared venture.

Shannon traced the lines on the blueprint with her finger, her eyes shimmering with a mixture of hope and trepidation. "Do you think this will work? That people will find healing here. That we'll make a difference?"

Daniel turned to her, his gaze steady as the foundation they were building. "I know it will. Not because of the walls or the rooms, but because of what you bring to them. Your fire. Your courage. Your heart. That's what people will see when they walk through those doors."

She swallowed hard, leaning closer as the weight of his words wrapped around her like a protective shield. "And you, how do you always know exactly what to say? It's like you see through all the cracks I try to hide."

Daniel smiled softly, his hand brushing against hers. "Because I've lived in those cracks. I know what it feels like to think you're too broken for the world. But you're not, Shannon. Together, we're building something stronger than all the pain we've survived."

Her voice broke slightly as she whispered, "You make me believe in the possibility of something whole."

Daniel reached out and cupped her hand, grounding her in the moment. "You didn't meet someone who understands. You met someone who survived. And together, we'll make sure Haven House becomes the sanctuary for everyone who needs it, just like we needed it once."

Shannon's fingers tightened around him, her lips curving into a faint, yet resolute smile. "Then let's build it—for them, and for us." She smiles faintly. "I never thought I'd meet someone who understood." Daniel touches her hand. "You didn't meet someone who understands.

Shannon's gaze lingered on the unfinished Haven House as she stood beside Daniel, the wind stirring strands of her hair. The building symbolized more than their shared dream; it was a tangible promise of healing, not just for others, but for themselves as well. The bricks felt warm beneath her palm, as though infused with every whispered hope that had been poured into their foundation.

Daniel stepped closer, his presence grounding her amid the swirl of her emotions. His hand brushed against her cheek, the warmth of his touch anchoring her in the moment. "Do you know why I believe we'll succeed?" he murmured, his voice hushed yet resolutely. "It's not just the vision, Shannon. It's you. You have a way of making people believe in second chances, in hope, even when they thought they'd never feel it again."

Her heart thudded against her chest, his words sinking deeper than she'd anticipated. "You make it sound like I'm the answer to everything," she whispered, her vulnerability laid bare. "But what if I falter, Daniel? What if this dream crumbles before it truly begins?"

His lips curved into a small, reassuring smile. "Then I'll be here to catch you," he replied simply, his fingers entwining with hers. "It isn't about perfection. It's about resilience. We'll build this together, brick by brick, and when it's done, it won't just be a shelter; it'll be a beacon."

Shannon felt the sting of tears pricking her eyes as her defenses crumbled. She leaned closer, her forehead resting against him, her voice trembling. "You've given me something I didn't think I'd ever feel again: trust. And now, you're teaching me to hope."

Daniel kissed her softly, the moment imbued with quiet intensity. It was a calm, unwavering commitment. "Hope is what brought us here," he murmured against her lips. "And love will carry us through."

As she pulled back, her fingers grazed his jaw, her touch tentative yet brimming with affection. "Daniel, you make me believe the world isn't as broken as I thought it was."

He took a step forward, the unyielding strength in his gaze matching the conviction in his voice. "You make me believe we're strong enough to fix the pieces we thought were beyond repair."

Together, they turned toward the building once more, the intertwined promise of healing and love fortifying their resolve. The storm ahead was inevitable, yet Shannon and Daniel's connection felt like the calm within it, a sanctuary built not just of walls and blueprints, but of daring to dream and daring to trust.

"Let's finish this," Shannon said softly, the fire in her eyes mirroring the passion in her heart.

Daniel squeezed her hand gently before releasing it to grab the next set of tools. "Together," he replied, his smile holding the weight of everything they had survived and everything they were yet to face. And just like that, amidst the dust and chaos of construction, the seeds of hope and love began to bloom. "You met someone who survived."

And just like that, amidst the dust and chaos of construction, the seeds of hope and love began to bloom. Shannon found herself drawn to the rhythm of their shared work, each hammer strike, each measured cut of timber felt like a heartbeat, steady and alive. Their laughter echoed between unfinished walls, a melody more precious than any song. It was here, in the quiet moments, that she began to see the depth of what they were building, not just a physical space, but a sanctuary for the soul.

One evening, as the sun dipped below the horizon and painted the sky in hues of amber and crimson, Shannon paused to watch Daniel at work. His figure shone in the golden light, each movement deliberate and precise. She marveled at him, not just for his strength, but for the kindness that radiated from him like warmth from a hearth.

"Daniel," she called softly, her voice carrying a weight she hadn't meant to reveal. He turned, his shirt streaked with dust, his smile patient and steady. "I never thought I'd feel this... this kind of peace again."

He stepped closer, wiping his hands on his jeans before brushing stray strands of hair from her face. "It's not just peace, Shannon. It's the start of something new for both of us. A foundation we can build stronger than anything we've known before."

The intensity of his gaze rendered her speechless. In that moment, she didn't just see Daniel; she saw every promise he had made silently through his actions, through his presence. She leaned into him, her forehead resting against his chest, the smell of wood and earth grounding her in the reality of it all.

As the last light of the day gave way to the cool embrace of twilight, Daniel whispered against her hair, "This isn't just a shelter for others. It's ours, too. A place where we can remind ourselves that we're capable of mending what's been broken."

Her hands gripped his shirt tightly, as if letting go would shatter the fragile beauty of the moment. "You've given me more than hope, Daniel. You've given me the courage to believe again."

He tilted her chin gently, his lips brushing hers in a kiss that was neither hurried nor hesitant. It was deliberate, a quiet declaration that spoke of love, commitment, and the unyielding resolve to weather every storm together.

Later, as they worked side by side beneath the stars, Shannon felt the weight of her doubts begin to lift. Daniel's steady hands placed the final beam, his words resonating like an anchor for her soul: "Together, Shannon, we'll finish this. Piece by piece, dream by dream."

As Shannon's sanctuary rose from the ground, so too did the foundation of their love, strong, resilient, and ready to face whatever came next.

Shannon's breath caught as they returned to the shelter, now bathed in the silvery glow of the moonlight. The sanctuary they had built together stood tall, its walls seeming to hum with the echoes of their shared efforts and unspoken promises. Daniel held her hand tightly, his warmth grounding her as her heart raced, not from fear, but from something far deeper and more consuming.

"Do you feel that?" he murmured, his voice low and charged with emotion. His gaze held hers, searching, as if he were trying to unravel every thought she had carefully tucked away.

"I do," she whispered, her voice trembling like the leaves in the night breeze. "It's not just the shelter. It's us. It's all we've done together, Daniel."

He stepped closer, the space between them evaporating until nothing remained but the pulse of their hearts beating in unison. "Shannon, you saved me as much as I ever saved you. This sanctuary is just the beginning, for us, for what we can be."

Before she could respond, his lips captured hers in a kiss that was fierce and consuming, like the rush of a storm sweeping through a quiet valley. She felt herself dissolved into him; her doubts and fears swept away in the tide of his unwavering devotion. His hands found the curve of her back, pulling her closer as if he feared she might disappear into the night.

When they finally parted, her voice was steady, her resolve unshaken. "I don't want to wait for a future that might never come. I want to build it here, with you, piece by piece."

Daniel's eyes softened with a tenderness that seemed impossible for a man who had weathered so many storms. "Then let's build it together, Shannon. No matter what comes, no matter how hard the road gets."

They spent the hours that followed weaving their dreams into the night, their voices blending with the symphony of crickets and the rustling leaves. Shannon's laughter broke through the silence as Daniel teased her about her crooked nail placement, and she retaliated by playfully smudging paint onto his cheek. Their relationship was intense and brought comfort to both individuals.

Later, as they lay side by side under the stars, Shannon traced invisible patterns on Daniel's chest, her fingers brushing over his heart. "You're my anchor," she said softly, her voice thick with emotion. "I don't know how I ever managed without you."

His arms tightened around her, his voice a whisper in the night. "You were always strong, Shannon. You just needed someone to remind you."

The sanctuary stood as a testament to their resilience, but the bond they had forged was the proper foundation of their future. Somewhere in the distance, the wind shifted, carrying with it the faint scent of rain, a harbinger of the storm to come. But for now, enveloped in the warmth of Daniel's embrace, Shannon felt ready to face whatever lay ahead.

It started on Sunday mornings.

Daniel made pancakes from scratch, not because he had to impress her, but because he loved the ritual of it. Flour dusted his forearms, and maple syrup always ended up on the tip of his nose. Shannon teased him endlessly, but deep down, it was the first time in years she felt safe enough to laugh in someone's kitchen.

"I never had this," she admitted one morning, barefoot, curled up on his barstool as he flipped pancakes with exaggerated care.

"What?" he asked, grinning.

"This. The softness. No drama. Just... being."

Daniel set the spatula down and walked toward her, wiping his hands on a towel.

He cupped her face gently, his thumb brushing the corner of her mouth.

"I'm not here to rescue you," he said softly. "But I'll stand beside you while you rebuild."

Shannon blinked back sudden tears.

"No one's ever said that to me before."

He kissed her then, slowly and deliberately. The kind of kiss that doesn't take but gives. That doesn't demand anything but invites.

Two Weeks Later – A Turning Point

They spent a weekend at a quiet cabin just outside of town, a place Daniel had gone to with his mother once a year until she passed. The fireplace was tiny, the bed creaked with every move, and there was no Wi-Fi, but Shannon had never felt more at peace.

They hiked, cooked, read in silence, and held each other under thick blankets as rain tapped softly on the tin roof.

One night, Shannon woke from a dream, one of the old ones, where Scott's voice invaded her mind, twisting her memories into shame.

She sat up, breath ragged.

Daniel stirred beside her, instantly alert, "You, okay?"

"No," she whispered.

He wrapped his arms around her from behind. "Do you want to talk about it?"

She hesitated, then nodded.

She told him about Scott. Regarding the manipulation, lies, and gaslighting that made her feel broken. About Christmas Eve, he gave her a re-gifted cheeseboard and told her to be grateful. About the women's numbers on his phone. About the ER visit after the breakup that nearly stopped her heart.

Daniel didn't interrupt. He didn't flinch. He just listened.

When she finished, she was shaking.

Daniel kissed her temple, "I wish I could've stopped him."

"You didn't even know me back then."

He tightened his hold. "I'd still go back. For you."

They Made Love That Night

The task was done diligently.

There were no masks, no performances, no fear of being too much or not enough. Shannon did not need to diminish herself to be loved. She didn't have to guess what he felt or wonder what price she'd pay for being vulnerable.

He interacted with her with respect and consideration, acknowledging her significance.

And afterward, tangled in sheets and each other, he whispered, "This isn't just love, Shannon. This is something I never thought I'd find."

She looked at him in the firelight, her heart trembling, "I'm afraid."

"So am I," he admitted. "But I'd rather be afraid with you than empty without you."

The Promise

A few days later, at Haven House, he took her to the site of the cornerstone installation.

"I want to name this room after your podcast," he said.

She blinked. "*Unmasked*? Really?"

"Because that's what you did for them," he said. "For women like my mother. Like the ones who live here now. You showed them it's okay to take off the armor."

Shannon swallowed the knot in her throat.

"You always say the right things."

"I don't," Daniel replied, pressing her hand to his chest. "But I feel them. Here."

They made love again that night, this time slow, aching, as if something in both knew what was coming. Like the universe was holding its breath, allowing one more night of peace before it shattered.

As Shannon drifted to sleep with her head on Daniel's chest, she whispered the words she hadn't said in years.

"I love you." Daniel's fingers brushed her hair.

"And I will never stop loving you. Not in this life... or the next."

Romance Grows

After that first weekend in the cabin, everything changed, not suddenly, but in slow, quiet ways, which surprised Shannon more than anything. She found herself waking each day not wondering what storm might hit, but instead anticipating the stillness that Daniel brought into her world.

They began taking weekend trips whenever they could steal the time, just the two of them.

No phones. No emails. No podcast deadlines.

Just wilderness, fresh air, and each other.

The Mountains

In the cool fall air, they hiked through dense pine forests in the high country. Daniel always walked behind her, not to lead, but to protect, watching her footing and holding out a hand when the trail narrowed.

At a rocky overlook, they paused to drink water, catching their breath. Below them, the trees stretched out in every direction, a rolling sea of green and gold.

Shannon leaned back against him, his arms wrapping easily around her waist.

"Out here, everything feels... quieter," she whispered.

"Out here," Daniel said softly, "no one's trying to take anything from you. Not your story. Not your strength. You're just... you."

She turned in his arms and kissed him slowly and full of gratitude. The world fell away.

The Winery

On another weekend, they visited a small vineyard tucked in the hills north of town. Daniel knew the owner, a widow who had once escaped an abusive marriage and rebuilt her life from vines and soil.

They drank Merlot under a string of hanging lights, sitting on a weathered wood deck as the sun dipped low behind the hills. A jazz trio played softly nearby, and Shannon's laughter came easier than it had in years.

"I've never laughed this much on a date," she said, swirling her glass.

Daniel grinned. "This is a date?"

"It is now."

He leaned closer, brushing his hand down her arm. "Then let me do this properly."

He kissed her, wine-flavored, dusk-drenched, and the world tilted beautifully.

Boating in San Diego

Summer brought warm days for Daniel and Shannon while working at the shelter, the Haven House, during the week. They spend long weekends escaping the heat in Phoenix in San Diego at San Diego Harbor. Daniel's boat, the Solace, anchored in the harbor, could sleep six people. Daniel took the helm with ease, navigating through quiet covers while Shannon lay back with her eyes closed, the wind in her hair, his hand resting on her ankle.

Daniel and Shannon swam in the middle of the ocean, laughing like teenagers while their bond continued to evolve and develop.

Shannon hadn't felt her body that free in years. For the first time, she felt free from judgment and shame in a relationship.

On the deck of the sailboat, Shannon basked in the sunlight and ocean breeze, lounging on the deck chairs atop damp beach towels. They sailed across the harbor to Coronado and picnicked on the shore of Coronado Island.

Then they spend the day walking through the tourist shops and enjoying the sights. For the first time, Shannon knew what it was to enjoy being in a realistic relationship with the future.

"I used to think this kind of peace was a lie," Shannon admitted.

"And now? Now, I think it's just rare. But real." Daniel smiled. "Let's make it less rare."

Their First Argument

Even the best love has edges.

One rainy afternoon, Shannon froze when Daniel offered to accompany her to a podcast taping. She pulled away, retreating into silence. Old instincts took over protection through isolation.

"You don't have to be there," she snapped.

"I *want* to be," he replied calmly.

"Well, I didn't ask you to!"

The room went still.

Daniel didn't raise his voice. He didn't retreat. He simply waited. Then said gently, "You're allowed to need me, Shannon. And I'm allowed to show up. That doesn't mean you're weak."

Her defenses cracked.

She cried.

He pulled her into his arms.

And after the storm passed, their love grew deeper, not just romantic, but resilient.

The Proposal That Never Came

One morning, while sipping coffee outside Haven House's back porch, Daniel said quietly, "I bought something."

Shannon raised an eyebrow. "Another kayak?"

He reached into his coat pocket and pulled out a small, velvet box. But he didn't open it.

"Not yet," he said with a smile. "Just… when the time's right."

She swallowed, heart pounding.

"Don't wait too long," she whispered.

He kissed her deeply.

"I won't."

That night, Shannon lay curled in Daniel's arms beneath the covers, listening to his heartbeat.

"Do you ever wonder," she whispered, "how we found each other after everything?"

Daniel didn't answer right away. Then:

"Broken things find each other. And maybe... sometimes, they heal better together."

She smiled against his chest, not knowing that these would be the moments she would replay endlessly.

Not knowing how close the storm already was.

He looked at her carefully. "I know that look."

"What look?"

"The one you have when a thousand people surround you but still feel completely alone."

Shannon felt the breath catch in her chest.

"You're not afraid to say the heavy things, are you?"

Daniel shook his head. "I learned not to waste time. My mother survived twenty years with a man who broke her spirit a little more each day. When she left him, she was free. But she also told me something I'll never forget."

"What?"

He stepped closer.

"She said the worst part wasn't the bruises. It was when she finally stopped expecting kindness."

Shannon blinked, and for the first time all night, she softened.

Daniel reached out, slowly, and tucked a strand of her hair behind her ear.

"I don't know what your story is, Shannon. But I see you. You haven't been around lately.

That's when her walls cracked. Not broken. Not shattered. Just... cracked, enough for light to get in.

She stepped forward, close enough that their breath mingled.

"I don't want another man trying to fix me."

"I wouldn't dare," he whispered. "I just want to stand beside you while you do it yourself."

And then, she kissed him.

Not out of need. Not out of impulse.

Out of recognition.

Out of a long ache, finally finding its answer.

Chapter 19
Daniel and the Tragedy

Just as Shannon begins to regain her trust, Daniel, who has been a reliable and supportive presence in her life, sustains severe injuries in a devastating car accident.

The trauma threatens to undo Shannon's hard-won healing, but they fight through it together. One year later, they opened a women's abuse recovery center, a sanctuary born from pain and resilience. Daniel was found dead outside the center during the mission.

The air had begun to soften with spring as Shannon and Daniel walked together through the quiet streets of their neighborhood. The chill of the past of Scott's past emotional abuse, the betrayal, and the podcast battles had finally started to thaw. Daniel was everything Scott wasn't. Gentle. Kind. Consistent. He never raised his voice. He didn't flinch when Shannon cried or tried to "fix" her pain with empty words. He just stayed.

"I've never felt this safe," Shannon whispered one evening, her head resting against his chest.

Daniel held her tighter. "Then let's build something from that safety. Not just for us, let's give it to others."

That's how *Haven House* was born.

A year later, they stood outside a small but vibrant building, freshly painted in warm creams and soft greens, with the words *"Haven House: A Sanctuary for Women in Recovery"* etched across the front in simple, elegant script. The podcast had grown into a movement, and with community donations, speaking engagements, and Shannon's unwavering drive, it had become a reality.

They opened their doors to survivors of emotional, psychological, and physical abuse, women who needed a soft place to land, just like Shannon once did. Every detail was intentional: the soft lighting, the healing gardens, the circular group therapy room. It was sacred ground.

But life, as Shannon had learned too many times, didn't give you peace without testing your grip on it.

On a rainy Thursday afternoon, Daniel was returning home from a county meeting regarding a new grant for

Haven House when his vehicle was involved in a head-on collision with a truck that had crossed the centerline. The impact crushed the front of his car and sent him spinning into a ditch. By the time paramedics arrived, he was unconscious, clinging to life.

Shannon arrived at the hospital breathless, screaming Daniel's name, her hands shaking as the ER nurse tried to calm her.

"He's in surgery," the nurse said quietly. "It's touch and go."

It was *too familiar*. The sterile walls. The smell of anti-septic. The helplessness.

She dropped to her knees in the waiting room and prayed—not out of religion, but out of desperation. "Please, don't take him," she whispered through clenched teeth. "I just got to know love."

He survived. Barely.

For weeks, Shannon lived by his side in the hospital, reading to him, playing his favorite jazz records, holding his hand even when he didn't respond. The recovery was brutal. Months of physical therapy. Memory gaps. Mood swings from the trauma. But Daniel was still Daniel, and when he returned to Haven House, in a wheelchair, the women clapped and wept as he entered the door.

He gave them a weak but genuine smile. "Good to be home," he said, and Shannon kissed his hand.

One year later.

They celebrated Haven House's first anniversary with an outdoor brunch, laughter filling the air. Local news covered the event. Shannon gave a moving speech about resilience, hope, and rebirth. Daniel, now walking with a cane, stood beside her.

That night, after everyone left, Daniel told her, "I've never been prouder of anything in my life than this place... and you."

She kissed him. "We made it."

But they hadn't.

Two days later, Shannon woke up to a gentle knock at her front door. When she opened it, she was greeted by two uniformed officers. One looked at her kindly, while the other shyly stared at the ground.

"Are you Shannon Sullivan?"

She nodded slowly.

"I'm sorry to inform you... Daniel Robinson was located this morning outside Haven House. He's... he's gone. We're investigating it as a homicide."

The world spun.

"No..." she gasped, grabbing the doorframe. "No, no, no—this can't—"

"I'm sorry, ma'am. He was a suspect."

The chapter ends with Shannon sitting alone in Daniel's office at Haven House. The walls echo with silence. His cane still rests by the chair. A grant proposal for an expanded trauma recovery program is the only document left open on the desk.

She stares at it, then at the framed photo of them both, beaming, unaware of the clock ticking down on their time together.

She clenches her jaw. The pain is back but this time, it has sharpened into resolve.

She picks up a pen.

And writes the first line of her next podcast script:

"They tried to silence him. Now they'll hear me louder than ever."

The morning air was crisp with the scent of renewal. Spring had broken through winter's hold, and for once, so had Shannon's heart. The past seemed like a distant storm cloud finally receding over the horizon. Scott's ghost no longer whispered in her ear. Her nights were free from panic attacks or doubts about her beauty. She had stopped apologizing for existing.

Now, she was building something with Daniel.

They sat on the back porch of their small farmhouse outside town, mugs of coffee in hand, bare feet brushing under a wool blanket.

Daniel's fingers traced absent patterns along the rim of his mug as his gaze drifted toward the horizon. "You know," he began, his voice tinged with that quiet determination Shannon had come to love, "it doesn't have to stop with Haven House."

Shannon tilted her head, studying him. "What do you mean?"

He leaned forward, resting the mug on the porch floor. "We've seen how your podcast gave women courage to speak their truths. Haven House gave them a safe place to heal. But what if we created something bigger? A network. A movement."

She blinked, her breath catching. "A movement?"

Daniel nodded, his eyes alight with the spark of inspiration. "Imagine... a community that connects women across the country with resources, support, stories and everything. A way to fight back together."

Her heart quickened as the enormity of the idea sank in. "That's... ambitious."

"And so was Haven House," he countered with a wry smile. "Look where we are now."

Shannon set her mug aside and burrowed deeper into the blanket. She thought of the nights she had spent alone in silence, the countless moments she felt invisible, powerless. A network, a movement, could be the answer to numerous prayers, the ripple that turned into a wave.

"I'll need to think of a name," she said finally, her lips curving in a faint smile.

Daniel laughed softly. "You'll produce something perfect. You always do."

They sat quietly for a moment, the peaceful silence gently interrupted by the distant whisper of wind rustling the trees. Even in that peaceful quiet, Shannon's mind was already bustling with ideas, weaving possibilities, and imagining what could be ahead.

And in that moment, she realized something profound: she wasn't just rebuilding her life. She was building a legacy.

"What if we started by hosting an event?" she ventured. "A gathering of women. Survivors, advocates, anyone who wants to be part of this... movement."

Daniel's smile widened. "A summit," he said. "The first of its kind."

Her pulse quickened. "The first of many."

As the sun gently sank lower on the horizon, casting the sky in beautiful shades of amber and crimson, Shannon felt her burdens lighten just a little more. She wasn't avoiding her past anymore; instead, she was shining a light to guide others. Together, she and Daniel were showing that even from the deepest heartbreak, something truly extraordinary can blossom.

And this... this was just the beginning.

"What if we gave this to other women?" Daniel said softly. "Not just the stories on your podcast. But a place. A real place. A sanctuary."

Shannon looked at him, stunned by the depth of his thought. "You mean like…a shelter?"

"No," he said. "Not just a shelter. A healing space. Somewhere, women can reclaim their voice and their dignity."

She stared out at the morning mist. "Yes," she whispered. "Let's call it Haven House."

A Year Later

The opening day of *Haven House* was more than symbolic; it was sacred. Built from donations raised by Shannon's now wildly popular podcast *Unmasked,* and with Daniel's legal savvy and heart, it had become a beacon for women across the state. The guest list included survivors, advocates, therapists, and a few brave women who had once slept in their cars to escape the fists of their partners.

The opening day of Haven House had etched itself into Shannon's heart. She had seen women walk through its doors with shoulders hunched, their stories written in the tremor of their hands and the hesitation in their steps. But by the end of that day, something shifted. There were smiles, laughter, and even tears of relief. Haven House wasn't just a building; it was becoming a lifeline, a haven.

Months passed, and Shannon immersed herself in work counseling, organizing events, and overseeing programs that empowered survivors to rebuild their lives. Daniel, ever the anchor, had taken on the legislative battles, championing funding and policy reforms that would protect women's rights and ensure Haven House could reach more communities. Together, they were unstoppable, their partnership a testament to resilience and hope.

One evening, as Shannon prepared to close the doors for the night, she noticed a woman sitting alone on one of the garden benches. The woman looked up, her eyes weary yet filled with an unmistakable spark of determination. Shannon walked over, her voice gentle, "Would you like to come inside?"

The woman nodded, hesitant but willing. She shared her story; a tale of survival that mirrored so many others, Shannon had heard. It carried its own unique heartbreak. By the time the conversation ended, Shannon felt an unshakable conviction. "You're not alone anymore," she said, grasping the woman's hand. "You're part of something bigger now."

That night, Shannon realized Haven House wasn't just her dream or Daniel's vision. It belonged to every woman who dared to step into its embrace, to reclaim her voice, her dignity, her life.

As they celebrated their first anniversary, Shannon stood at the podium again. This time, the crowd was even larger, the applause deafening. Her gaze swept across the audience, catching glimpses of familiar faces, women who were now thriving, unshackled from their pasts. And by her side, Daniel's unwavering presence reminded her that together, they had forged something extraordinary.

But life had a way of testing even the strongest bonds. The crash came like a thief in the night, stealing away their sense of invincibility. Shannon's grip on the phone tightened as the voice on the other end delivered the gut-wrenching news. Her world tilted, but she couldn't let it collapse. Not when so many others depended on her strength.

For Daniel, and for everything they had built together, Shannon vowed to fight harder than ever, even as the weight of grief threatened to pull her under. Haven House was not just their shared dream; it had become a lifeline for countless women seeking refuge and hope. Shannon resolved that Daniel's dedication and unwavering belief in their mission would live on, woven into every corner of the sanctuary they had nurtured.

The days following the crash were a blur of anguish and resilience. Shannon found herself both mourning and rallying. Shannon was able to channel her heartbreak into an unyielding drive to keep Haven House thriving. She doubled her efforts, pouring her heart into counseling sessions, outreach programs, and legislative advocacy. She wanted every woman who crossed the threshold of Haven House to feel the enduring presence of Daniel's spirit, his compassion, and his commitment to justice.

Shannon's determination inspired those around her, from the staff to the women Haven House served. She mentioned Daniel in every meeting and speech, emphasizing that his impact was evident through the lives he influenced and the efforts he made.

On a quiet evening, Shannon found herself standing in the garden of Haven House, surrounded by the soft glow of twilight. She gazed at the bench where she had once offered comfort to a weary survivor, and the memory filled her with renewed purpose. Haven House was more than bricks and mortar; it was a tribute to resilience, a testament to the power of hope and unity. Despite the pain, Shannon knew she had to carry forward the torch they had lit together.

Months later, Shannon stood at another podium, her voice steady and resonant. As she recounted stories of transformation, of women reclaiming their lives, she felt Daniel's presence beside her, quiet but unwavering.

Her words echoed through the hall, "Haven House is not just a shelter; it is a movement, the sound of a thousand women rising to take control of their futures. And this movement, this sanctuary, will continue, for Daniel, for all of us."

The applause roared like a tidal wave, but Shannon's heart remained anchored in the memory of the man who had believed in her, in them, and in the countless lives they had set out to change together.

Shannon stood at the podium, her hand on Daniel's.

"I didn't survive to stay quiet," she said. "I survived to make noise. Haven House is the sound of a thousand women rising." Everyone should hear it clearly.

The applause was deafening. Shannon felt reborn. And beside her, Daniel smiled, quiet, proud, and hers.

The Crash

Three months later, it happened.

Daniel was returning from a late city council meeting when a black SUV ran a red light and T-boned his car on the driver's side. The impact crushed the entire front cabin and sent his car careening into a utility pole.

Shannon got the call at 11:47 p.m.

"This is County General," said a voice. "Are you the partner of Daniel Robinson?"

The word *partner* lodged in her throat like a knife.

"Yes... what happened?"

"There's been an accident. It's serious. You should come. Now."

She barely remembered the drive to the hospital. Just her hands locked around the wheel, her heart pounding with such force it made her dizzy. By the time she got there, Daniel was already in surgery. Skull fracture. Three broken ribs. Internal bleeding. A punctured lung.

"He may not make it through the night," a doctor told her. "I'm sorry."

Shannon collapsed into the hospital chair, the sterile fluorescent lights buzzing overhead. But then, she stood. Walked to the edge of the surgical unit. Pressed her palms against the glass.

She stood slowly, her movements deliberate, and walked to the edge of the surgical unit. Pressing her hands against the glass, she leaned forward, balancing herself so she would not pass out from shock.

She whispered through clenched teeth: "You are *not* leaving me, Daniel. We have not yet completed our work.

The Recovery

Daniel's survival was nothing short of a miracle, but miracles, Shannon thought bitterly, came with complications. The days after the surgery blurred into an exhausting rhythm of hospital visits, insurance calls, and sleepless nights. Every beep of his monitors sent her heart racing; every flicker of his eyelids brought a fragile hope.

When Daniel finally opened his eyes, the first thing he asked was, "Who are you?"

The question cut deeper than Shannon expected, but the doctors had warned her. Memory loss could be common with trauma of this magnitude, they explained, and Shannon plastered on a brave face even as her stomach churned. It was only partial amnesia, that's what they said.

But it wasn't just the memories of her; he'd lost parts of himself that seemed to be missing, too.

Shannon couldn't let it go. The photograph lingered in her mind, presenting an enigma that required resolution. Daniel's behavior, once charmingly enigmatic, had turned guarded, even evasive. She spent hours staring at the group photo, searching for clues, something to latch onto in a sea of confusion. The words scrawled on the back, **_Don't trust anyone,_** lingered like a dark cloud over their fragile attempts at normalcy.

One night, as Daniel slept fitfully, still recovering from the physical and emotional toll of the accident, Shannon found herself drawn to his desk. The pile of papers from before was gone, cleared away as if Daniel had anticipated her curiosity. The drawer below had a brass lock that reflected the light from the window.

Her heart hammered in her chest, guilt and determination warring within her. But the phrase from the photo whispered again in her head, a warning, or a plea. She searched the room quietly and found a paperclip, bending it into a makeshift tool. Minutes felt like hours as her trembling hands worked at the lock until it clicked open.

Inside, she found a notebook. The leather cover showed signs of wear and scratches, concealing its interior. Shannon opened it cautiously, her breath catching as she began to read the chaotic scrawl within. The notes contained fragmented and unclear messages, including unknown names and phrases such as "*They know* and *Keep them safe*."

Among the scattered words, one phrase stood out: *The incident was intentional.*

Shannon froze, the blood draining from her face as the room seemed to close in around her. What did he mean? Was Daniel in danger? Was she? And why had he hidden this from her?

The sound of movement behind her made her spin around, clutching the notebook to her chest. Daniel stood in the doorway, his silhouette cast in shadow, his eyes sharper and darker than she had ever seen them.

"What are you doing, Shannon?" His voice was low, and there was something new in it that made the hairs on the back of her neck stand on end.

"I should be asking you the same thing," she replied, her voice trembling but resolute. "What aren't you telling me, Daniel? What really happened to you?"

Once home, their lives became a delicate dance of navigating his new reality. He forgot the simplest things: the smell of coffee in the morning, the way her voice softened when she spoke his name, even the reason he kept a scar above his left eyebrow. Yet, Shannon told herself they could rebuild. This wasn't the end of them. It couldn't be.

But then, subtle cracks began to appear. Daniel, once open and warm, began to withdraw. His gaze darkened during quiet moments, his movements sharper, less certain. The man Shannon once knew seemed different now, and it was not solely due to the trauma he had experienced.

Late one evening, she awoke to the sound of papers rustling. She found Daniel hunched over his desk, illuminated by the faint glow of his desk lamp. He turned slightly as she entered, quickly shoving a photograph under a pile of documents.

"What are you doing?" she asked.

"Nothing," Daniel replied too quickly, his voice tight. "Just... sorting some old things."

But the tension lingered.

Days later, the photograph surfaced again, this time slipped between pages of a well-thumbed book on the coffee table. A group photo, faded and frayed at the edges.

Daniel stood in the center alongside two other men Shannon didn't recognize. The scrawled handwriting on the back read: ***Don't trust anyone.***

She confronted him. "Who are they?"

Daniel's face pales. "Old friends," he murmured, but his eyes betrayed him. "It's nothing... just the past catching up with me."

The words froze Shannon in place. The past. The very thing Daniel seemed desperate to leave behind. Something he was hiding began to resurface, linked to his fractured state of mind.

As the days turned into weeks, Shannon couldn't shake the feeling that someone, or something, was watching them. Footsteps echoed too long in the driveway. A car idled down the street late at night, its silhouette casting shadows through their curtains. And then, the letters began arriving.

At first, Shannon thought they were standard junk mail. But the sharp scrawl of the handwriting on the envelopes, paired with their ominous messages, made her blood run cold. She read them in the empty kitchen while Daniel slept upstairs, her hands trembling. *She doesn't know what you did.*

Shannon's world tilted. *What had Daniel done? Who were the men in the photograph? And how far was the past willing to go to reclaim him?*

The next morning, she decided she couldn't wait for answers to come to her. If Daniel wouldn't, or couldn't, tell her the truth, she would find it herself.

Weeks have passed. Then months. Daniel learned to walk again, speak again, and even laugh, but it came in fragments. Shannon nursed him through every moment, feeding him with a spoon, cleaning his bandages, holding him while he shook from night terrors.

But some things didn't return.

His memory was patchy. He forgot words. He became suspicious, even paranoid at times. Shannon chalked it up to the trauma.

However, he then began locking his office door.

Then came the anonymous letters.

"You should've stayed gone, Daniel."

"She doesn't know what you did."

Shannon found them in the mailbox at Haven House. No return address. No explanation.

She confronted him one night. "Is there something I don't know?"

Daniel's hands trembled as he reached for her. "There are things from before we met. Work I did. People I exposed. I thought it was over. I thought they moved on."

"Who?" she demanded.

"I don't know," he whispered. "But I think someone wants to finish what the accident didn't."

One Year Anniversary of Haven House

Shannon pushed aside the fear. The threats. The shadows. That day was about celebration.

Haven House had helped over four hundred women in one year. The event was well attended. Shannon gave another moving speech. Daniel stood next to her with a cane, smiling faintly, but his eyes were always scanning the crowd.

After the event, he leaned in and whispered, "I need to tell you something tonight."

But he never got the chance.

The Murder

Two days later, Shannon woke at dawn, alone in bed. Daniel had left early for a zoning board meeting. By 9 a.m., there was a knock at the door.

Two officers. One young. One grizzled and pale. Ma'am," the older one said, removing his hat. "Are you Shannon Sullivan?" She nodded, heart already splintering.

"There's no straightforward way to say this. Daniel Robinson was located early this morning. Outside Haven House. He was... murdered."

Shannon couldn't breathe. It was as if someone turned the world inside out. "No," she gasped. "He was okay. He *survived.* He wasn't supposed to die."

"We have reason to believe this was targeted," the younger officer said.

"We have reason to believe this was targeted," the younger officer said. "There were no signs of robbery or a random act of violence. Whoever did this knew exactly where to find him and waited for the right moment."

Shannon's hands trembled as she clutched the doorframe for support. "Targeted? By whom? Why? Daniel never—he wouldn't have enemies."

The older officer's gaze softened, but his voice was steady, professional. "We're still piecing everything together, ma'am, but there's evidence suggesting Mr. Robinson was involved in uncovering some... sensitive information. There were documents found in his car, and they pointed to something much bigger. Larger networks, powerful people."

Shannon felt the weight of their words sink like a stone into her chest. She glanced toward Daniel's office through the doorway, where his chair sat slightly turned, as if he'd just stood from it. The life they had built together, the things he had poured into his soul, all seemed to tremble on the edge of unraveling.

Her knees buckled. "No, no, no…"

The Aftermath

Inside Haven House, Daniel's office was untouched. His last cup of coffee was still sitting at the desk. Shannon ran her hands along the wood; her grief wrapped in rage.

She opened the drawer and found a file labeled **"Contingency."**

Inside: names, dates, and an unsigned sworn statement.

Her heart dropped.

Daniel had been investigating someone. A powerful man in their city. A donor to their cause. A man with secrets tied to a network of abusive physicians. Some are still practicing. And some were tied to Scott. The pieces clicked all together.

The accident. The letters. The silence. This wasn't random. This was murder.

That night, Shannon sat in front of her podcast microphone, the red light pulsating steadily. Her audience, numbering in the hundreds of thousands, waited in hushed anticipation. The silence was heavy, electric. Then, her voice cut through the void—raw, deliberate.

"You think you can bury the truth? Do you think your money, your power, your secrets are untouchable? Let me tell you what happens when you try to silence justice. It doesn't fade away, it grows louder, sharper, more relentless."

She leaned forward, her fingers brushing the microphone as if daring her words to fall harder. "I know who you are. I know your faces, your lies, the way you hide behind your charities and your influence. You've built walls around your crimes, thinking you're safe in the shadows. Let me promise you those walls are crumbling."

Her tone dropped, icy and unwavering. "You wanted silence. You wanted control. But what you've unleashed is a fire you cannot contain. I am out for you, out for every name, every secret, every piece of evidence that will shatter your safe havens of deceit."

Shannon's eyes hardened, and her voice was like steel. "This is for Daniel. This is for every woman you sought to silence. This is not just justice, this is reckoning. And trust me, it's coming."

The folder on her computer glowed faintly, a testament to the weight of her claim. Files, images, testimonies, all neatly exposed.

She took a deep breath.

"This is Shannon Sullivan. This is *Unmasked*. And I'm coming for you."

"You think you can bury the truth?"

She leaned closer to the microphone, her voice dropping to a whisper that felt more menacing than a scream. "You thought you could erase the past. But history doesn't forget; it waits. And now, the reckoning begins."

Chapter 20
Silence and Secrets

The silence was no longer comforting. It was heavy now, thick with secrets, dripping with the echo of things left unsaid. Shannon sat alone in the darkened podcast studio, lit only by the dull red glow of the *"record"* light that she hadn't pressed. Her fingers hesitated over the button as she experienced a profound sense of grief, anger, and fear.

Daniel was gone.

Shot in broad daylight, just steps away from Haven House, the shelter they had both dreamed would become a refuge for women like her. Like the ones who had called into her show. Like the version of herself she'd finally begun to shed. Now his absence pressed down on her chest like a stone.

Her breath came shallow.

Her mind, always spinning, kept returning to the image of him lying in her arms, blood staining her hands as sirens wailed in the distance.

She hadn't cried yet. Not really. Not the way she had after Scott.

That pain had come in sobs and storms. But this loss was colder. Deeper. Like someone had ripped her heart out and left an echo chamber in its place.

She turned to the wall where Daniel's jacket still hung, left from a night he'd come to surprise her with wine and take out after a rough podcast recording. She couldn't bring herself to move it. Touching it would make it real.

But there was no denying it.

Daniel's death is under investigation. And the whispers Shannon had started chasing, of cover-ups, of medical fraud, of powerful men hiding behind white coats and boardrooms. These were no longer whispers. They were sirens.

She finally hit the record button.

Her voice cracked as it came through the mic. "This wasn't supposed to be the next episode," she said, swallowing down the fear. "But I can't stay silent anymore. The truth got someone killed."

A long pause.

"His name was Daniel Robinson. He was kind and brilliant. A philanthropist. A woman's son, whose mother experienced abuse and silence for many years. He believed in healing. In second chances. And he believed in me."

Another pause, as Shannon steadied herself.

"And now he's dead. It wasn't random. It was a warning. To stop asking questions. To stop digging. To stop exposing the connections between the abuse we survive... and the institutions that protect the abusers."

She inhaled sharply.

"Well, I'm not stopping."

She leaned in closer to the mic, her voice gaining strength.

The title of this episode, *Mask of Silence*, signifies the experiences that many individuals have endured. We've smiled through the pain. We've minimized our trauma. We've let men like Scott, doctors, fathers, husbands, lovers, gaslight us into believing we were crazy, dramatic, unstable."

Her voice was low now. Controlled.

"But silence is complicity. And I won't be complicit anymore."

She clicked a folder open on her laptop.

Inside: anonymous files, hospital records, sealed lawsuits, voice messages from former nurses and residents. Each one another crack in the mask. Each one another thread in the tangled web Daniel had started helping her unravel before he was killed.

She hit play on the first one button.

A nurse's voice, trembling: "We weren't supposed to talk about the overdose. He said the board would bury it. Is that the woman, Sharon? She wasn't stable anyway. But it wasn't her fault. Dr. Hargrove made the call…"

Shannon leaned back, heart pounding. She could feel it the truth was getting closer. But so was danger.

They had taken Daniel. But they had underestimated her.

This time, the silence would not win.

Shannon didn't remember driving home that night. She didn't remember locking the door or turning on the lights. All she knew was that at some point, she ended up curled on the floor of her living room, Daniel's favorite flannel wrapped around her like a burial shroud, his scent barely clinging to the fabric.

The grief was not loud.

It was suffocatingly quiet.

It crept into her bones like winter, leaving her numb in places she hadn't realized could still feel. She couldn't stop thinking about the way his body had crumpled. The confusion in his eyes in those final seconds, he hadn't expected it. He hadn't even had time to run. She hadn't either.

A thousand thoughts raced through her mind, each one a blade slicing her sanity. *What if we hadn't gone to Haven House that day? What if I had walked out with him? What if I'd made him stay in the car?*

The guilt was as poisonous as it was irrational, and still, she drank it down like a drug.

She replied to their last moments as if it were a prayer and a punishment. Daniel brushes her hair back, whispering that he has something to tell her, something big. He never got the chance. Her hands trembled. *What had he meant to say?* Had he known something? Had he discovered something so damning that it got him killed? Grief twisted into fury.

Shannon rose from the floor like something feral awakening. She stormed into the studio and opened the digital file Daniel had started, a folder innocently named "HH Research."

But she remembered now, he had smiled oddly when he created it, as if it were more than just data for Haven House.

Inside the folder was chaos, audio clips, redacted reports, medical records and names. So many names. Some she recognized from her past interviews. Others made her stomach churn.

Scott's name appeared repeatedly. In dismissed malpractice reports, in patient complaints that vanished. In files of women who'd died during "complicated procedures," their deaths were always swept away by the hospital's legal team. Shannon gasped as she scrolled faster.

There was a note from Daniel, hidden in metadata, one she hadn't seen before:

"If something happens to me, start with Brighton. And follow the money."

Brighton Medical was the private research firm Scott once casually mentioned during a drunken evening, dismissing it as a "vanity project." Shannon had brushed it off at the time. Now it felt like a ticking bomb. Her chest seized with another wave of grief and rage.

Daniel had been onto something. He was trying to protect her. Attempting to safeguard the women affected by the actions of influential men in authoritative positions within the medical field. And now he was dead, and he was not here to tell us.

Suddenly, her vision blurred. She stumbled to the bathroom and collapsed beside the toilet, but it wasn't nausea; it was panic that her body was finally reacting. Tears erupted from some ancient place in her soul. The sound that escaped her wasn't human. It was like an animal, raw, wounded, and primal.

She wept until her throat burned. Until her voice cracked and her ribs ached. Until she had nothing left but silence and the sound of her heart breaking into pieces too jagged to fit back together.

She crawled to her bedroom, clutching the audio recorder like a crucifix. Not to sleep, but to make sense of the madness of the weeks prior without sleep. She recorded her pain. Every gasp. Every fragmented thought.

It wasn't for the podcast. Not yet, it was for her. To survive the pain of Daniel's death.

Then her phone vibrated. An unknown number. She hesitated, then answered. A man's voice in a low, gravelly and controlled manner said, "You need to stop digging, Ms. Sullivan. You've already lost one man. Don't make it two." The line went dead.

Shannon's hand shook so violently that she dropped the phone. But the fear no longer paralyzed her. It transformed into anger and determination.

They thought Daniel's death would silence her. But the truth had just become personal. She opened a new episode file.

"This is *Unmasked*. And if you're listening, you need to know: the mask is slipping. And behind it… is a monster."

The nightmares came in waves.

At first, there were disjointed fragments of screams behind closed doors, blood in her hands, Daniel calling her name from somewhere she couldn't reach. But as the nights passed, they sharpened into brutal clarity.

In one dream, she stood in an operating room, frozen, while Scott stood over Daniel's lifeless body, with scalpel in hand, grinning. In another, Haven House burned in the distance while a faceless man whispered, *"You were warned."*

Each time she woke up gasping, drenched in sweat, her screams swallowed by the empty walls of her apartment. The city outside moved on, but inside, time had ruptured.

And then came the threats, real ones.

The first was a note left on her windshield. Simple, typed. *"This isn't your story to tell."*

The second came two days later, a photo slid under her door. It was a blurry surveillance still of her outside Daniel's grave, standing alone. The back of the photo had one word in block letters: *ENOUGH.*

By the third incident, Shannon stopped calling the police. They didn't care. The officer barely even wrote down the report, offering her a condescending smirk. "Could be a prank, Ms. Sullivan. You're a public figure now. These podcasts stir up all kinds of drama."

No patrol car. No follow-up.

Just more silence.

She tried to keep recording, but her voice began to falter. Every time she leaned into the mic, she could hear someone breathing in the back of her mind or just outside her apartment. Was she imagining it? Her therapist said she might be experiencing trauma-induced paranoia. But Shannon knew better. She wasn't paranoid. They were watching her.

She kept the blinds closed. Carried pepper spray. Slept with her laptop beside her bed. But none of it felt like it was enough. She was unraveling, and whoever they were, Scott, his network, the hospital, they wanted exactly that. To break her.

Until she remembered someone.

Maya Delano.

It had been years since they spoke. Back when Shannon still wrote for the local features desk, Maya had been a rising star in investigative journalism, fearless, brilliant, and burned more than once by digging too deep.

Last she heard, Maya had gone freelance after exposing a pharmaceutical cover-up that nearly got her killed.

Shannon sent one message:

"Need help. It's about Daniel. They're watching me. I think I'm next. Please."

Five minutes passed. Then ten. Then a reply.

"Address. I'm coming now."

Shannon felt something shift in her chest like air returning after drowning. Two hours later, there was a knock at the door. Three taps. Then two.Just like they used to do.

Maya stood in the hallway, dressed in all black, a messenger bag slung over her shoulder, sharp eyes scanning the corridor.

"Hell, Shannon," she said, stepping in. "You look like hell."

"I feel worse," Shannon replied, voice brittle.

Maya dropped her bag and pulled out a recorder, a notepad, and a burner phone. "Start from the beginning. Don't leave anything out. If we're going to take on ghosts in white coats, I need the whole damn haunting."

For the first time since Daniel died, Shannon felt steady.

She exhaled and began to talk. The files are now encrypted.

Shannon had found them buried in Daniel's "HH Research" folder, dozens of documents with indecipherable names: patient initials, timestamps, medical codes. But Maya knew exactly what she was looking at.

"These are hospital trial logs," she murmured, eyes darting across the screen. "Unregistered. Off-record. No FDA signoffs."

Shannon blinked. "You mean... illegal?" Maya nodded grimly. "Experimental hormone injections. Neurological treatments. Drugs not approved for human testing. All tied to Brighton Medical."

She clicked open a document labeled **"Subject K.S. | 2001"**.

Shannon's blood went cold. *K.S.*, her own initials.

It was a psych evaluation. The tone was clinical, detached. Her childhood medical records, long thought lost, were there in horrifying detail. The trauma-induced dissociation, the self-harming episodes. Her father's name was redacted, but his "psychosexual dominance" was noted in a margin. It read like a case study in abuse and silence.

"Why would this be in Daniel's files?" she whispered.

Maya frowned. "Because they were following you. You were part of this. You were observed longer than you realized."

It made sense in a sick, twisted way. Her father's connections. Scott's casual interest in her therapy history. The way he'd always asked strange questions after her hypnosis sessions. He had known something. And so had Daniel, before he died.

Shannon stood, nausea curling in her gut. "I need air."

They decided to head for the mountains the next day to clear their heads, to sort through the files without eyes on them. Maya had a friend with a remote cabin near Flagstaff. No Wi-Fi. No GPS. The silence would be useful. For once, safe.

Or so they thought.

Halfway up the winding road to the cabin, with the pine trees towering like sentries on either side, Shannon noticed the SUV.

It had been behind them for at least twenty minutes. No headlights. No license plate. No attempt to pass. "Maya..." Shannon said, her voice barely audible. "I see it," Maya replied, her knuckles whitening on the steering wheel.

They sped up. So did the SUV. Maya took a sharp turn. Gravel sprayed like shrapnel. The vehicle stayed close to its headlights, suddenly flaring on. It bumped into the back of their car. Shannon screamed. "They're trying to run us off the road!" Another hit to the back of their SUV and it started to fishtailed. Maya fought to stay in control. "There's a turn-out coming. Hold on!"

The road narrowed, hugging the side of a cliff. A single guardrail separated them from a thousand-foot drop into darkness. The other driver surged forward, attempting to push them from the inside. Another final shove to the SUV.

Maya jerked the wheel. The car skidded sideways, crashing through a cluster of trees just off the shoulder. The metal shrieked. Then stillness.

They were alive. Breathing heavily, shaken and bruised.

The other vehicle didn't stop. It disappeared into the woods like a phantom.

Shannon's hands trembled as she unbuckled herself. "They're not just warning me anymore," she whispered. "They're trying to kill me."

Maya climbed out, scanning the area with her phone light. "We must go dark. No tech and no trails. From this point forward, they don't get to know where we are."

Back at the cabin later that night, Maya decrypted another file. And what they found turned Shannon's blood into ice.

It was a list of names. Former patients. Test subjects. Many of them are women. Some had died in mysteriously overdoses, suicides, or car accidents.

One name stood out. Daniel Robinson. Next to it: "Subject D.R. – Terminated." Date: The day of his murder.

Shannon fell to her knees, the room spinning.

This wasn't just a conspiracy. It was an execution list.

They returned to Shannon's apartment under the cover of night. Windows stayed shut and locked. Phones powered down. Neither of them slept. They took turns looking at the door, waiting for something to come.

It arrived at dawn. A small brown envelope, at the front door. No postage. No name. No return address.

Shannon stared at it for a long time, her breath shallow. Her hands shook as she picked them up. Inside was a single item: a black flash drive. No markings. Just one word scribbled in Daniel's handwriting on a tiny white sticker: *"If I'm gone."*

She dropped to the floor. The room felt airless.

Maya knelt beside her. "Play it. Now."

They inserted the drive into Shannon's laptop. One file. An audio recording. Shannon hit play. Daniel's voice filled the room.

"Shannon... if you're hearing this... it means I didn't make it." Her hand flew to her mouth. A strangled sob escaped.

"I've been trying to protect you—ever since I realized who Scott really is. And what he's part of. Brighton isn't just a private research firm. It's a shell company. The real work...

It's happening in the basement of St. Elora's Medical Hospital, the wing that's been 'under renovation' for three years." Maya's eyes widened. Shannon froze.

"They've been running unauthorized drug trials. On vulnerable women. Some from shelters. Some from psych words. Some... like you. Scott's name is all over the documentation. He was the chief physician for two of the trials. But it goes deeper than him. There's a network of doctors, hospital board members, and even law enforcement. They've been burying complaints. Silencing whistleblowers."

Daniel's voice faltered as he continued recording the tape.

"I confronted Scott, two nights before I recorded this. He laughed. Said no one would believe me. That your past made you 'an unreliable narrator.' He said he'd already started the process of 'neutralizing the threat.' You, Shannon."

The room spun. Shannon curled forward, her entire body shivering.

"I thought I could outrun it. I thought I could get the evidence from someone who mattered. But if you have this... then I failed. And now you have a choice."

A pause. His voice softened.

"You can run. Disappear. Start over. Or... you can finish what I started. Tell the world. Expose them. Unmask every monster hiding behind those surgical masks and medical boards. But if you do, know that they will come for you. Just like they did for me."

Another pause.

"Shannon... I love you. I loved you from the moment I saw you standing in that godforsaken auditorium, trying to smile through your pain. You are braver than you believe. Stronger than you think. And whatever happens next don't let my death be in vain."

A breath. One final sentence.

"Unmask them all."

The recording ended.

The room was dead silent, except for Shannon's quiet, steady weeping. Maya placed a hand on her shoulder.

"We have enough to start burning the whole damn thing down," Maya whispered.

Shannon looked up, her face streaked with tears, but her eyes burned with resolve. "No," she said. "We're not starting a fire. We're starting a war."

Just after sunset, the buzzer rang. Shannon and Maya froze.

They hadn't told anyone they were back. The building had no door attendant. No one should know they were here. Maya reached for her stunned baton. Shannon gripped a kitchen knife. Heart hammering in her chest, she pressed the intercom. Static. Then a voice.

"My name is Dr. Alina Cross. I was a friend of Daniel's. He told me to find you... if anything ever happened to him."

Maya exchanged a sharp glance with Shannon and nodded once. They opened the door slowly.

The woman standing there looked nothing like Shannon had imagined. No lab coat, no polished professionalism. Just a slight, haunted woman in her forties, wearing a hoodie and jeans, her hair tied in a haphazard bun. Her eyes darted nervously down the hall.

"I can't stay long," she said breathlessly. "I'm being followed."

They let her in. Maya bolted the door. Shannon didn't even wait before asking: "How did you know Daniel?" Alina's face softened. "We were interns together at St. Elora's. Years ago. I was the one who brought him into Brighton study. He didn't know what it was not at first. None of us did. They called it a 'harmless sleep aid trial' for PTSD patients. But they were lying. They were always lying."

She pulled a small folder from her coat. Inside were hard copies photos of sedated women strapped to gurneys, charts listing undocumented side effects, and internal memos. A memorandum has been forwarded to Dr. Scott Barragan. Subject line: **"Subject 6B—severe dissociative episode. Consider medical redirection or discharge."**

Alina's hands trembled as she handed the file over.

"They called it *medical redirection*. But it wasn't a treatment plan. It was code for chemical sedation. Or worse. Some women... they didn't leave the hospital alive."

Shannon turned pale. "Are you saying they were murdering patients?"

Alina swallowed hard. They were conducting experiments on women who would not be noticed missing. Drug addicts, runaways and abused women from shelters. Patients with no families. Daniel began his investigation upon noticing discrepancies where police reports listed individuals as deceased, but their families were unaware. The remains were cremated shortly thereafter and their organs sold on the black market.

Maya's voice was grim. "And Scott was involved in this?"

Alina nodded. "He was one of the most powerful gatekeepers in the program. I heard him refer to it once as unavoidable for 'medical evolution.' Like we were gods, I tried to walk away. Daniel begged me to go public. But I was terrified." She looked at Shannon now. "But when I saw the news... that he died... I knew it was time."

Shannon's eyes welled with tears. "What do we do with this?" she whispered. Alina looked between them. "If you go to the police, it'll vanish. You'll vanish. But there's a file. A main list. Names, dates, payments and signatures. Daniel was close to finding it. He believed it was concealed in St.

Elora's server archive. You get that file... and the world will finally believe you."

Maya asked, "Why hasn't someone done it already?"

Alina's voice dropped. "Because every person who's tried... is either dead, missing, or suddenly very wealthy."

She stood, zipping her coat. "I've told you what I know. Now, I have disappeared. You should too before they erase you." And with that, she was gone. The door clicked shut behind her.

Shannon stared down at the file in her hands.

Maya whispered, "Do you believe her?"

Shannon didn't hesitate. "Every damn word." She walked into the studio. Sat at the mic. Pressed record.

"Tonight's episode was supposed to be about grief. But grief isn't the whole story. It never is. Behind it... is betrayal. And behind that? A system built to keep women like me silent, sedated, and buried. But we're not going quietly anymore."

"Daniel's death was not the end. It was the beginning. And if you're listening, if you're scared, if you're alone, if

someone's told you to shut up and sit down, this is your invitation to speak. Because I'm not done, I've just begun."

Chapter 21
The Fallout

By morning, it had already begun. The episode had aired for barely eight hours, no music, no guests, only Shannon's brittle but steadfast voice, exposing the shadows behind Daniel's murder and the secret experiments buried within Brighton Medical Group.

As dawn slid into day, the ripples began. Rumors leaped from inbox to inbox, hashtag to hashtag. It was as if an underground stream suddenly broke the surface, and what had once been whispered in hospital basements and late-night phone calls now roared in the bright glare of public scrutiny.

Shannon watched the notifications multiply, her hands shaking over her keyboard. Every ping meant another voice, another story and another survivor who refused to be erased.

It wasn't just the usual listeners who heard it this time. It was a vast community, looking for answers.

A popular true crime journalist picked up the story within hours. Then came the retweets. The reactions. Survivors from around the country began tagging Shannon online, sharing their own chilling experiences from St. Elora's or similar hospitals.

Unmasked Truth was trending by noon. Shannon sat frozen in her studio, watching the chaos unfold on her screen.

"Is this real?"

"Brighton Medical is a front? Hello, who would have guessed that? How many women did they do this to?"
"I remember a girl from my group home who went to a 'clinical trial' at St. Elora's and never came back. Her name was Kayla. This can't be a coincidence."

And then, someone uploaded a clip of the recording. Daniel's voice.

"If you're hearing this… it means I didn't make it."
It went viral.

By late afternoon, Shannon's inbox was flooded with messages from survivors, doctors, former hospital staff, and journalists. Some offered thanks. Others begged for protection. A few sent warnings.

"Be careful, Shannon. You've stirred a monster."

The phone rang. She let it go to voicemail. She no longer trusted unknown numbers.

Maya paced behind her. "You've lit the match. Now we must survive the fire. "There was a knock at the door. Not a soft one. Maya peered through the peephole and froze. "It's media. Channel 7. And I think, yes, the *Tribune* is out there too. Hell, Shannon." She didn't answer. She couldn't move. Her heart thudded with something between terror and vindication. She had told the truth. And now, everyone knew it. But the celebration was short-lived.

A new email landed in her inbox. No subject. No signature. Just a single link. A private, password-protected server.

She hesitated. Then clicked. The screen lit up with a live feed from a camera in a dark room. The angle shifted slightly, and I focused on it. A woman. Bound to a chair. Bloodied. Her face was bruised and barely recognizable. But Shannon knew that face. Dr. Alina Cross.

A message popped up under the feed:

"You've gone too far. This is your only warning. Stop the podcast. Delete the files. Or she dies.

Shannon stared at the screen, her pulse hammering in her ears. The threat was clear, but the stakes were even clearer; she couldn't back down now. Her fingers trembled as she typed a response into the anonymous email portal.

Maya gasped behind her. "Oh my God." Shannon's knees buckled. It wasn't over. It was only the beginning.

She had become a threat. And now... they were coming for everyone. Shannon didn't wait.

Within an hour, she and Maya were driving through the backroads toward the nearest FBI field office just outside Phoenix. They said nothing for most of the trip.

The video of Alina played repeatedly in Shannon's mind, looping with Daniel's voice: *"If you're hearing this... it means I didn't make it."*

The car hummed softly as they approached the city limits. Shannon's grip on the wheel tightened with each passing mile. Maya finally broke the silence, her voice barely above a whisper. "What if they don't believe us?"

Shannon glanced at her, her jaw set. "They'll believe the files. They'll believe the evidence. It's too damning not to."

Maya nodded, though doubt shadowed her face. The memory of Alina's battered face haunted both of them; fueling their resolve even as fear clawed at their edges.

When they reached the FBI office, Shannon parked in a secluded corner of the lot, scanning for anything unusual. Were they under observation? Watched?

The office building in Phoenix was faceless with gray concrete, tinted windows, and no identifying sign beyond a steel plaque. As they stepped inside, Shannon's stomach churned with unease.

As they entered the lobby, Shannon noticed the sterile atmosphere, the subdued sound of printers and the murmur of voices from behind frosted glass partitions. The tension was palpable. She was risking everything, but the truth needed a voice louder than fear.

At the security checkpoint, she asked to speak with an agent. Preferably, I would be assigned to medical fraud or organized crime, as I have some evidence in this area and need to discuss it with someone who oversee these matters.

"Name?" the guard asked.

"Shannon Sullivan."

That name carries weight now.

She was escorted to a quiet interview room with glass walls. Inside there were chilly air and a cup of stale coffee. Maya sat beside her, with her hand resting protectively on her bag.

A receptionist glanced up and offered a polite smile. "Can I help you?"

Shannon stepped forward, her heartbeat thrumming in her ears. "I need to speak to someone in charge of medical fraud and organized crime. Urgently." The receptionist hesitated; her fingers poised over the keyboard. "Do you have an appointment?"

"No," Shannon replied firmly, clutching her bag as if it were armor. "But you'll want to hear what I have to say."

Several minutes later, a door opened, and Agent Bryce Kendrick strode through the door in his sharp suit and piercing eyes radiating authority. Behind him was a younger woman, her face calm but alert, clutching a legal pad. Bryce extended his hand, his lips curving into a knowing smile.

"I've heard your podcast," he said, his voice measured but intrigued. Shannon's throat tightened. This was it; the crossroads where her truth and their willingness to act would determine everything. What she had in her pocket could either ignite a revolution or bury them all under a tidal wave of danger.

"I hope you're ready to hear what comes next," Shannon replied, her voice steady despite the storm raging inside her.

She clutched the flash drive in her pocket like a talisman.

It held everything from Daniel's recording, Alina's documents, and the encrypted Brighton files they had uncovered. The main list was still out of reach. But this was enough to start a war.

Shannon's eyes flickered with hope. "Then you know why I'm here."

He nodded once. "We've been following Brighton Medical for a while, but without any hard proof, our hands have been tied. What you brought could be the first real break."

Shannon slid the flash drive across the table.

"Daniel Robertson died for this," she said softly. "And now Alina Cross is being held somewhere. They sent me a live video feed. They know what I've uncovered. They're threatening to kill her if I don't stop."

Kendrick's jaw tightened. The female agent leaned forward. "Do you have the source of the feed?"

"I don't know how to trace it," Shannon admitted. "It was a private link. Disappeared after five minutes."

Kendrick nodded to his partner. She stood and left the room to run the flash drive and begin the trace. He turned back to Shannon. "We'll investigate Alina's whereabouts immediately. But you should understand something."

"What?" "If what you're saying is true, this isn't just a hospital scandal. It's organized and well-funded syndicate. With legal and political insulation. We've suspected for years that Brighton is the public face of a much larger machine."

Shannon's heart sank. "How high does it go?" He hesitated.

"All the way to state-level health regulators and higher. We have reason to believe they've paid off prosecutors and judges."

Maya cursed under her breath. "So, you're saying we're going up against a syndicate."

"I'm saying you've kicked a hornet's nest. And they're going to come after you with everything they've got." He leaned forward, lowering his voice.

"You need protective custody. Both of you. We can relocate you until we dismantle this." But Shannon shook her head. "No. I'm not disappearing. That's what they want. That's what they did to Alina."

Before Kendrick could argue, his phone buzzed. He stood, walked to the hallway, and took the call just outside the door. Through the glass, Shannon could see his body tense. His eyes flicked toward her. Then back to the phone. He returned moments later, face unreadable.

"Excuse me. There's... been an incident," he said. Shannon stood. "What kind of incident?"

Kendrick didn't meet her eyes. "Dr. Alina Cross was found. In an abandoned house outside Tucson. Dead. Self-inflicted gunshot wound, according to initial reports." The words landed like a gut punch. Shannon staggered back into her chair. "No," she whispered. "No, she wouldn't. She *wouldn't.*"

Maya slammed her fist on the table. "You think we're going to believe that was suicide? That's how they clean up their mess!" Kendrick sighed. "I agree. And I'll dig deeper. But I'm warning you, this gets more dangerous from here."

Shannon stared out the window. Her reflection looked hollow. Ghostlike. But inside her, something sharp was awakening. Something ancient, loud, and furious.

"No more threats," she said, her voice steady. "No more whispers. I'm going public. The names. The files. All of it. I'm releasing it on the podcast tonight."

Kendrick paled. "If you do that, you'll be a target?" "If I don't," says Shannon, "I'll be next."

Shannon and Maya left the FBI field building for her apartment to release the last podcast that would reveal everything. They were going to blow up the Phoenix community with the biggest scandal of the century and they had the evidence to prove it.

By nightfall, Shannon's face was everywhere.

News clips spliced her podcast audio over stock footage of hospital corridors, courtrooms, and body bags.

Headlines screamed across every social media platform:

"Whistleblower Found Dead."

"Podcast Host Alleges Human Experimentation."

"St. Elora's Named in Shocking Abuse Claims."

The world was listening loud and clear. Shannon sat in her studio, exhausted but alive, her voice hoarse from the recording she had just released. This time, she had held nothing back: names, locations and documents. She had dropped it all into the public domain. The files were now available to anyone. After the downloading, the story would go live. There would be no more silence.

Maya watched the download numbers climb like wildfire. "You just broke the internet," she said quietly.

Shannon's eyes carried a deep shadow of exhaustion, yet they sparkled with unwavering determination. Her presence, both strong and unshaken to the world, had just uncovered the biggest scandal. She had inspired a movement that went viral, and the excitement was exhilarating. She and Maya understood the danger they were involved in and they both agreed that there would be no rest that night.

At dawn, FBI Agent Kendrick called. His voice was tight and forced. "You need to come in immediately. Now. It's urgent." Maya's eyes narrowed. "Something's wrong." Agent Kendrick stated on the phone, "I am picking you up to drive you to the field office, be ready when I get to your apartment."

Agent Kendrick drove Shannon and Maya to the FBI field office. They both new that they needed to finish what Daniel started. They knew something was wrong. Still, they went with the agent driven by instinct, adrenaline and the conviction to finish what Daniel started. As they entered the field office, both Shannon and Maya sensed immediately that something wasn't right. The faces behind the security desk were unfamiliar, their smiles too tight, and the air felt heavy with unspoken warning. Their check-in dragged on, filled with unnecessary questions and sideways glances.

When they were finally cleared, they were escorted down stark corridors to a wing, neither of them recognized: dimly lit, unnervingly silent and cut off from the usual bustle.

Maya leaned in, her voice just above a whisper. "This doesn't feel like standard procedure, Shan."

Shannon nodded, her nerves prickling beneath her skin. Every instinct screamed caution.

Shannon glanced over her shoulder, half-expecting someone to emerge from the shadows or a camera to pivot in their
direction. The hum of distant voices was absent; even the
familiar clatter of office equipment seemed to have been
swallowed by the silence.

They exchanged a look, reaching a silent understanding:
stay alert, don't trust anything at face value. The elevator at
the end of the hallway dinged, but no one emerged.

Instead, their escort gestured briskly for them to keep
moving, his face betraying nothing.

As they resumed their uneasy walk, every step felt like
crossing a threshold into unknown territory. The doors they
passed were closed, the blinds drawn. The fluorescent lights
overhead buzzed with anxious energy. In the silence, their
footsteps sounded too loud.

The corridor finally bent toward a dead end, stopping at a
heavy, reinforced door. Their escort keyed in a code, the lock
disengaged with a mechanical thud, and he pushed the door
open.

They were motioned into a windowless room and left
alone. The click of the lock outside echoed in Shannon's
chest. She exchanged a glance with Maya, an intuitive
glance between them. Something was wrong here.

Inside, the air was cool and stale, the decor sparse with
just a table, three chairs, and a surveillance camera blinking
quietly in the corner. Without a word, the escort motioned

them inside and retreated, the door shutting behind them with a finality that made the hair on Shannon's arms stand up. The ventilation system's steady hum was the only sound breaking the oppressive quietness in the room. Shadows pooled in the corners, making the sparse furnishings seem even more unwelcoming.

Shannon paced once around the table, her fingers drumming nervously atop the metal surface. The air was thick with anticipation. Then, footsteps approached from the corridor, measured and deliberate, growing louder.

The handle rattled. Instinctively, Shannon and Maya straightened, bracing themselves as the door swung open. Moments later, the door opened and a stranger stepped in. His suit was immaculate, his expression unreadable. "Ms. Sullivan, Ms. Delano. I'm Agent Crowley. Agent Kendrick has been reassigned."

Shannon's heart pounded. "What? Why?" Internal protocol. He mishandled evidence and breached secure files. He's been placed on administrative leave."

Maya pushed to her feet and gazed sharply at him. "We want to speak to Agent Kendrick." "I'm afraid that won't be possible," Crowley replied, his smile thin and insincere. "We're here to debrief you both. After that, we'll escort you to a secure location. For your protection. "The chill in his words made Shannon's stomach twist. She realized, with a surge of clarity, that the walls were closing in on them.

But Maya was already moving. Without hesitation, she pulled her phone and thumbed a shortcut Daniel's encrypted livestream app. In seconds, their words and faces were beamed out to the world.

Agent Crowley turned, startled, but Maya's voice rang out strong: "This is Maya Delano. We are inside the Phoenix FBI field office. They've just told us that the agent working on our case has been reassigned. We believe we are being silenced."

Crowley's eyes flashed. "Turn that off." Maya's jaw set. Strongly towards him. "Make me, " she replied to him.

A beat of charged silence filled the room. Then, in the halls beyond, footsteps thundered closer.

Shannon raised her chin, the fire in her eyes reignited. "If we're going down, the world is coming with us. "Somewhere, a siren blared. The livestream viewer counts spiked. And on the other side of the world, a new wave of allies began to mobilize.

Shannon felt it too. "I'm afraid that won't be possible." A long silence fell over the room.

Crowley smiled, but there was nothing warm about it. "We're here to debrief you both. After that, we'll escort you to a secure location. For your protection."

Shannon's stomach dropped. It was happening. The cover-up. Shannon stood tall, her voice steady and commanding. "This is what corruption looks like. They don't want you to see it, but you are in real-time." A second later, armed agents burst into the room. Guns drawn. Shannon froze. Maya didn't blink. Crowley growled, "This stream ends now."

And then there was a voice from the hallway. Loud. Furious. "STAND DOWN."

Agent Kendrick appeared, flanked by two federal marshals. "You're all out of line," he barked. "Crowley, this is above your clearance. You've been compromised; we have the wire transfers. Crowley paled. "This is a mistake," but the marshals restrained him.

Kendrick turned to Shannon, breathless. "I had to move fast. They tried to shut me down from the inside, but I got the proof. Crowley's connected to Brighton. He's one of them."

Shannon collapsed into the chair, the shock washing over her. Even the FBI was corrupt and not a safe place.

Kendrick approached, softer now. "You just became the most dangerous woman in America. And the most protected." He held up a flash drive.

"This is the master file. The original Daniel tried to find. I pulled it from the St. Elora's archive last night. We've got them, Shannon. The whole damn network."

Tears welled in her eyes. She took the drive, gripping it like a sword. "Then let's finish this," she whispered. Shannon gripped the flash drive tightly, her gaze flickering between Kendrick and the agents outside the door. The weight of the truth pressed down on her shoulders, as heavy and unyielding as the storm brewing in the hallway. For a moment, silence hung thick in the room with the hum of tension filling the air.

Then the sound of distant footsteps thundered closer. Kendrick's face hardened. "They're coming," he said, his voice low but urgent. "Brighton's people. They'll stop at nothing to keep this buried."

Shannon's throat tightened. "What…what do we do?" The master file sat like a live grenade on the table between them. Shannon stared at it, her pulse thudding in her ears. The names. The payments. The cover-ups. Everything Daniel died to uncover is all here. Evidence that could tear down the walls of Brighton Medical Group, dismantle St. Elora's, and expose the rot eating away at the heart of the medical system."

Kendrick moved closer, his voice barely audible. "Shannon, if we don't act now, this all goes back underground. They have eyes everywhere. You've seen what they're capable of."

Shannon's throat tightened. "What…what do we do?" "Kendrick, we can't do this alone. There must be someone we can trust."

Kendrick shook his head, his expression grim. "Trust? That's the first thing Brighton strips away."

Shannon tightened her grip on the flash drive, her mind racing to sort through possibilities as the tension around her crystallized into raw urgency. "Kendrick," she murmured, meeting his unwavering gaze, "we can't just sit here. If we wait for them to surround us, it's over."

"I know," Kendrick replied, his tone clipped. He glanced toward the vents above an escape route, perhaps? "But if we're going to get out, we need misdirection. Something to stall them. They're trained to corner us."

Shannon's heart pounded, her instincts pulling her toward action even as fear clawed at her determination. Her eyes darted to the small window overlooking the alley below, then back to the grenade-like tension in the room. She reached into her bag, pulling out a lighter and a half-empty bottle of medical-grade alcohol.

Kendrick frowned, realizing dawning. "You're thinking a diversion?" Shannon nodded, her movements swift but calculated. "We light it up with smoke and flames. Anything to shift their focus. It'll buy us enough time to get to the stairwell, but only if we're fast."

"Will it work? We are running out of options here, girls. Let's go for it." The master file sat like a live grenade on the table between them.

Agent Kendrick locked the door behind them. "We need to move fast. Once this gets out, they'll unleash everything."

"I'm not scared anymore," Shannon said. But even as she said it, the lights flickered.

Once, twice, and then the emergency lights flashed red along the floor. Somewhere deep inside the complex, an alarm blared high-pitched and shrill. Kendrick cursed, pulling his weapon. "We're on lockdown," he hissed.

Maya bolted to the window checking out the commotion outside. This wasn't an accident."

Shannon clutched the flash drive. "They're here." Footsteps echoed in the hallway. Boots. Many of them. Coming fast.

Maya opened her bag and pulled out a second flash drive. "Copy it. Now."

Shannon inserted both into Kendrick's laptop, fingers flying. The file began to transfer, **17%... 32%... 49%...**

Kendrick braced against the door, gun drawn. "I swear to God, if Crowley brought in a cleanup team." Gunshots are being fired close by. Kendrick shouted into his radio. "This is Agent Kendrick. We are under assault. Unauthorized breach repeat, we are under." Then Static.

The laptop beeped **87%, 92%, and 99%.** Then everything freezes. The transfer bar stopped. The screen went black.

"What happened?!" Shannon screamed.

Maya checked the drive. "It's dead. The system wiped mid-copy. "A voice crackled from the overhead speaker, low, distorted and synthetic. "You should have walked away, Ms. Sullivan."

The lights returned, but not the overhead fluorescents. Spotlights with blinding light were focused on them from outside through the window. Three red lasers danced across the glass. Maya dove. "SNIPERS." The window shattered as bullets tore into the room.

Kendrick grabbed Shannon and tackled her to the floor, shielding her body as the door blew open behind them. She couldn't hear anything now. Just her heartbeat. Just Kendrick shouting Maya's name. Just Maya screaming. And the lights went out again, and Darkness and Silence settled in the room.

And the sound of someone whispering into Shannon's ear: *"They've taken Maya."*

Acknowledgement

I want to acknowledge the following people who help to make this book a reality. Thanks to all the people in my Writer's Club at Terravita Community who assisted me with the editing of this book including my assistant Judy Bartel-stone.

Thanks to Diane Nowak for encouragement to write and publish

Thanks to my nephew Richard Carlos DePascale who encouraged me to write about the shadows in my past and all my past students who believed in me.

Thanks to my son Jason Logan for the courage to write about mental illness.